Seven Nights of Sin

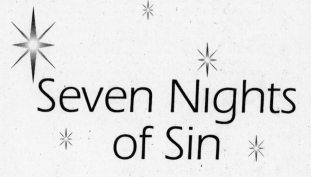

Seven Nights
of Sin

Lacey Alexander

HEAT

Heat

Published by New American Library, a division of
Penguin Group (USA) Inc., 375 Hudson Street,
New York, New York 10014, USA
Penguin Group (Canada), 90 Eglinton Avenue East, Suite 700, Toronto,
Ontario M4P 2Y3, Canada (a division of Pearson Penguin Canada Inc.)
Penguin Books Ltd., 80 Strand, London WC2R 0RL, England
Penguin Ireland, 25 St. Stephen's Green, Dublin 2,
Ireland (a division of Penguin Books Ltd.)
Penguin Group (Australia), 250 Camberwell Road, Camberwell, Victoria 3124,
Australia (a division of Pearson Australia Group Pty. Ltd.)
Penguin Books India Pvt. Ltd., 11 Community Centre, Panchsheel Park,
New Delhi—110 017, India
Penguin Group (NZ), 67 Apollo Drive, Rosedale, North Shore 0632,
New Zealand (a division of Pearson New Zealand Ltd.)
Penguin Books (South Africa) (Pty.) Ltd., 24 Sturdee Avenue,
Rosebank, Johannesburg 2196, South Africa

Penguin Books Ltd., Registered Offices:
80 Strand, London WC2R 0RL, England

First published by Heat, an imprint of New American Library,
a division of Penguin Group (USA) Inc.

First Printing, April 2008
1 3 5 7 9 10 8 6 4 2

Heat is a trademark of Penguin Group (USA) Inc.

LIBRARY OF CONGRESS CATALOGING-IN-PUBLICATION DATA
Alexander, Lacey.
Seven nights of sin / Lacey Alexander.
p. cm.
ISBN: 978-0-451-22314-2
I. Title.
PS3601.L3539S48 2008
813'.6—dc22   2007042244

Set in Centaur MT
Designed by Alissa Amell

Printed in the United States of America

To Chris in Hawaii—hope you enjoy this one!

THE ORIGINAL SIN

"Really to sin you have to be serious about it."
—Henrik Ibsen

One

"I don't need a man. I don't need a man. I don't need a man."

Usually, Brenna did her morning affirmations at home, but the alarm had gone off late, and just like breakfast, her affirmations had been forced to wait until she got to the office. Fortunately, she was stealing a few minutes alone in the break room with a donut and the self-help book she'd been reading, aptly titled, *You Don't Need a Man to Be Happy*.

She lowered her voice even further for the next set. "I don't need a penis to pleasure me. I don't need a penis to pleasure me. I don't need a penis to pleasure me."

Maybe she should drop that one from her repertoire, though. Saying it only made her think about penises.

"I am responsible for my own pleasure. I am responsible for my own pleasure. I am responsible for my own pleasure." Which, of course, meant masturbation. And she had nothing against that—it could get a girl through many a long and lonely night. But to tell herself it would be *enough, forever*—well, that was challenging. She'd have to work on *feeling* that one more as she said it.

Still determined, however, she started the first repetition. "I don't need a man. I don't—"

"Spoken just like someone who needs a man."

Flinching, she looked up to find her friend and coworker, Kelly

Mills—blond, fairly glamorous, and someone with plenty of men in her life. Kelly did PR for Blue Night Records, the indie music label that employed them both, and she also held a degree in psychology, which she claimed she needed in her line of work.

"I don't," Brenna reassured her about needing a man. Despite having little in common, the two had been good friends since Brenna had moved to L.A. three years ago, so if someone had to intrude on her affirmations, she was glad it was Kelly.

Kelly gave her head a scolding tilt. "People who *don't* usually don't need to say it."

"Huh?"

Kelly crossed her arms beneath ample breasts. "Take my next-door neighbor, Ms. Freeland, for instance. She's seventy-five and never been married. She's an artist, she traveled the world in her youth, she loves her Scottish terrier, Fiona, and she's never needed a man. She's never told me that, but it shows in everything she does. It's simply a part of her. She doesn't feel the need to go around explaining why she's not married or that she doesn't need a man—because she's so truly comfortable not having one.

"On the other hand, there's Ms. Nelson, three doors down." Kelly dropped her chin derisively and shifted her weight from one pointy red pump to the other. "She's forty-five and clearly lonely. She tells me all the time how she doesn't need a man to fulfill her, but what ruins it is how darned bitter and angry she sounds every time she says it. She might not *want* to need a man. But she obviously needs one."

"Your point again?" Brenna asked, eyebrows raised.

"Saying you don't need a man over and over indicates that, like it or not, you do. And there's no crime in that, by the way. Most women are wired to desire love and commitment."

Brenna only rolled her eyes. "Love and commitment—bleh." She didn't have to say more since Kelly knew all the nasty details about her cheating husband and recent divorce. "The last thing I'm interested in is commitment. And that's the truth."

Kelly nodded. "I believe you. You have trust issues. But I'll tell you what you *do* need."

"What's that?"

"To paraphrase the immortal words of John Mellencamp, you need a lover—who won't drive you crazy."

A lover? Brenna had had relationships, and guys she'd dated, and of course, a husband, but she'd never been the confident, carefree sort of woman who could have someone she thought of as a *lover*. So she pointed to her book. "According to this, a good vibrator will provide the same fulfillment."

Kelly raised her eyebrows matter-of-factly. "Do you have one?"

"No."

"Why not?"

Brenna pursed her lips. "Besides the fact that I'm too shy to go into one of those stores? Well, because somehow an evening with a vibrator just sounds a little . . . empty, as in boring. I know some women talk a good game about it, but—"

Kelly held up her hands in a *stop* motion. "Say no more. And listen to me. You *need* a lover. How long has it been since you've had one, by the way?"

"Does Wayne count?" Her smarmy ex.

Kelly grimaced. "Don't tell me he's the last? I mean, you've been divorced for, what, six months now?"

Brenna sighed. "And separated for a year before that."

Kelly looked as if Brenna had just announced the death of a loved one. "Oh dear God, you poor girl. Stand up."

Brenna blinked her surprise at the command, but the imposing look in Kelly's eyes pushed her to her feet. Placing her hands on Brenna's hips, Kelly positioned her in front of the small mirror above the sink in one corner of the break room. Reaching around her from behind, Kelly deftly undid the top two buttons on Brenna's blouse, then firmly cupped the undersides of her breasts to hoist them higher. "We've got to get you a man, and we're going to start by showing off your assets a little more."

Sadly, it had been so long since anyone had touched Brenna intimately that even Kelly's unexpected grasp aroused her a little, sending a tingling sensation shooting straight to her panties.

But she still had no desire for some meaningless affair. Or some meaning*ful* affair. Which pretty much cut out affairs. And brought her back to the book. "I don't know, Kel. I just don't think men or sex are on my personal menu anymore. That's why I'm doing these affirmations. I want to get them out of my system."

Kelly stepped back to the table, peering down at the book still lying open. Then she let out a huge *harrumph*. "Oh my God! Trust me, honey, you *do* need penises. We *all* need penises. Penises are one of God's gifts to women. Sure, He gave us labor pains. And periods. And kept us oppressed for centuries. But He did give us the penis, and that makes up for a lot."

Brenna simply sighed. Then buttoned up her blouse, hiding the cleavage Kelly had just revealed. This was pointless—the cleavage *and* the conversation. "Did you come in here just to harass me or did you have a purpose?"

"Oops, sorry—I almost forgot. Your moratorium on men totally sidetracked me. Jenkins wants to see you in his office." Their boss and the CEO of Blue Night. "Word in the halls is that he's got some big announcement to make, but no one knows what it is. So go check it out and end the suspense for all of us."

An announcement, huh? It was the first Brenna had heard of it, and being Jenkins' right-hand gal, she usually knew what was going on around here. So, after wiping away donut crumbs with a napkin, stowing her book in her desk drawer, and checking to make sure she'd rebuttoned her blouse correctly, she grabbed up a notepad and pen and headed toward Jenkins' office, knocking gently on the open door as she peeked inside.

"Brenna, come in," he said with what she thought a rather devious smile. "And close the door."

Carl Jenkins was exactly the kind of man people commonly referred to by his last name. Smart and calculating, no nonsense, all business— more the kind of guy you'd expect to work at one of the majors than a small indie label. That said, Blue Night had grown fast the last few years, in no small thanks to him. Sporting slicked-back hair and rather beady eyes, he was also the kind of guy you never felt completely comfortable with, and Brenna still didn't, even after three years as his administrative assistant.

After pushing the door shut, she eased into the chair across from him, wondering exactly what the big news was. "Kelly said you wanted to see me. There's some sort of big announcement afoot?"

Her boss's gaze widened as he chuckled lightly. Clearly, he was surprised but not startled to hear his employees suspected something was up. "An announcement? Sort of, dependent upon this conversation. But first, a secret. And I know I can trust you to keep a secret—right, Brenna? Especially when it's in your best interest professionally."

"Of course," she said, hoping he didn't see her nervous swallow. Brenna *hated* secrets. Professional, personal—either way, she just didn't like them. She'd gotten *divorced* over a secret, after all—a secret affair. But it sounded as if she was about to have one dropped on her anyway.

"I've watched you grow in this business the last few years, Brenna. You're a quick learner, smart, responsible, and people like you. Plus, you're nice. In a city like L.A., you don't always *find* a lot of nice, and that makes you a commodity."

She was a commodity? When had *that* happened? But no matter— maybe this meant she was getting a raise. Maybe a *secret* raise no one else was getting? A secret like that she could probably keep. "Thank you, Mr. Jenkins. I've really loved learning about the music business since coming to work here."

"You may not realize this, Brenna, but you probably know the ins and outs of this company better than most people in this office. I hear you on the phone with everyone from our artists to our distributors, and you know what you're doing. To a degree that I think it's a sin to keep you in your current position."

At this, Brenna blinked. This wasn't just a raise?

"I want to groom you to be Blue Night's next A&R rep," Jenkins said—and she struggled not to let her jaw drop.

He wanted to give *her*—little Brenna Cayton from Centerville, Ohio—the most coveted position at the label? Most of the people who worked there, from the mailroom guy on up, had taken jobs at Blue Night with the aspiration of someday advancing to the glamorous post of artist and repertoire representative, scouting for and signing new talent. She, on the other hand, had not. She'd simply needed a job, gone on an interview. She found it fulfilling enough just to work at a cool record label. But to be that cool label's A&R person—wow, talk about a head rush.

Then it hit her. "Is Damon leaving? Going to one of the majors?"

Damon Andros *was* Blue Night Records to the industry—and the paparazzi. His heart-stopping sex appeal combined with his rock star persona to make him deliciously photo-worthy, especially when out partying with rock bands or on the arm of the latest female pop sensation. He was also Blue Night's sole A&R rep—so successful and well-known in the biz that there was no need for anyone else. Brenna attributed the label's accomplishments just as much to Damon Andros as she did to Jenkins.

Whose smile stayed in place but stiffened. "That's where the secret comes in."

"Oh?" Brenna held her breath, waiting.

"It's like this," her boss said, tilting his head. "Despite Damon's obvious success, over time he's started to . . . become a liability. If you don't believe me, just ask Kelly—she takes the calls from the reporters, fields the rumors. But I'm sure you don't *have* to ask her—because everyone knows."

Brenna nodded shortly, sighing. There *were* rumors. That Damon Andros ran a modern-day casting couch—signing women only after they'd slept with him. That he partied illicitly hard with the musicians he hung out with. He was the L.A. music scene's official bad boy. "I just didn't realize Damon's behavior had any significant impact on Blue Night's business." After all, it was a rock-n-roll lifestyle and this was La La Land.

"Fortunately, it's been a slow-coming thing. But now I've got Claire Starr threatening to sue us, claiming he wouldn't give her a contract until she had sex with him." Starr was a recent Blue Night one-hit wonder whose bad attitude had gotten her ousted from a label that usually nurtured performers and stuck with them through ups and downs. "Could be sour grapes since we dropped her, but on the other hand, it's the kind of publicity that could kill us, and whether or not it's true, his general behavior makes it plausible." A hopeful smile slid back onto Jenkins' face. "So, would you like to hear my proposition?"

Sadly, despite how exciting it was, this whole thing was suddenly making Brenna break out into a sweat. Still, she said, "Sure."

"I want to announce that we're adding you as an A&R rep due to our growth over the last couple of years, and I want Damon to begin training you—starting on his scouting trip to Vegas next week. You'll shadow his every move. He'll show you the ropes, introduce you around, teach you how to spot a star as opposed to a flash in the pan.

"As for Damon's fate, I'm holding steady until we see what happens with Claire. But the minute she sues, he's gone. That might be next week, next month, or never—we'll have to let it play out. Either way, I want you ready to take over. And . . . if it works out that Damon can clean up his act and put a more professional face on Blue Night, I won't leave you out in the cold. If I end up keeping Damon on the payroll, it's safe to say we'll continue making good money, and I'll need you *both* out there finding new talent.

"In the meantime, everything I've told you about Damon stays between you and me. To the rest of the world, you're training for a *new* position, not Damon's existing one. Got it?"

She drew her lips together, again trying to hide the nervous swallow. "And that includes Damon? He has no idea he's going to be grooming me to take his job when you fire him?"

Jenkins answered with a succinct but conclusive nod.

Okay, regroup. Your boss has just offered you the opportunity of a lifetime. And to get it, all you have to do is lie your ass off to the sexiest guy you've ever encountered. For a week. Maybe longer. Oh, and you have to lie to everyone else about it, too.

Her stomach churned.

"Can I count on you, Brenna? Are you on board?"

For a dream job? "Definitely." What else could she say?

Two

She knew she'd just promised to keep a big, ugly secret from everyone, but the moment Brenna rose from her chair, she planned on making a beeline to Kelly. She could trust Kelly. And she had to tell *somebody* or she'd never survive this.

Yet as she exited Jenkins' office, eyes cast toward the floor, her gaze fell on a pair of masculine black boots, small silver buckles on the sides. She stopped, looked up slowly, and found none other than Damon Andros standing before her. Her blood ran cold even as her body tingled with unadulterated lust. Except for the blood running cold part, because of the impending lie, it was her usual reaction to him.

Of course, she'd learned to push that down. Because it only made sense. Every woman in the office—or on the planet, for that matter— went gaga when Damon Andros walked into a room, all sexy ripped jeans and vintage T-shirts, his wavy black hair brushing his shoulders, and his dark eyes looking like a place where you could easily drown. There was no point in wallowing in it, so she'd simply learned to look away, not let herself get lost in that intense brown gaze, not let herself imagine how it would feel to be pressed against that bulge behind his zipper.

And even after three years, she barely knew him. He worked from home—or from local clubs, or various scouting locations—only stopping in once every week or so to meet with Jenkins behind a closed door. He didn't come to office happy hours or luncheons or Christmas parties—he just sauntered in, all rock star hot and confident, scarcely glancing at her as he went by. Of course, she usually got a short, not-unfriendly "Hey." Which is what he gave her now—as her eyes met his and her panties dampened.

"Hey," she said in return, trying to hide her reaction.

"He's in?" He motioned behind her to Jenkins' office.

"Yeah." It was the most complex answer she could muster.

He gave a short nod in response and headed inside, shutting the door.

And she stopped, turning to stare at the slab of wood that had just separated them, her heart still beating too fast.

Soon, very *little* would separate them. She was going to spend a week in close quarters with the man—Damon Andros, Greek god—soaking up his knowledge, practically breathing his very breath.

And probably lusting. A lot.

Because it would be way harder to push it down when she was with him all the time, looking at that gorgeous face, wanting to run her fingers through that soft mane of hair.

But she'd just have to be professional about it. And sometimes, when you knew a guy was *that* completely out of your range, it was just easier—healthier—not to think of him sexually at all and concentrate on the business at hand. In this case, stealing his job without his knowledge.

She cringed, remembering the deal she'd just made with the devil—and found it surprisingly effortless to think of her boss that way. Then she made the intended beeline to Kelly's office down the hall, where *she* was now the one closing the door.

"Did you get the scoop?" Kelly glanced up from her computer screen, still looking model-perfect in her fitted red suit, her blond hair swept up on top of her head.

Brenna blinked nervously in reply. "Oh yeah, I got it."

"Then spill."

"It's a secret."

"But you're going to tell me anyway, right?"

Brenna leaned closer. "Just swear you won't tell anyone, Kel. Jenkins would probably fire me if this gets out—from *both* my jobs." She rolled her eyes at the craziness of it all.

Kelly raised her eyebrows. "Both?"

Brenna let out a breath, then sat down on the corner of Kelly's tidy desk and told her everything, concluding with her impending trip to Vegas, on which she would be leaving in only four ridiculously short days.

To her vast surprise, when she finished Kelly was smiling. "Problem solved," her friend said. "Instant lover. Just add lust and stir."

Brenna's jaw dropped. *"What?"*

"You heard me. Damon is the perfect lover for you. No fuss, no muss, no long or messy attachment. What happens in Vegas stays in Vegas. It's the perfect fuck."

Brenna blinked again, barely knowing which aspect of this to tackle first. "Okay, to start with, Damon Andros has barely ever even looked me in the eye—so I'm pretty sure he's not dying to get me into bed. And to end with—*are you even listening to me?* Jenkins intends for me to baldly lie to Damon for an entire week during which I will be with him during every waking second! That's seven full days and nights of lying."

Kelly appeared unfazed. "Let's focus on the nights. And on the fucking, not the lying. Because trust me, with a few tweaks, he *will* be dying to get you into bed. You're a very lucky girl, Brenna," her friend said with a confident smile, as if this were a done deal. "You get to have down and dirty sex with Damon Andros, something most women only dream about. I mean, doesn't the man just make your pussy quiver?"

Brenna simply slapped her hand to her forehead. "You're crazy. No, wait—you're driving *me* crazy. I need your help with a moral dilemma and all you can talk about is sex."

But it was as if Kelly was in her own little world now. "I'm taking you shopping this weekend. Block out all of Saturday and plan to get an early start at the Third Street Promenade. Wear your most supportive bra. Or, actually, never mind. We'll get *new* bras—you're going to need some very hot lingerie. And I'll wrangle you an appointment with my hairdresser. He's always booked solid, but for me, he'll squeeze."

Brenna merely sighed, exhausted even though it wasn't yet 9 A.M. "I can't *afford* your hairdresser. And what's wrong with my clothes?"

"Nothing. They're great for sending out that I'm-going-through-a-bad-divorce-leave-me-alone message. Not so much, though, for the do-me message."

Brenna sucked in her breath. "I don't want to be *done*. And even if I did, Damon would not be the guy." He was totally hot, but just as totally out of her league. Out of her *universe*. To the point of being intimidating. She'd be embarrassed to even express interest in him since surely he'd find it laughable. Or maybe pathetic.

Then she shook her head, thoroughly exasperated. "But to get back to the actual *point*—I'm not concerned about sex. I don't need a man, remember? What I'm concerned about is . . . this is sort of like I'm stealing his job. And lying to him about it—to get him to *help* me steal his job. It's despicable."

Kelly shrugged, finally shifting her focus to the problem at hand. "Maybe, maybe not. It's all in your perspective. On one hand, he brought this on himself. It's not that he's really doing anything other people aren't, but he's failed to use even a modicum of discretion and now it's coming back to bite him in the ass. On the other, you *are* going to be participating in a big lie that benefits you, which *does* make you guilty as charged." Then she leaned slightly forward, narrowing her gaze on Brenna. "That said, we're talking about a dream job here, and Jenkins wants *you* for the part. It's an enormous opportunity, and you'd be a fool to pass it up. So that's why you need to get your head on straight about this. You have to commit to the lie, commit to the sin."

Brenna drew in her breath, chest tightening. "I *hate* lying." Now that she thought about it, it had been a lot easier to listen to Kelly's plans for an imaginary seduction than to remember she was going to have to lie to a guy who'd done nothing wrong to her.

"How about this?" Kelly suggested. "How about we don't think of it as lying? Instead, we'll think of it as . . . ambition. Going after the brass ring. Getting something you really want. Because as mild-mannered as you are, my dear Brenna, I can see it in your eyes already. You want this job—bad."

God help her, she did. She loved music. She'd come to love it even more since landing at Blue Night. To help determine what people listened to, and to have the power to give musicians a real shot at stardom, at making their dreams come true—it would be amazing. And already she could taste the thrill—and the fulfillment—it would bring her. "I just wish I didn't feel so guilty about how I'm going to get it."

Again, Kelly shrugged. "Look at it this way. Where better to do something wrong than Sin City?"

THE FIRST NIGHT

"Sin is geographical."
—Bertrand Russell

One

Brenna arrived in Las Vegas with a new wardrobe, a new hair color, and a new attitude. Not about sex with Damon Andros, but about the job. She'd talked herself into believing Kelly was right—that this was just the way business was done in the entertainment industry. It wasn't an ethics issue—it was simply how the game was played. Damon Andros would surely view it that way if the situation were reversed.

Damon had flown from Los Angeles to Vegas on the same day that Brenna made the five-hour drive across the Mojave Desert. Good old Jenkins—happy to make her lie, and just as happy not to offer her a plane ticket, explaining that they were still an indie label, after all, and money didn't grow on trees. "Once you're in the A&R seat, though," he'd promised her, "the red carpet will be rolled out for you."

God knew this wasn't where she expected to find herself at the age of thirty—starting a whole new career, and crossing a desert to do it. But maybe a big, new, high-profile job would somehow give her back the sense of security her divorce had stolen.

She'd tried to concentrate on that as she'd prayed her car wouldn't overheat in the hot May temperatures, and as she'd driven, she'd actually spotted more than one mirage—tricks played by the sun, convincing her she saw a large, smooth body of water, only to discover as she grew nearer that it was simply more flat, brown land.

So it was a relief, even if a bit overwhelming, to finally hit the Vegas

Strip. She'd never been to Sin City before, but a drive up the ten-lane street revealed it to be all she had imagined. Even during the daytime hours, millions of lights flickered and danced to either side of the famous boulevard. She passed enormous fountains, roller coasters that sped by high above her car, and even whole buildings that changed colors at will. She spied the Brooklyn Bridge, an Egyptian pyramid, the Eiffel Tower, the Roman Coliseum, and an erupting volcano—and thought it was as if the whole world had collided here, reshaping itself into pure spectacle.

Pulling in at the Venetian, where side-by-side rooms had been reserved for her and Damon, she followed a winding lane to the front doors. She was astounded by the scope of the place even *before* driving up under the awning that covered at least a dozen lanes of one-way traffic: a busy but efficient menagerie of cars and luggage carts and suitcases manned by guys dressed in the stripes and neck sashes of Italian gondoliers.

One of them rushed to open her car door. "Welcome to the Venetian. Checking in?"

"Yes."

She was checking in to the Venetian. And checking in to Las Vegas—the place where people came to sin.

And already, as she strolled through the doors into the ornately huge lobby complete with frescoes on the arched ceiling high above, a change somehow began to come over her. It started slowly, yet it was easy to recognize, and . . . shockingly easy to embrace.

It wasn't about the new clothes. Or the new hair. And she wasn't even certain it was about the job she'd come here to steal.

Because it seemed to grow from within her, echoing outward from her very core.

She could scarcely explain it to herself, but . . . she simply felt different here.

Filled with a strange, new energy. Ready to make changes in her life.

Maybe it *was* about the new clothes and hair, for all she knew. Maybe it *was* about the job. The truth was, she'd told herself that this *had* to happen, that she *had* to become the sort of person who could play this game. Yet something about the very aura of this place was—that quickly—helping the process along, making it suddenly feel smooth as silk, and at the same time exciting as . . . sin.

As she stepped up to the lavish registration desk and gave her name to the clerk, a heady sense of freedom coursed through her veins. A sense of *newness*. And if ever there had been a time in her life when it would be beneficial to be someone new, it was now.

Because this was Vegas, baby. Enormous, overwhelming, a stunningly bright oasis built in the desert purely for the pursuit of pleasure—and like it or not, she was about to immerse herself in it.

Two

The room was plush, not to mention enormous, quickly making her decide maybe she was going to like this being an A&R rep thing—even without the airplane perks just yet.

She was busy gaping at the huge, tiled bathroom when she noticed—from the corner of her eye—a blinking light on the room's phone, informing her she already had a message. Perching on the edge of the bed and pressing the message retrieval button, she found herself blown away by the mere sound of Damon's deep voice. "Brenna. You've had a long drive, so take the afternoon to relax. Then meet me tonight at Mon Ami Gabi in front of the Paris at seven. I look forward to working with you."

He never identified himself. Because he didn't have to.

Arrogant, she thought, rolling her eyes.

But also sexy. And sexy could make up for arrogant in a lot of ways. She supposed she'd never actually heard him string together so many words before, and his voice alone, even without his looks to accompany it, had just made her nether regions go warm.

Not that she could afford to think about him being sexy. Or about him making her warm in the panties. Nope, to Brenna, Damon Andros was now simply a means to an end, a stepping stone to an exciting new career. And Kelly had made it clear: he'd brought this on himself. Soon this week of subterfuge would be history, and she'd have a shiny new job to show for it.

Of course, by the time she was getting ready for dinner a few hours later, she'd grown nervous. Like her old self, her *real* self—nervous little Brenna who answered phones and processed contracts and generally stayed in the background, nervous little Brenna who was afraid to be around an ultra-hip guy like Damon for more than a minute or two.

But a look in the mirror reminded her that she'd decided *not* to be nervous little Brenna anymore. Hair that had been mousy brown a few days ago was now a warm, sexy shade of auburn, done in a stylish cut that fell straight but angled around her face and shoulders. And the body she generally kept covered in fairly conservative clothes now appeared much curvier than usual in well-fitted jeans, pointy-toed ankle boots, and a fitted white blouse that revealed the beaded cami underneath, along with a shadow of cleavage. Kelly had officially declared this Brenna's confident-cosmopolitan-chick-on-the-move look, and she couldn't deny that it actually made her feel that way. A pair of new sunglasses completed the image.

She knew the Paris Hotel was far enough away to warrant driving or taking a cab, but she decided to walk. As fabulously luxurious as the Venetian was, she felt hungry to see more of Vegas and figured doing it by foot was the best way to take in the details.

What she discovered as she set out was a strange city of walkways and escalators and bridges that seemed to lead in every direction without necessarily making it clear where they would take you. So she followed her instincts, *and* the crowds, and felt miniscule in comparison to it all. She'd never been to the Grand Canyon, but she'd heard people talk about feeling small there, like an incidental speck. She thought she'd just discovered the *urban* Grand Canyon, a place at once grand and opulent yet also gaudy, emitting an underlying sense of seediness that somehow wafted around her in the air.

Pausing on the sidewalk, she found herself staring across wide, bustling Las Vegas Boulevard at the grandeur of Caesars Palace with its manicured lawns and pristine white Roman-style structures—when the view was suddenly obscured by a moving billboard being pulled up the Strip by a truck, displaying a busty woman in barely-there lingerie and the words WANNA PARTY WITH ME? along with a phone number. Something in Brenna's chest tightened, and indeed, already she understood that she'd landed in a place of true contradiction—more specifically, a place where manicured lawns and hookers coexisted peacefully.

Continuing on, she passed families complete with baby strollers followed by groups of young women in slinky dresses clearly headed out clubbing. Limousines sleekly traveled the same streets as crowded city buses. Mexican men stood on corners foisting cards bearing pictures of nude call girls and their phone numbers at every person who passed by, regardless of age or gender. When Brenna unknowingly accepted one and on it found *Bambi, age 21*, she flinched and let it drop, only then realizing the walkway was littered with them. Sin literally covered the ground here.

Approaching the Paris Hotel, Brenna spotted the café that fronted the building, looking much like she imagined the cafés that lined the Champs-Elysées in the *real* Paris, where she hoped to go someday. The Vegas version of the Eiffel Tower shadowed the streetside eatery, and she couldn't help being delighted by Damon's choice of restaurant. She knew it wasn't really Paris, but she was willing to enjoy the imitation and happy to be reimmersed in the more opulent aspects of Sin City.

That's when she spotted him, already seated and perusing the menu. He wore two small hoops in both earlobes, and even sitting down, his muscular frame made his simple vintage Ramones T-shirt and ripped, faded jeans look like the height of fashion. The mere sight of him caused her breasts to swell within the confines of her bra, her jeans feeling snugger at the crux of her thighs and making her tingle.

He didn't see her, of course—because she looked so different from the last time he'd encountered her—but that gave her a chance to pause and study him privately, from a distance, for longer than she ever had before.

When he raised his eyes to a waitress, pointing to a selection from the wine list, his brown gaze sparkled so vibrantly that Brenna's heartbeat kicked up. The way the young waitress smiled down at him, Brenna knew *she'd* caught that heart-stopping twinkle, as well. He smiled back at the girl, another thing Brenna had never witnessed, at least not at length, and—oh my—it was so stunning she nearly melted into the sidewalk.

And she had to spend a *week* with him? Concentrating on *work*? Trying to hide her *lust*? Trying to *fight* it?

She let out a sigh—just as Damon's gaze fell on *her.*

He must have felt me looking at him.

Except he clearly didn't recognize her, still. Which was at once embarrassing . . . and thrilling.

Because his expression was blatantly sensual, sexual, the look of a man silently making a move on a woman using only his eyes. And very effectively, too.

Oh God, Kelly was right—Damon Andros actually thought she was *hot!*

Trying her damnedest to be "new Brenna," she took her best shot at offering him an easy smile, then made her way inside the hotel to reach the gated patio enclosing the café. On her way, she lectured herself—but not with her usual *I don't need a man* mantras. Now she had switched over to: *You can do this. You can be cool and confident and sexy. You can be new Brenna.*

Not that it would lead anywhere, of course. Once he realized who she was, it would be strictly business between them.

And that was okay. Because she might not be doing her affirmations right now, but despite everything, she remained resolute about not needing a man, least of all one she couldn't realistically have. She simply wanted Damon to respect her, see her as an equal, as someone who could do this job. And if he suddenly thought she was attractive, too . . . well, that was just a perk that would add to her confidence.

She exited back out into the warmth of the night in the café area, making her way past couples at small round tables until she reached Damon and sat down across from him, smoothly lifting her sunglasses to the top of her head.

Then she watched him blink.

"Brenna?" His dark brows drew slightly together. God, he was beautiful.

"Surprise," she said, pleasing herself with how confident and comfortable she sounded. "I'm a redhead now. I figured—new job, new look. What do you think?"

"You look fabulous," he told her, and their eyes met again, and this time it was almost fatal.

Because she was so *close* to him now. And that look—that intense, oh-so-sexy look—was pinning her in place, almost holding her down, taking control of her. If she'd suffered the first twinges of arousal a moment ago upon spotting him... well, that had been nothing compared to this. The juncture of her thighs spasmed as she—almost involuntarily—thrust her breasts forward and ran her tongue along her upper lip. Casting her most provocative smile, she said a low, cool, "Thanks."

Despite all the times she'd seen him in the office, this was the first time they'd really been face-to-face, the sole focus of each other's attention—and it was also the first time in her life she'd ever had such a visceral, physical reaction to a man. One of Kelly's many raw, out-there comments suddenly came back to her: *Doesn't the man just make your pussy quiver?* Brenna seldom thought of her body in such terms, but... maybe *new* Brenna did. Because her pussy was definitely quivering *now*, no doubt about it.

Damon's small smile looked slightly predatory, but she didn't mind at all. "I was surprised when Jenkins informed me you were coming on board in A&R," he told her. He was talking business, yet his eyes still said *sex, sex, sex.*

Something in it inspired her to be saucy—apparently another part of the new her. She raised her eyebrows, flashed a playful grin. "Afraid of a little competition?"

He laughed—a deep, throaty sound that kept the spot between her legs humming. "Not at all, babe. Just didn't know you had those aspirations."

Normally, she hated it when a guy called her *babe* or *honey* without really knowing her. But like everything else about him, when Damon did it, it was sexy as hell. Even the remaining last hints of a New York accent sounded seductive coming from *that* mouth.

"I didn't," she answered, "and frankly, I was just as surprised as you when Jenkins offered me the position. But I love Blue Night, and I have a passion for music, so it seemed like the opportunity of a lifetime."

Damon nodded slowly, his warm chocolate eyes narrowing. "It is. And though I had doubts about how you'd fit in the role, I'm not worried anymore."

She tilted her head, getting almost comfortable with the new her. "A new hair color and a few new clothes make that much of a difference?"

"It's not the clothes," he said with a soft head shake. "It's the attitude. You've got it. I can tell. You've embraced this."

"Completely," she told him. *I've embraced wanting this job. And lying to get it.*

And there was something else Brenna was on the verge of embracing, too. Her lust for him. Her plan had *not* been to spend time ogling him, wanting to get in his pants. But she clearly did, with a force unrivaled.

Yet that still didn't mean she planned to do anything about it. It was one thing to be "new Brenna" in looks, in her job—but it was another altogether when it came to men, and sex. So she would just have to lust *quietly*, her nipples jutting through her bra, her cunt veritably vibrating against her jeans. And, wow—it looked like new Brenna used even *more* blunt, naughty words. Too much time spent with Kelly this past weekend, clearly.

Just then, the wine arrived—a nice Pinot Grigio—and they ordered dinner, both starting with onion soup. Conversation turned in the direction she'd expected—to the music biz, and Damon explained how indie labels differed from the majors, what kinds of talent he sought for Blue Night, and the tasks a typical week might include.

"Scouting trips are fun, but once an act is signed, your job will include a lot of hand-holding. You'll answer questions, pump them up when they're worried, do your damnedest to make sure the work stays true to their vision and ours, accompany them to media gigs, celebrate with them when their CD hits the shelves, and be available to take phone calls at two a.m. when they're just not feelin' the love. You're basically the performer's connection to Blue Night. Professionally. Artistically. Emotionally. And while you're holding all these hands, you're still out there listening for the next new sound that might be a little too left of center for BMG or Sony. Think you can handle all that?"

The truth was, Brenna hadn't realized the far-reaching aspects of the job. But she *could* handle it. In fact, old Brenna had always been a pretty good hand-holder by nature. So she said, "Absolutely," and he flashed a sexy grin in reply, making her pussy surge anew.

"Good answer," he said. "Because all that was designed to make you balk, even though it's true—and you passed the test."

She raised her eyebrows, still confident, almost even flirtatious. "Will there be lots of these? Tests?"

He leaned back slightly, brown eyes seeming to size her up. But this look was about more than sex appeal—it was about whether she could do the job. He finally gave a succinct head shake. "I can already tell you're a pro. From here on out, it's all about teaching you the business."

Brenna's chest tightened with the pleasure of having earned his respect. Not to mention the pleasure of just being able to look at him and soak up all that male beauty.

After their entrees arrived, Damon regaled her with stories behind some of their biggest successes—where he'd found them and what had made him want to sign them. "I can't teach that kind of instinct," he said, cutting into his filet mignon, "but I can tell you what I was thinking, feeling—and hope you'll glean something from it."

Darkness was falling, the bright lights of the Vegas Strip starting to make the night glow, and traffic on the boulevard grew heavier as people set out for the evening. When another of those moving billboards came to a stop just beyond the sidewalk next to them, Brenna couldn't help glancing up to see a doe-eyed brunette, topless, her hands barely covering her voluminous breasts. LONELY? CALL ME, the sign said.

Like before, it jarred her. It wasn't surprising that Las Vegas was crawling with "escorts," but it *was* somehow surprising to see the evidence so very *out there,* a blatant reminder that people came here to sin among the neon.

"Something wrong?" Damon asked, drawing her gaze back to his.

Swell—she'd been caught gaping at an ad for prostitution. "Just a little taken aback," she admitted. "I've never been to a place like this before."

"You've never been to Vegas?" He sounded surprised.

"No, I'm a Sin City virgin. Or I was until today."

"So what do you think of it?" He tilted his head, appearing truly curious.

Glancing up the Strip, where she could see New York, New York and the Excalibur, spires and towers gleaming in the night, all that light somehow beckoning, she said, "It's glossy on the top, but dirty underneath. It's . . . seamy, yet somehow alluring."

He pressed his lips together, nodding, clearly absorbing her response.

"It's got a bit of a wreck-on-the-highway quality to it," she went on. "With a wreck, you know you won't like what you see, but you still have to look. Here, you know what you find may not be pretty, but you're going to immerse yourself in it anyway."

Draining his second glass of wine, he asked, "And how is it that an L.A. girl has never been to Las Vegas?"

Indeed, Vegas was a quick weekend getaway from the coast for lots of people, and sort of a home-away-from-home for the entertainment industry. "I'm not really an L.A. girl," she explained. "I just moved west from Ohio three years ago for my husband's job."

"I didn't know you were married." Had she imaged that hint of disappointment in his voice? His gaze dropped to her left hand, curled casually around the stem of her wineglass.

Despite relishing his interest, her hand felt naked, and she still hated having to tell him, "I'm recently divorced."

Keep being new Brenna, she told herself. But the dissolution of her marriage had been the greatest devastation of her life. If it hadn't gotten dark out, she'd have slid her sunglasses back on to hide her eyes.

"I'm sorry," Damon said.

"Don't be." She swilled a drink of wine for courage. "He was a jerk. The cheating kind, to be exact."

"Hell," he said. "That sucks."

She raised her eyebrows, tried for a smile, and wondered if *he'd* ever cheated on anyone. "Yeah, it does—*did*. But it's very over now, and I'm very ready to move on."

Yikes, what had she just said? Had it sounded like a come-on? *Please, God, don't let him think it sounded like a come-on.* And what had happened to *I don't need a man?* She took another sip of wine, her whole body still whirring with the potent arousal he inspired.

"Well, Vegas is a great place for moving on," he told her.

Oh geez—he thought she wanted to party. Maybe not necessarily with *him,* but just in general—and that was bad enough. Even though *he* definitely liked to party, she wanted him to see her as cool, confident, *professional* Brenna—not as a party girl on the rebound.

Regroup. Put your cosmopolitan face back on. Pretend you're not getting drunk.

To her surprise, it actually succeeded. She sounded utterly at ease when she said, "I'm here to work. Play will have to wait for another time."

"Another good answer," he told her. "But I wouldn't complain if you wanted to play just a *little.*" His eyes sparkled again, and she feared she would come in her panties.

Staying cool was becoming more of a challenge every minute, and it was all she could do not to choke on her answer, but she managed to get one out. "To be honest, I'm . . . not sure Vegas holds the kind of play I'm interested in."

He cast a skeptical look. "You can get just about anything your heart desires here."

Not true, she wanted to say. *You couldn't get love. You couldn't get a husband who didn't cheat.*

Oh boy, she *was* drunk. This was bad.

Whatever you do, don't go all maudlin on him. Carefully, she concocted an answer. "Let's just say . . . sex seems a little too . . . out in the open here. For my taste anyway."

"Ah. And you like it in private."

Okay, she should have been *more* careful. Why on earth had she mentioned sex, of all things? But she had to go with it now, so she answered honestly. "Afraid so."

And then it happened—a vision flashed through her head.

Her, having sex, with *him.*

His naked body atop hers, moving, pounding into her, his hard cock filling her with each deep stroke.

Jesus, when on earth had she started using words like "cock"? She wasn't even sure she could blame Kelly for this one. It was the wine, she decided, even as Damon reached to refill her glass.

"Just half," she told him quickly, and he stopped pouring but emptied the rest of the bottle into his own.

"This is a very man-centric place, isn't it?" she heard herself asking without even weighing it. Damn wine.

He tilted his head, his expression indulgent. She hoped it meant he liked her openness, as opposed to thinking she was some kind of kook. "I guess that's a fair assessment."

"I mean, I just don't think that kind of thing appeals to women—selling sex on a billboard."

His eyes glimmered with quiet amusement. "Hey, if you're gonna sell sex, isn't that as good a place as any?"

"Point taken, but maybe it's the whole idea of *selling* sex that turns me off. I suppose men just aren't as offended by that."

He shrugged, grinned. "I'll admit it takes a lot to offend me. But you know, there are billboards with guys on them, too. Male strippers, that kinda thing. Maybe you'd like *that*."

She shook her head instantly, the honesty spilling from her now, like it or not. "I just think it's weird when sex is so . . . on display, like any other ad." She let her tone shift into that of a TV commercial: "Try our new wireless plan. See Celine Dion in concert at the Mirage. Buy an hour of sex with a stranger."

He offered a knowing smile. "Look at it this way. Las Vegas is . . . Disney World for adults."

"But instead of Mickey and Minnie, here they have . . . strippers and whores?"

He laughed lightly. "Something like that. Anything goes here." He lowered his voice, looked her in the eye. "Anything."

And something in the way he said that last word made her wet all over again. Wet and hungry.

She suffered the insane urge to reach across the table, grab him, and tell him she wanted him, in private or even in public—that despite all her claims, that part didn't even matter right now.

Yikes, talk about your visceral physical reaction to a man!

New rule: Don't drink in his presence—it brings out the bad girl in you.

Interesting, because she'd never known there *was* a bad girl in her.

"More wine?" he asked. "I can order another bottle."

She held up her hand. "Thanks, but no."

"You sure?"

"*Very* sure." *Sure I'm going to self-combust before the evening is through.*

Because that bad girl she'd just found was barely holding herself in check. Her whole body pulsed with wanting—and an uncharacteristic sense of wild abandon. And maybe it was the wine. And maybe it was Damon. And maybe it was this place, this lusty, lavish, sinful place.

But worse, maybe it was *all* of it—mixing and gelling together to bring out an untamed sexual response she'd never before experienced.

And if that was the case, it was going to be a very long week.

Three

The cab ride back to the hotel was too hot—the windows were down, no AC going—but Brenna's main focus was the fact that Damon sat with his legs apart, the way guys often did, and his denim-clad knee touched hers.

Insane how a tiny touch like that could make her so hot *inside*, too.

They didn't speak—the cabbie had techno music blaring, making the car's seat pulse beneath her. But as they passed through the Venetian's vast floral-scented lobby a few minutes later, Damon told her to come to his suite the next morning. They would order breakfast in the room, he said, then spend the day going over Blue Night's various contracts—she would learn what she could offer, which terms were flexible and which were not.

She tried to concentrate on their conversation but found it difficult as they made their way onto the elevator with three young, good-looking, jock-type guys. As the elevator rose skyward, she found herself *feeling* all the "maleness" around her, and at the same time feeling so utterly "female" that she could barely understand it.

She liked sex, of course, but she had never been a woman who got *hungry* for it. Hungry without rhyme or reason, as if she simply had to have it and would take it in any form in which it came. But that's how she suddenly felt in the confines of the elevator that seemed to swirl with testosterone. That's how she felt after spending a mere couple of hours with Damon Andros. She knew he was hot, but she couldn't believe she was suffering such a crazy reaction to the guy!

When the elevator doors opened on their floor, she stepped out, her body moving with that fluid sense of ease that came with just a little intoxication. Only now she didn't know if she remained drunk from the wine, or if she was only drunk on Damon.

When he walked her to her door, she turned to look up and found him standing close, his gaze on her mouth.

It made her want to kiss him. Hard.

Made it so that kissing him, pressing against him, rubbing her body against his, seemed the only natural, sensible thing to do.

And when he lifted his eyes to hers, that only made it worse. Because his expression said that if she *did* kiss him right now, he would respond. He was so near that she could almost feel him without touching him, and his musky masculine scent filled her senses.

But kissing him would be stupid, stupid, stupid. You have to work with him day and night for a week—possibly longer. And you're stealing his job. You cannot *kiss him.*

"Ready for this?" he asked.

Her pussy flooded with possibility. "For what?"

"The world of A&R," he said smoothly.

"Oh, of course," she replied with an airy quickness, at once relieved and disappointed to be pulled back from the sexual precipice she'd been hovering upon.

"Get a good night's sleep."

Fat chance of that. "All right."

His voice went lower. "And I'll see you in the morning."

"Mmm-hmm," she murmured as Damon took her key card from her hand, their fingers brushing, and unlocked her door.

"Good night," he said softly.

Her eyes remained glued to his. "Good night."

And then she was stepping inside and the door was closing and he was gone, and she had the distinct feeling that she'd ended up in the wrong room. Or he had. Either way, they should have gone into one of the two rooms *together* and fucked like animals.

She let out a heavy breath and reminded herself once more why that couldn't happen.

Sex on the job was bad enough. Sex on the job with someone you were lying to was . . . freaking *heinous.*

And yet as she took off her clothes and slipped into a white cotton cami and fresh panties—because her others were soaked—desire still held her in its grip. And as she stood before the wide bathroom mirror washing her face and brushing her teeth, she grew keenly aware of her nipples pointing through her top, hard and sensitive, and of her cunt, swollen with want inside her bikini panties. And as she climbed beneath the fancy bedcoverings, she found herself lost in a mishmash of images: visions of her and Damon Andros, bodies naked and intertwined.

This was awful. There seemed no good answer. Having sex with him was a moral impossibility. But *not* having it, especially now that she sensed he'd be amenable to the idea, seemed insane, not to mention torturous. How had this even happened? Sure, she'd wanted to be someone new and different here—but not different *like this.* She could scarcely fathom the effect one mere evening in the man's presence had had on her.

But then Brenna remembered how you got through tough things. You didn't let yourself obsess over the big picture—you handled one moment, one problem, at a time. And the problem right now was getting to sleep, having a peaceful night.

So she bit her lip and let her hand ease under the covers, over her mound. She cupped herself, relieved to have any sensation there at all—*finally.* She wished, suddenly, that she'd been brave enough to buy a vibrator, and smart enough to travel with it. She wanted something inside her, deep.

She swirled two fingers across the engorged nub at the front of her pussy and let the pleasure melt through her. God—it was like having walked across the hot, barren desert and finally finding sweet water. Now she wanted to gulp it, so she pressed her fingers harder, lifted her pelvis against them.

She sighed and licked her upper lip and needed more. Yet she didn't *have* more, so instead she turned to fantasy. She imagined if Damon could see her right now. She imagined him knowing he'd *done* this to her, gotten her this hot. She wondered if there was any way he *could* know just how hot she was right now, and she envisioned him lying in bed on the other side of the wall that separated them, picturing her this way.

But, damn it, she *still* needed more, some other kind of stimulation. All of Las Vegas lay outside this room, sin upon sin upon sin taking place. How many people were doing something naughty right now within one short mile of her? Thousands, she would bet. So to lay in her bed rubbing herself somehow seemed . . . too simple, too drab, not befitting the atmosphere.

Strangely restless, she rose from the bed without a plan. Wandering the spacious room, she found herself standing before the minibar. Normally, she never even *opened* the minibar, outraged by the price gouging, but that was immaterial now. Peeking inside, she spied a row of tropical-flavored wine coolers. She pulled one out and twisted off the top, then took a long swallow, letting the alcohol warm her chest. Almost *any* physical sensation felt good at the moment, like a step toward relief.

Then she walked to the drapes that lined the outer wall of the room and, locating the center, opened them up. Wow! The move revealed a window wall that looked out over the Vegas Strip and its nightly show of lights. Dear God—how had she not realized this before now? She experienced it again—that sense that someone had built this city purely for people to be bad. And she wanted to be bad now, too—to somehow commune with this place.

Setting her wine cooler on a table, she lowered her panties, letting them drop to the floor, and stepped free of them. She sat down on the carpet, facing the window, legs spread. She still yearned for Damon to be here, touching her, fucking her, but her mantras, she tried to convince herself, were true. She *didn't* need a man—she could take care of her own needs.

Looking out on the lights, she stroked her fingers through her parted slit. Wet. Soft. She shivered, then reached for the wine cooler. Still touching herself with one hand, circling her fingers over her clit, she used the other to lift the bottle to her breast—hard, cold, moist against her nipple. The bottle's dewy sweat left her top damp, her nipple visibly darkening the white fabric, even with the lamps off. The Las Vegas Strip provided enough light in the room on its own.

Brenna's fingers slid down into the folds of her pussy, petting deeply, wanting to truly *feel* herself, *all* of herself, the way a man would explore her. The way *Damon* would surely explore her.

She pushed first one, then two fingers inside herself, then moved them in and out of the warm tunnel. Oh God, she wanted them to be Damon's cock—bigger, harder, sturdier, and more powerful than anything she could do to herself, even if she *had* brought a vibrator.

Withdrawing her fingers a moment later, she whirled them once more around her swollen clit, then reached inside her cami to squeeze one breast full in her hand. Then she lowered her open bottle between her thighs, pressing it there.

Mmm, God. So cool. And so wonderfully hard. Way too big, wide, but it still felt incredible as she began to move against it. She felt so dirty now. Dirty in a way she wanted to share with someone. Because she feared being this dirty by herself could also make her feel pretty damn lonely if she let it.

But she *couldn't* let it. So she looked out on the Vegas lights and imagined again that Damon was with her. Not only was he with her, he was telling her what to do. *Move the bottle up and down on your pussy. That's right. Faster. Faster. Yeah.*

Now take it away. Take it away and splash just a little wine on your cunt. To make you even wetter.

Biting her lip, she withdrew her gaze from the neon spectacle beyond the window and glanced down, spilling just a little of the cooler over her parted slit. She gasped at the cold splatter, then imagined Damon's deep, commanding voice again.

Touch yourself, Brenna. Stroke your fingers through your pussy.

She did. Extra wet now, like he'd wanted.

Yeah, like that. From the bottom all the way to the top. Press your fingers into the moist folds. Feel yourself. Feel yourself.

Now rub your clit for me.

She did that, too, moving two fingers in tight, hot circles overtop the protruding little nub.

Thrust against it.

She obeyed.

Rub harder, harder. Make yourself come. Look out on those lights, imagine all the dirty things people are doing out there, and make yourself come harder than you ever have before.

"Oh!" The orgasm was brutal, causing her body to buckle, her head to drop forward as her pelvis jerked in rough response. Each sensation echoed through her like a small explosion, ripping her apart, stealing her senses, her reason. All that mattered was pleasure, hard and consuming . . . until it ended.

And then she realized she was sitting half naked before a large window and had just gotten herself off with the help of a glass bottle.

Dear God.

This city was stealing more than her senses. She feared, already, it was on the verge of stealing . . . her soul.

Making of her something she wasn't.

Or . . . was it, more accurately, maybe just *redefining* her?

Showing her parts of herself she'd never known before?

Whatever the case, the really scary part was . . . she almost didn't care about all the reasons she couldn't have sex with Damon. She almost wanted to call him, listen to his deep-voiced hello, and say, simply, "Fuck me."

Setting the wine cooler aside, and not even thinking about her panties, she rose and went to the bed. Sitting down, she grabbed up the receiver. She looked at the instructions for dialing another room and keyed in the numbers.

Then she slammed down the phone before the call could go through, her heart pounding against her chest.

What had she been thinking?

She'd truly been *calling* him? To beg for *sex*?

Thank God she'd come to her senses.

Apparently, the relief the orgasm had provided had finally sunk in.

The relief, and the bit of shame from having to be so dirty alone. What insane behavior!

Suddenly, she was *glad* she'd been alone.

Just go to sleep. Don't think about this anymore. It never happened.

You don't need a man. You don't need a man.

You need a fabulous job.

Tomorrow, you will meet with Damon and you will think about the job, not sex. You will do the job, without sex. The job is what's important here, the thing you really want.

I don't need a man, I don't need a man, I don't need a man.

THE SECOND NIGHT

"If it were possible to have a life absolutely free from every feeling of sin, what a terrifying vacuum it would be!"
—Cesare Pavese

One

The good news was that Brenna had, surprisingly, gotten a good night's sleep, after all. An orgasm could do that for you.

The bad news was that she woke up horrified to remember the previous night. Again, she felt relieved that she'd been by herself. But that wasn't stopping the horror. As she scurried to the window to snatch up her panties and put them on, then made her way to the bathroom, she thought about primal needs. And she finally understood how sex could turn people crazed and desperate sometimes. She'd never quite gotten that before now. Last night, however, sex had made her do something which, a mere day before, would have seemed unthinkable.

But it's your little secret. Your secret sin.

No one will ever know. Thank God!

She wasn't sure whether to blame Damon Andros or this place. One minute she'd been shocked and appalled at the city's seaminess, the next she'd been wanting to be a part of it, to somehow revel in it. Such opposing emotions made no sense to her.

Yet, again, she had to break it down and deal with the problem at hand. Which was that she had a whole week of Damon *and* this city ahead, so it didn't matter which one of them was causing her erratic reactions. She had to put last night behind her and focus on the work—nothing else.

Of course, when she stepped into the shower, she discovered that her body still felt ... overly sensitive. As she ran the soap over her skin—her breasts, her stomach, her thighs—she found herself also wanting to run it between her legs. The warm water beating down on her felt too good. Her own curves, as she washed, felt too lush.

Shit. This was not good. But she still had to deal, and she had to get serious about it.

So with that in mind, when she stepped out of the shower, she didn't put on any of the new clothes she'd brought with her. In fact, she dressed as plainly as she could, in a pair of jeans and a plain pink tee she'd packed more with an eye toward sleeping in it than wearing it out. And after blow-drying her brand-new auburn hair, rather than run the flatiron through it, she instead shoved it back into a small ponytail.

She considered not wearing makeup but decided that was going too far. She wanted to be plain, not totally unattractive—although she kept it to a minimum, applying just a little powder and lipstick and brushing on a bit of mascara.

Leaving the bathroom, she cringed at the sight of the open wine cooler still sitting on the table across the room. Rushing over, she closed her fingertips gingerly around the narrowest part of the bottle, twisted the lid back on, and deposited it in the nearest wastebasket. Yuck.

Then, looking to the door, she took a deep breath. *Last night's silliness is over. Done. Past. Today is about the serious business of learning your new job. So go over to Damon's room, but do not think of him sexually anymore. He is your trainer, your teacher, that's all.* With any luck, he wouldn't look so good in the morning, either.

As she grabbed up the leather portfolio she'd brought for taking notes, then grabbed her room key and headed for the door, she began to murmur, "I don't need a man. I don't need a man. I don't need a man."

Two

Damon opened the double doors to his deluxe suite to find Brenna on the other side. She didn't look like she had last night—but she was still damn cute in a tight little T-shirt that hugged her breasts well enough that he could see her nipples poking through. Of course, that made him wonder about her bra. Exactly what kind of bra did Brenna Cayton wear? Given that every time he saw her she looked entirely different, it was an impossible call, which made the question even more intriguing.

"Hey," she said, casting a small smile—and looking sheepish. He had no idea why. Just because there had been some chemistry flowing between them last night? It was undeniable, but neither had acted on it, so he didn't see it as a big deal.

"Hey," he said easily. "Come on in."

As she stepped into the tiled foyer, her eyes widened, taking in the place. "Oh my God."

"What?" he asked, laughing lightly.

She turned to look at him, a wisp of auburn hair falling free from her ponytail to frame her face. "I thought *my* room was great, but yours is . . . freaking fabulous."

She was right, but he'd stayed here so often that he sometimes forgot the sixteen-hundred-square-foot suite, featuring a dining table and a huge living area in addition to a bedroom and deluxe bath, wasn't your average hotel room. "Believe it or not, I need the space. If we find any acts we want to court or sign, I need a good place to talk business with them. And besides, before today is over, we're going to have contracts spread all over the living room." He'd brought along a file containing every contract variance he could think of to show her.

"Still . . . wow," she said, and he couldn't help enjoying her innocent exuberance. That bit of innocence had leaked out a little last night, too, when they'd talked about Vegas, and sex, even if she'd tried to hide it behind professional coolness. Maybe that was what he'd liked about her so much last evening—that she could be so professional and at the same time truly genuine.

"There's a room service menu on the table." He pointed to the dining area. "Let me know what you want and I'll place an order. Then we'll get to work."

"Sounds fun," she said, her expression filled with nothing but sincerity.

"Contracts—fun?" Arching one brow, he shook his head. "Not exactly. This is the tedious, boring part. But I promise it's the worst aspect of the job. That's why I figured we should get it out of the way, so everything else will seem better by comparison."

She gave her head a playful tilt, shoving that stray lock of hair behind one ear. "I'll have you know I've already *read* most of the contracts—just for fun, when I processed them—so this won't all be completely new to me. Although I don't know what it all means, I'm actually *interested* in this part, which means . . . if the rest is even better, I'm in great shape."

Damon's jaw dropped. "You read contracts for fun?"

She nodded enthusiastically—and looked cute as hell.

"No wonder Jenkins promoted you."

He kind of wanted to kiss her. Like he had last night, standing outside her door, looking into her pretty green eyes, feeling the heat moving between them. Without meaning to, he let his gaze drop to her breasts again, to the delectable sight of her nipples jutting against that pink fabric, and his dick went half hard.

But then he pointed back to the menu. "Pick something for breakfast," he said again to break the tension that had just grown so quick and invisible between them. Because fucking someone you worked with closely was never a good idea. That had been the only thing to keep him from inviting her back to his room last night, and it was a good enough reason this morning, too. Damn, when had Brenna the office girl turned into Brenna the hot chick? How the hell had he missed it?

He gave his head a slight shake, trying to clear the lust out, and turned away from her to grab some files.

The truth was, he wasn't well-practiced at pushing down his desires. He was single, he liked to have fun, and he'd never seen any reason not to indulge in good, hot sex when he found the opportunity—which, in his world, was often. What he never understood was why such news made the damn papers. When had he become a celebrity? Why did anyone give a shit who he slept or partied with?

Whatever the reason, though, it seemed his social life *did* qualify as entertainment for the masses these days, as well as good fodder for the rumor mill, and he knew his image needed an overhaul. He didn't care what people thought of him, but he sensed Jenkins feared he was starting to give the label a bad reputation, and if there was one thing he didn't want to risk, it was his job.

And fucking the girl he was training probably wouldn't do a lot to convince anyone he was a decent guy who *didn't* demand sex of female performers before signing them.

Not that Brenna would fuck and tell. He knew that instinctively. It went back to what he'd felt from her last night—a professional maturity mixed with an underlying . . . *realness* that was almost sweet.

But he still couldn't do it. And spending this week with her *without* doing it would be good practice.

"Know what you want yet?" he asked, turning back to face her.

"Blueberry pancakes," she said.

And their eyes met. And he experienced it again, that urge to move closer, lean into her, press his mouth to hers, press his hardening cock to the crux of her thighs. He still couldn't believe this was the same girl who'd been sitting outside Jenkins' office the last few years. "Sounds good," he said, trying to keep his voice from coming out raspy. "Think I'll have the same thing."

He strode to the phone, thinking what he really wanted to have right now wasn't on the room service menu.

Three

They ordered lunch in, too. They scoured contracts, Damon talked, Brenna asked questions, and he sometimes quizzed her on what she'd learned. And by the time they finished working late that afternoon, several things were clear to Brenna: she'd already understood the Blue Night contracts better than she'd realized, she was catching on fast, she enjoyed working with Damon and thought him a far nicer guy than she'd ever expected—*and it was impossible not to think of him sexually.*

The man *dripped* sex, after all. From his dark good looks and bedroom eyes to the workout-chiseled body that his clothes couldn't begin to hide. From the very moment he'd answered the door that morning, she'd been permeated with a raw lust that surpassed anything she'd ever experienced. And this time she couldn't blame it on wine. Or atmosphere. Or anything except pure animal magnetism.

Every time he smiled at her it sliced right to her core. Every time his eyes sparkled on her, she felt it between her legs. And the way his toned muscles had filled out his Violent Femmes "Gone Daddy Gone" T-shirt had turned her warm all over. She'd been aroused by his very presence all damn day. And finding out, even more than she had last night, that she actually liked him—and thought him intelligent, shrewd, and amiable—wasn't helping the situation. It would have been a lot easier to ignore the animal magnetism if he'd been the smug jerk she'd always envisioned.

But you got through the day okay, she reminded herself as she changed clothes for the evening. They were going to an underground club called Fetish—"which," Damon had promised her with a wink, "isn't as scary as it sounds."

"So I don't need to wear black leather from head to toe to fit in?" she'd asked.

He'd tilted his sexy head, a glint of flirtation in his eyes. "No—but I wouldn't *mind* seeing you in some black leather."

Of course, her nether regions had gone completely hot, even as she'd felt a warm blush climb her cheeks while she tried to laugh it off.

You got through the day okay, and you'll get through the night, too. And then you'll get through all the other days to come. And she really believed she could. Because even as hot and bothered as she'd been today, she *had* managed to stay focused—mostly—on the work, and she'd learned a lot.

In addition to teaching her what the contracts *meant*, Damon had also schooled her on when certain points should or shouldn't be offered, which ones were the very last she should promise a performer, and how wild about them she should be before giving in to certain demands. "But," he'd also told her, "the beauty of being with an indie label is that most of our acts are first-timers, open-minded, hungry, and willing to take what we can offer. You won't be faced with many artists making contract demands, and if you are, you need to take a good look at whether they're worth it."

So now she was extra excited to see how this whole process really began, and she would witness it tonight. Appearing at Fetish was an alternative girl band called Blush—the group had sent Damon a CD, he'd happened to pluck it from the many he received on a regular basis, and he'd been impressed. The band didn't know Damon would be there— he'd simply found their web Site, with club dates. He'd explained to Brenna that he often liked to "sneak up" on an act and watch them quietly, unnoticed, in case he didn't like what he saw. "Makes it easier for everyone," he'd said. "No dashed hopes or heartbroken singers. Plus I can see how they perform on any given night."

As it happened, Brenna *was* wearing black leather for the outing—at least a little. A black leather miniskirt, with high-heeled boots, and on top a slightly sheer leopard-print blouse with a black bra underneath.

Everything was new, bought on her shopping excursion with Kelly, including the bra and the silky black thong beneath her skirt. She hadn't chosen the outfit because of where they were going, and she hadn't chosen it to look sexy for Damon—she'd chosen it for the same reason she'd selected her apparel the previous evening: because she had to look the part of a hip, cool A&R rep if she was going to represent Blue Night Records.

And even if the idea of looking hot while she was with Damon appealed on a gut level, she would just have to ignore that. They'd be going out to *lots* of clubs this week—it's why they were in Vegas—and she couldn't wear a plain T-shirt every time she saw him.

Her greatest fear was that an evening of feeling sexy with Damon, and *wanting* Damon, would lead right where it had last night—to a desperate masturbation session alone in her room. And frankly, now that the day was waning and her body had felt wired for hours, just from being in Damon's company, she was beginning to remember exactly what had made her indulge in such an extreme form of self-pleasure.

Oh well, if that's where the night led, then that's where it led. But as she finished her makeup, going daring with the eyeliner, she decided to stop worrying and instead resume looking forward to all that would come beforehand.

Just then, a knock sounded on the door. Damon.

Her pussy went moist just knowing she was about to see him. Which was bad. Very bad.

But she took a deep breath and hurried to whisk the door open. He stood before her looking...masculinely beautiful. No other way to describe it. His raven hair fell in beautiful waves to his shoulders. His beautiful eyes captivated her with a glance. And his beautifully hard body made a simple black button-down shirt over black jeans look like haute couture. A small silver cross hung on a chain at his throat.

She bit her lip and lowered her gaze, trying to hide the physical reaction that rushed through her body like a river of heat. "No vintage tee tonight, huh?" she asked, working to raise her eyes back to his.

He grinned in reply, then gave her a not-very-subtle once-over. "Good thing I put on a real shirt or I'd look like a slob next to *you*."

His gaze stuck on her skirt, which stopped halfway down her

thighs, and the eye-to-thigh contact made her whole body tingle. "Nice," he said.

"I decided to do . . . a *little* leather," she explained.

"I like." Then his look reconnected with hers. "Ready?"

"Very." Oh crap, had she just said that? "I'm really anxious to do some official scouting," she added, trying to cover her lust.

"You mentioned liking Mexican food, so I made reservations at Taqueria Cañonita downstairs along the Grand Canal. Good people watching," he added with a wink.

But as they headed up the hall, Brenna couldn't help thinking *they* might be the people who would be watched. She'd kept herself feeling Vegas cool and confident while getting dressed, but the fact was—she'd never worn such a racy outfit in her life. And she couldn't deny that something *about* the raciness made her feel a bit more in keeping with the man at her side—like maybe, just maybe, little Brenna Cayton from Ohio might actually be a worthy companion for him.

Ten minutes later, they were seated at a table for two at the edge of the canal where it ran through the Venetian's indoor shopping area. But the lighting and the blue-sky-and-white-cloud ceiling above had the effect of making Brenna feel as if they sat at another outdoor café. "This is wild," she said, leaning back to look at the "sky."

"This is Vegas," he said, taking a sip of the wine that had just been poured.

Just then, they both heard a snap and flinched at the bright flash of a camera. Brenna turned her head to look.

"Don't," Damon warned before she was even able to spot the photographer, reaching to touch her hand where it rested on the table. She shivered inside at the contact. "If you ignore them, they'll go away."

Which is when she realized—dear God, some member of the Vegas paparazzi had just taken a picture of *her* because she was with *him*. How utterly strange.

"Don't be surprised if you turn up on the Internet tomorrow above some caption like 'Damon Andros' mystery woman.' Sorry about that."

The truth was, she didn't mind. In fact, she found the notion sort of exciting. But she didn't say so; she just shook her head. "It's all right. No big deal." Then she lowered her chin. "But is that weird for you? To have strangers taking pictures of you all the time? Or are you used to it by now?"

"Honestly, it's still pretty fucking strange," he replied, his expression wry. "And I still don't get it. This shit doesn't happen to other A&R guys—how did *I* get so lucky?"

Because you're beautiful. It all came back to that. Surely he knew how enjoyable he was to look at. But thank God she hadn't blurted it out, and she certainly wasn't going to bring it up. "You hang with a lot of rock stars and starlets," she reminded him with a smile. "Maybe that makes you a celebrity by association."

He shrugged. "Still, it's bizarre when people you don't know think they know stuff *about* you." Then he tilted his head, his brown eyes intense upon her. "I assume you've heard the rumors."

"About womanizing? And sex for a contract?" She pursed her lips and answered succinctly. "Yeah." She saw no reason to lie about it.

He nodded, then gave her an easy smile. "The upside is I'm saving a hell of a lot of money on clothes. People I don't know keep sending me T-shirts with band logos on them. Saw me wearing them in pictures, I guess. Now I get a new one in the mail every few days."

She grinned. "From admiring fans? Or bands wanting you to walk around wearing their T-shirt?"

"Some of both—they come from everywhere. Hell, Hugh Hefner's people sent me a Playboy tee last week with a note thanking me for stopping by the mansion."

Brenna blinked and sat up straighter. "You've been to the Playboy Mansion?"

He shrugged again. "Yeah."

"What was *that* like?"

He took another sip of his wine, and Brenna decided she could use a little alcohol in her system, as well, so she reached for her own stemmed glass. Because cool new Brenna shouldn't be intimidated or freaked out by the idea of what probably went on behind those particular doors, but old Brenna *was* and she'd forgotten to disguise it.

"Pretty damn fun," he said, eyes sparkling once more, a bit lecherously this time.

Her stomach churned with a blurred mix of repulsion and excitement imagining what sort of *fun* he might have experienced there. Indeed, it seemed that Damon Andros had the same effect on her that all of Las Vegas did.

"Will *I* now be . . . uh, required to go places like that?" she asked.

He lowered his chin. "Required, no? But it's the kind of place where people in entertainment congregate, so . . . if you get an invitation, you'd be smart to accept."

"Ah," she said, still stuck in *old* Brenna world. Then she swallowed nervously. It was one thing to put on a leather skirt and see-through blouse. But when it came to walking the walk and talking the talk, could she really do it? She'd never even thought about having to go to places where she might be uneasy. Even this bar tonight—would she be comfortable going to a place called Fetish by herself, without Damon as an escort?

"What's wrong?" he asked, clearly reading her face.

She thought of faking it, claiming nothing was amiss, painting herself as cool, confident Brenna again. But she'd spent the whole day with Damon now, and she truly liked him—so she couldn't help being honest. "Maybe I shouldn't tell you this, but . . . I'm not sure I could handle that."

Damon replied by propping his elbow on the table, planting his chin in his fist, and pinning her in place with his eyes. "Oh, I bet you can handle a lot more than you think, babe."

Four

Fetish was a dark but not dumpy building on the edge of town. They'd taken a taxi and now exited into a crowded parking lot lit with dim streetlights. Red gothic neon announced the bar's name above the door, beneath which hung a sign with black plastic lettering that said, simply: BLUSH.

Despite the bold new Brenna she'd been trying to become, her stomach swam with nerves. She'd been to plenty of clubs in her day, but never one like this. While she could see that Damon had not steered her wrong—many of the people coming and going could have been at *any* bar, judging from their appearance—at least half the patrons sported a goth look that made her glad for her leather skirt. Now if only the terror in her eyes didn't give her away.

As Damon paid their cover charge to a big bald guy at the door with a spider tattooed on his neck, the man squinted at him and said, "Hey, aren't you . . . that guy?"

Damon just smiled slightly and replied, "Nope, I'm not him," and placed a hand at the small of Brenna's back to usher her inside.

The interior of Fetish was even darker—she could barely see the people who packed the place even as she and Damon squeezed through, and deafening music blocked any chance of easy conversation. And that's when it hit her—this was her life now, her job. Going to clubs,

Listening to loud music. And to her surprise, she suddenly felt rather adrift, not sure where to go or what to do.

That's when Damon's palm closed warm over her shoulder. "Listen," he said in her ear.

And again, she was reminded why they were there. The music. Blush. She looked over her shoulder at him. "Is this them playing now?"

He nodded.

The sound was fast, hard, funky, and—when she forgot the fact that it was blaring—undeniably appealing.

"Initial impression?" Again, he leaned near so she could hear him, and the warmth of his breath buffeted her neck.

"They're good," she replied. "They have a quality that's somehow both modern and . . . a little 'new wave' retro."

His nod, along with the look in his eyes, made her think he liked her answer.

"Let's go get a drink," he said.

As they wove their way through the crowd, she caught a glimpse of the band on a small stage off to the right.

"Don't look at them yet," he instructed, yelling over the music. He'd explained to her last night that in the indie world, sound was everything. "We're not going for Britney Spears and Jessica Simpson, people that become pop stars largely because of how they look," he'd said. "If they have that kind of appeal, great. But we're more concerned with what they can do." He'd gone on to tell her that he sometimes liked to hear someone for a while before seeing them—he didn't like to let their appearance influence him too soon. She'd thought that sounded smart, and respectful of the music, so she followed him to the bar without glancing toward the stage.

The more she listened—as they ordered two Long Island iced teas—the more she liked. Blush's sound struck her as hip, confident, fun, and *very* sexy.

In fact, certain words in the lyrics began to leap out at her. "Creamy." "Soft." "Dirty." "Night." Words that might mean little on their own, but somehow the commanding female voice turned them sexual, and

Brenna became aware of a dewiness between her thighs that hadn't been there a few minutes before.

Of course, maybe it was also because the dark room was so crowded, which meant she and Damon were shoved together tight at the bar, their arms touching, their hips, too. He smelled good, a mixture of soap and musk and just a little perspiration.

And though she still heard the music, she somehow quit listening very closely, letting the next slower, sensual-sounding song lull her into a warm, quiet sort of titillation. The alcohol content of the drink quickly contributed to a feeling she could only describe as a . . . relaxed lust. She wasn't sure if that even made sense, but she grew strangely at ease with her desires, letting them leak to the surface, no longer trying to push them down.

Still crushed close to her mentor as a large biker type squeezed past, she leaned closer to Damon, absorbing the sheer pleasure when one of her breasts pressed against his arm. At the same time, she slid her free hand up onto his shoulder. To help her balance on her heels. But also sort of just to touch him. So warm, solid.

And as the biker passed, making a little more space, she didn't move away, didn't draw her hand back down. Damon felt too good. This was too nice.

He turned to look at her, his eyes only a few inches away and as captivating as ever. His gaze said he knew. What she felt. What she wanted.

That was when she backed away.

It was all suddenly a little too immediate, intimate.

And even as beautiful as he was, as heated as his expression, she *couldn't*. For so many reasons. She had to work closely with him right now, had to learn a job. And she was *stealing* his job, more or less lying to him. And see-through blouse and new confidence aside, deep down she was still old Brenna and, sadly, maybe she just didn't *truly* believe she was in Damon Andros' league.

She blinked and averted her gaze, then took a long sip of her drink. "This is strong," she said unthinkingly as liquid warmth moved down through her chest.

"Hard to get a Long Island that's not," he reminded her with a soft, teasing grin.

Of course it was—she knew that. Why on earth had she ordered something with four or five different kinds of alcohol in it? Because *he* had, and because it had been easy to just say, "The same." But she was beginning to regret the choice if it made her this loopy this fast. Of course, she'd had wine at dinner, too.

"Let's go see the band now," he suggested, and as she followed—letting him lead the way through the crazy-thick crowd—she found herself wanting to touch him again, wanting to curl her hands over his shoulders, press herself against his sturdy back.

Then she thought, *Dear God, since when do you get turned on by a guy's back?* Too much "iced tea," that was for sure—nervousness had made her sip too much too rapidly. She set the drink aside as they passed a table littered with empty glasses.

Just then, Blush came into view and Damon pulled her by the hand into the masses standing before the stage. She instantly sized up the band with one glimpse: they weren't gorgeous, or even conventionally pretty, but they were sexy and they knew it. It was in their confidence, and in their music.

The four young women varied in appearance, but all were in their twenties and wore skimpy tops resulting in ample cleavage. The lead singer possessed long blond hair, board straight, with dramatically harsh bangs that matched her dramatically harsh makeup. She belted out an old Joan Jett song, "Do You Wanna Touch Me (Oh Yeah)," moving provocatively with the standing microphone. She sported a black leather bustier and a ragged denim mini that started low on her hips and stopped high on her thighs.

"What do you think?" Damon asked in Brenna's ear, now standing behind her.

She kept her eyes on the singer, afraid to look at Damon—in case she accidentally kissed him or something. Her whole body hummed with lust. "A little rough around the edges, but confident, and sexy as hell. In control of the audience and knows how to work them." Despite the intoxication rushing through her veins, her brain continued to churn. "We could market them like a smarter, hipper, more modern Courtney Love."

But then she *did* turn to look at him, because she had no idea if she was on the right track or if she, conversely, sounded like a total newbie, and she wanted his honest reaction.

His eyes shone warm on her. "Very good."

But then his gaze dropped to her mouth.

And her cunt spasmed.

So she bit her lip and turned to face forward again, watching the band.

"Although," she said, still speaking her thoughts aloud, "isn't Blush too soft a name for them?"

She peeked over her shoulder to see Damon give his head a quick shake. "It's *ironic*," he said. "Or maybe it means they *make* you blush. But either way, it *says* something about them. Most band names these days are just words somebody thought sounded good together, but they don't say anything about the music or the band. *This* says something about their image, and that makes it a built-in marketing tool."

"Ah," she said, getting it. "Cool."

All around them, the mixed mainstream-and-gothic crowd moved to the music, and without thought or decision, Brenna found her hips beginning to sway back and forth, as well. She kept her eye on the blond singer, watching her seduce fans with her heavily outlined eyes and the way she thrust her breasts forward or swung her hair dramatically over one shoulder.

"What does the crowd tell you about this band?" Damon asked near her ear. But his voice came a little lower now, raspier. His breath on her skin made her tingle below.

She shifted her focus from the lead singer to the people around her, trying to think. But it was difficult because the room was still too full, keeping her close to Damon, and now that she was moving with the music, she was also moving slightly against *him*.

On one side of her stood a young couple who looked like they could live next door to her—average, middle-class—dancing wildly. On the other she found a girl with bright pink hair, shrouded in black from head to toe. And she knew the answer.

Only this time, instead of turning to face Damon, she merely leaned back, resting her head on his shoulder to speak up into his ear. "A cult following that's gone mainstream. Crossover appeal."

Again he said, "Very good," but *also* again, his voice went lower, his eyes shaded as he peered down at her, and it would have been damn easy to kiss him because their faces, mouths, were so dangerously close.

So Brenna promptly lifted her head back up, watched the band. She didn't want to talk anymore—talking, even about business, seemed perilous at the moment. She just wanted to be quiet now, listen to the music, soak up the atmosphere. And maybe dance the alcohol out of her system before she did something stupid.

Still observing the crowd, though, her gaze stuck on two girls kissing, passionately making out near the stage. Both were young, pretty, not particularly gothic, and, if she had to guess, not really lesbians. In fact, she suspected the two good-looking guys standing by watching lustfully were their boyfriends.

Their eyes were closed, their tongues meeting in languorous abandon as their hands ran caressingly over each other's body. Brenna didn't *want* to keep watching, but something about the sight hypnotized her. And despite her shock, she couldn't help feeling a little excited by the blatant sexuality of the act. Just like those stupid moving billboards—she didn't want to be aroused by it, but to her astonishment, she was.

So much softness. So much sex.

Just *out there*.

And somehow, that was the point of it.

Would the two young women be taking such delight in each other if they were alone? Or was it about doing it in front of their boyfriends and in public? Brenna didn't know for sure, but she *felt*—to the marrow of her bones—that behaving so outrageously *without* going behind closed doors was a big ingredient in their desire.

A quick glance over her shoulder revealed that Damon had followed her eyes and noticed the two girls, as well.

Old Brenna was embarrassed. To be caught watching something like that. And by Damon of all people. She instantly wondered if he could see how much it aroused her—her pussy felt positively huge beneath her skirt, as if, at this moment, it was the biggest part of her.

But *new* Brenna simply asked him, "Does that turn you on?"

God, what was she doing? After all, she'd decided it was safer not to talk anymore. Yet she couldn't help being curious. Wanting to know what he felt, yearning to understand the way he thought about things. *Sexual* things.

"Yeah," he said simply. Blunt about it, just like during their conversation last night.

She bit her lip, her breasts seeming to swell within the cups of her bra. He was aroused, too—right now, right here, next to her.

Did that mean he was hard? She suffered the urge to find out, to reach out and press her hand to the front of his pants. "Tell me why," she murmured instead.

He watched the girls a moment more, drawing Brenna's gaze back to them, as well—and then finally turned to look her squarely in the eye. "*Two* of everything. *Two* sets of soft female lips. *Two* pairs of round breasts. All those curves . . . moving together."

Ah. Maybe that made sense. And maybe that explained why *she* was excited, too. Her gaze stayed locked on his, but she couldn't summon an answer, so he went on.

"I like women who are free enough to follow their urges, lose their inhibitions."

Now she found her voice, to say, "I'm not sure they *have* inhibitions," and they both laughed, but it faded quickly because the mood taking over the club was pervasive.

To Brenna's left, the couple she'd noticed dancing before were now also kissing. Their bodies moved rhythmically to the music, their mouths grinding together as sensually as their pelvises. And a goth guy now nibbled on the neck of the pink-haired girl on Brenna's right. The girl smiled, letting her tongue slide slowly across her upper lip. It was as if sex was filling the room, floating in the very air, almost as if it were somehow being pumped into the building the same way casinos were rumored to pump extra oxygen into the gaming areas. Brenna's skin prickled, soft but powerful sensations echoing through her body, making her want to get lost in it all.

Yet her attention was drawn back to the stage when Blush broke into a new song with a steamy, sexy beat. Unfamiliar with it, she assumed it was an original. And like the last song—like *many* of their songs, it seemed—it was about sex.

Through a pumping chorus, the band repeated the words "best

hands" again and again, leaving Brenna to conclude that must be the title. The blonde sang about the hands easing their way across her skin, about fingers dipping into private places, and eventually about the hands reaching, reaching, for ecstasy. The whole crowd soon focused on the young woman, who began to move against the mike stand as she had before.

Brenna realized that not only was she watching the singer ease the microphone between her legs, thrusting gently with the beat of the song, but she was watching it *with* Damon. They were witnessing it *together, experiencing* it together. In fact, they were experiencing it with every person in the room. *More blatant sex on display.*

Yet as time passed, she grew less repulsed than she'd been last night—and more fascinated.

The whole club seemed to pulsate with the beat now, and Brenna continued moving her hips back and forth, surrendering herself to the intoxicating strains.

She should have been alarmed when she felt Damon's hands mold to her hips, but she wasn't.

It was too incredible to be touched by him, even just in that small way, pleasure spreading rapidly through her.

And then, then—*oh yes!*—he was pressing into her from behind, enough for her to realize he was going hard against her ass. It felt like a dream, a fantasy, but it was shockingly real.

Low in her ear, he rasped, "Dance with me, Brenna. Move with me."

It would have been smart to step away, or to tell him to remember they were professionals here, doing a job. That this was a mistake.

Yet she simply couldn't. More than just the song was intoxicating her. More than the alcohol she'd consumed. She was drunk on Damon Andros, and she *had* been for the last twenty-four hours. And she'd tried to play this smart, be bigger than her lust—but now it was consuming her.

So she moved with him, drank in the heat of his body as he leaned closer, felt the power of his hot erection against her rear.

Had anything in her life ever felt better?

She didn't think so.

She didn't think any physical sensation had ever pulled her in so quick, so deep, leaving her helpless to fight it.

Together they swayed as the blonde on the stage purred the provocative lyrics that added fuel to their fire. Brenna never looked at him after that, simply kept her eyes straight ahead, feeling it all, trying to survive it, trying to believe it, and wondering what would happen now.

But she *knew* what would happen, of course. The song would end. The song would end and they'd stop moving together and they'd pretend things were normal again, that he hadn't touched her, that she hadn't experienced the deep, raw pleasure of his stiffened cock against her ass.

And it was just as she drew that conclusion . . . that something else entirely took place.

The warm masculine hand curving over her right hip eased upward, over the gauzy fabric covering her stomach and higher, higher, coming to rest beneath her breast, his thumb arcing up onto the rounded flesh while his fingers played about the bottom of her bra. The intense delight combined with intense need to make her sway more sensually, her breath turning labored, her cunt throbbing madly.

Which is when his other hand snaked downward onto her thigh— and up under her skirt. That quick, that smooth. His fingertips eased between her legs, caressing the silk there.

Her breath hitched and she involuntarily moved in a whole new way, beginning to undulate, as if she were having sex. She met his touch in front and pressed her ass to his hard-on in back. His right arm now circled her waist to keep her steady—he must have realized he was making her weak, her whole body nearly convulsing from the hot strokes his fingers delivered.

Did anyone around them see what was going on, the way he was touching her? Surely not—the crowd remained tight, the spaces between bodies mostly dark, private even though in public.

She'd long since ceased paying attention to the song but glanced up at the stage in time to catch the last line: *The best hands are mine.* It was an end-of-song twist—the lyricist had no lover, but was touching *herself.*

Damon kissed Brenna's neck now, sending fresh spirals of pleasure all through her. Oh God. *Oh God.*

And when the song ended, the crowd cheered—and Damon leaned near her ear to rasp the words, "Come with me."

She turned to find that meeting his gaze now was different—even more paralyzing. Because his hands were on her. Because he wanted her as much as she wanted him. And Kelly's words came back to her. *Instant lover. Just add lust and stir.* She'd never dreamed it could really happen.

Damon's hand closed firm around her smaller one as he pulled her through the crowd. She didn't see the people they passed, didn't hear the next song begin—she could focus on nothing but him and the need that burned through her.

They broke away from the masses near the back of the club, and he led her briskly down a low-lit hallway. He twisted the knob on an unmarked door, but it was locked. "Damn," he muttered under his breath, then tried another across the hall. This one opened and he pulled her inside. Shut the door behind them. Flipped on a light switch to illuminate a dim bulb overhead.

They stood in a supply closet amid buckets and brooms and shelves filled with cleaning products. Her heartbeat pulsed everywhere as their gazes met, both hot and ready.

Damon lifted his hands to her face and kissed her, pushing his tongue warm and moist between her lips. Her mouth, her whole body, responded—she was on autopilot now, following urges, vaguely recalling how Damon had told her that turned him on. Pressing her palms to his chest, she curled her fingernails into his shirt as one heated kiss turned into another.

Then his mouth dropped to her neck and his hands to her skirt. Blush's music made the whole closet vibrate, but the main thing Brenna could hear was her own labored breathing as Damon pushed up under the leather to find her panties. One rip and her thong dropped, a *whoosh* of air cooling her pussy.

He breathed heavy now, too, and they both worked hurriedly at his belt and pants. Part of her couldn't believe she was letting this happen, yet it was beyond her to stop.

And when his zipper parted and Damon pushed his underwear down, too, Brenna went weak at the sight of his cock. Oh God, it was big! So thick and long and rock solid—for her.

She wrapped her hand full around it, making him moan. She wasn't usually so aggressive, but she also wasn't usually in a closet making out with Damon Andros.

Gazing down at his erection empowered her, and the very way it felt in her fist—silk over steel—had her pulling it toward her, closer, closer, needing it inside her more than she could understand.

"Wait," Damon whispered, and a hint of panic paralyzed her—*please don't let him be stopping!*—until he yanked his wallet from his back pocket and pulled out a square foil packet.

"Oh," she sighed in relief. Then, "Hurry."

She held his enormous cock upright between them as he rolled the condom snugly down over it.

The next thing she knew, his hands were closing on her bare ass, she was wrapping one leg around his waist, and he was thrusting himself deep into her hungry cunt.

"Unh!" she cried at the impact, and their eyes met as he began to move in her.

She'd never done anything so animalistic in her life, but that's what she felt like right now—an animal, out of control, reckless with heat. She'd also never been with anyone so large before, and the fullness was almost overwhelming, especially standing up.

"So wet," he growled—and she wrapped her arms around his neck and held on tight as he pumped into her welcoming flesh.

"All day," she admitted between breaths. "And last night. Oh God!" she cried as he filled her again, again. "Fuck me," she whispered in his ear.

She never said things like that during sex—but again, she'd never been with Damon Andros. He clearly drove her to new heights—or maybe depths.

"Fuck me," she said again. "Fuck me."

"I'm fucking you, babe," he assured her. "I'm fucking you hard."

They moved together, firm strokes that echoed through every inch of her body, and she met them, pressing down, her moves rubbing her clit against him in front.

"So big," she breathed. "So big in me."

"Ah, baby—*yeah*," he said, his voice filled with a dirty arrogance she felt to her soul. And then he thrust even deeper, and she knew he wanted her to feel every hard inch, wanted her to know exactly how big he *was*.

Intense pleasure reverberated through the small of her back and down her thighs, and weakness threatened to make her collapse. Damon kissed her roughly, and their ragged breathing nearly drowned out the echo of music through the door.

"Let me see your tits," he demanded, the words darting jaggedly through her. He couldn't reach them himself since he had to hold on to her with both hands to keep their bodies interlocked—and she never could have dreamed she'd find such a command *hot*, but she did. She hurried to yank at the buttons of her blouse, then reached up to shove both bra straps off her shoulders. The cups dropped and her breasts tumbled free, and she instantly loved having revealed herself to him.

He let out a groan as his eyes dropped to her chest, and she found herself arching involuntarily forward. "Suck them," she said.

Another rough growl left him as he bent to take one turgid nipple into his mouth, pulling on it hard.

"Oh God," she murmured. "Oh God, yes."

She was getting closer, closer—she was going to come.

"Fuck me," she pleaded again. "Fuck me."

He continued driving his cock deep and suckling her breast as she moved against him in the hot, tight circles that brought her the most pleasure.

"Oh . . ." she moaned, lost to the sensations, eyes shut now. She forgot they were in a closet half undressed, forgot she barely knew him, forgot this was the most illicit sex she'd ever even come close to having—and exploded in orgasm. She cried out as it rushed through her, pulsing outward from her cunt all the way to her fingers and toes. "Yes, yes, yes," she sobbed until finally the waves began to calm and total weakness pervaded her body.

Opening her eyes, she caught a glimpse of the bare lightbulb above her, another of her pointed nipples below, glistening from his ministrations—and felt like someone else. Until she met his gaze, her arms resting around his neck, and then she felt like no one but herself, living out the naughtiest of fantasies—naughtier, in fact, than any she'd ever even had. "Oh, God," she breathed.

"Good?" he asked, those sexy brown eyes still filled with saturating heat.

"Mmm," she sighed with one slow, well-pleasured nod. "Now . . . fuck me some more. Fuck me 'til you come." Brenna hadn't been herself since arriving in Sin City, and she saw no reason to change that now.

With their gazes still locked, he tightened his grasp on her bottom, his fingers digging in slightly. Then, teeth clenched, he drove into her—once, twice, again, again—slow, hard thrusts that reached her very core. Her body jolted with each, her breasts jiggling. At moments, her head dropped back, her eyes shutting, but when she opened them again, Damon's gaze always met hers, and such stark intimacy enhanced every sensation. And it was only when he said, "God, God—now," that *his* eyes fell shut in ecstasy.

Brenna watched the climax take him, transform him, watched the pleasure and pain steal over his expression, and almost thought *she* could come again from the severe joy of having delivered him there.

But it was when he opened his eyes and she knew the sex was over that she began to feel just as she had upon coming into the club tonight—a little adrift, unsure. "Good?" she asked, as he'd asked her.

"Perfect."

And then . . . nothing. She had no idea what to say, how things would be now.

Gently, he pulled out of her, leaving her to stand on her own. God, her legs were wobbly. And her body suddenly empty. Struggling to stay on her feet, she instinctively reached to put her bra back in place.

"Shit," he said, then, "Sorry."

She balked slightly. "Sorry?"

"It's a bad idea to fuck someone you work with."

"Oh. Yeah. I had the same thought." She buttoned her blouse, watching as he removed his condom to drop it in an empty wastebasket resting conveniently on the floor behind him.

This was starting to feel a little surreal. She'd just done it with Damon Andros.

But no, wait—it had *already* felt surreal. This was more than that. *Un*real. Dizzying.

"Although," she added, thinking aloud, "it's not as if this is the first time you've had sex with someone you worked with." Singers, she meant.

A small, cynical smile took him. "All completely consensual, without contract promises, by the way."

"I believe you," she said softly. And she did. She couldn't imagine Damon would have to make promises to get *any* woman into bed.

"And . . . a habit I was trying to break."

She bit her lip. "Then what went wrong?"

He zipped his pants, met her gaze. "You're too damn hot."

It probably indicated some flaw in her character that, even as she stood totally absorbed by this man and what she'd just done with him, she could also mentally step back and take wild pleasure in the fact that *the* Damon Andros truly thought *she* was too hot. But as a girl who'd always felt very middle-of-the-road and pretty-on-her-good-days, it thrilled Brenna to the tips of her toes to feel, for once in her life, as if she was truly that attractive and exciting.

"Maybe we should call it a night," he suggested.

"What about the band?"

"What's *your* take? If you were here without me, would you be prepared to offer a contract?"

She didn't hesitate to nod. "Yes."

"Good. Because that's exactly what I'm gonna do. On the way out, we'll introduce ourselves and set up a meeting." He grabbed the doorknob, but stopped to look back. "Ready?"

She gave herself a quick once-over and realized her panties lay looped around the ankle of one boot. "Except for those."

A fresh sultriness invaded his gaze as he stooped to remove them, dropping them in the waste basket, and before rising, he peered up her skirt to murmur, "Mmm—nice, babe."

It was enough to get her hot all over again, that fast.

So when he reached back for the doorknob a few seconds later, she closed her hand around his wrist, wondering aloud, "Damon, about what just happened . . ."

"Yeah?"

"Since we both agree it was a mistake, does that mean . . ."

"That we won't do it again?" He gave his head a sexy tilt and flashed those bedroom eyes. "Look, babe—we could say we won't, and torture ourselves the next few days. But you know what they say."

"What's that?"

"What happens in Vegas stays in Vegas." He concluded with a seductive wink.

"Oh," she said, her voice a little too soft.

Kelly had said the exact same thing when they'd discussed the then-impossible-seeming notion of Brenna having sex with Damon. And so he was saying he wanted to fool around with her while they were here, but forget it had happened once they returned to L.A. And maybe something about that would have offended *old* Brenna, but in new Brenna's world, it seemed like a perfectly acceptable idea as still more of Kelly's words came back to her. *No fuss, no muss, no long or messy attachment.*

Of course, the truth was that it would probably be *impossible* for her to work with him on a long-term basis after this. Because every time she looked at him, she'd remember fucking him. And she'd want to do it again.

But she probably didn't have to worry about that. Because he was probably going to be losing his job.

A thought that made her stomach churn for a whole *different* reason—her deception.

Yet she simply couldn't think about that now. There was no good answer or solution, so what was the point? She had no intention of letting Jenkins' underhanded ways ruin the best sex of her life with the hottest guy she'd ever encountered.

And given her precarious situation, enjoying this now and cutting it off at week's end sounded . . . well, like the perfect plan.

Five

Damon led Brenna up the hall, hand in hand, as Blush's lead singer's smoky voice resonated over the club's loudspeakers. "We're gonna take a little break, but don't go anywhere 'cause we're just gettin' started." He headed toward the stage, wanting to intercept the band and get out of there.

Damn, Brenna had gotten him hot, fast. So much for not fucking the girl he was training. Hell, he guessed that was just the kind of guy he was—he thought life was too short not to indulge in pleasure so long as it didn't hurt anybody. And even if this *seemed* like a bad idea, maybe it wasn't. Since she wasn't a potential Blue Night artist, surely no harm would come to him or anyone else if they had some dirty fun together.

Fortunately, he came face-to-face with the Blush singer as she descended the few steps at the side of the stage. He held out his hand. "Hi, I'm Damon Andros of Blue Night Records."

The saucy blonde, so slick and cool up to now, suddenly looked like she would faint, her eyes widening and jaw dropping. "Oh God. You *are*."

"This is my associate, Brenna Cayton, and we've been enjoying the show tonight." *So much that we just did each other in a closet.*

Damon knew the mood the band set was only part of what had drawn him to Brenna tonight, but he also couldn't deny that Blush's particular style of entertainment had pushed their mutual attraction along at a breakneck pace.

As the singer, Candy Lark, introduced herself and the rest of the band, Damon watched all the girls' eyes light up, then wasted no time telling them he wanted to sign them. A few of the band members jumped up and down, squealing their excitement, while Candy Lark did her best to act professional and thank him for coming to see them. Passing her a business card on which he'd already written his room number at the Venetian, he set up a breakfast meeting the next morning in the suite.

He still loved that part of the job—giving someone a chance to make their dreams come true. He'd been trained—and he had to train Brenna, as well—to remember this was a business, about money and profits, but he thought it was important to keep your heart in the job, too.

Five minutes later, he slid into a cab next to Brenna, glad to be alone with her again, although he wasn't sure why. Granted, there'd been no time for pillow talk after their frantic coupling, but he wasn't especially a pillow talk sort of guy. Maybe it was the sexy little smile she wore in the dark confines of the taxi that made him enjoy just being with her.

"Why the smile?" he asked as the cab sped away from Fetish. "Excited about offering the contract?"

She bit her lip and looked cute as hell, even in the shadowy light, and kept her answer low so it would be just between the two of them. "Oh, that was fun, but the truth is . . . I'm just thinking about the fact that I'm not wearing panties."

His groin tightened, and he couldn't hold in a small grin. "You smile when you're not wearing panties?"

"I've never not worn them before," she confided.

It surprised him a little. Because she'd seemed so carefree about the whole thing. And despite their discussion last night about keeping sex private, tonight she'd seemed like a girl who . . . well, who might have done it in a closet once or twice before. "Ever?" he asked.

"Ever."

He tilted his head, still trying to get to the bottom of what he now knew was a *naughty* smile. "And . . . ?"

She weighed her answer, looking strangely young and girlish and pleased with herself. "It makes me feel . . . wild. Sexy. Free."

Damn, there it was—that *genuine* part of her again. That part of her so real he could almost taste it. And he liked it. A lot. In all his thirty-five years, many of them spent enjoying women, he wasn't sure he'd ever met anyone quite like her.

Without planning it, he leaned over in the cab to kiss her. "Stay in my room tonight," he said low in her ear.

Pulling back to look at him, she cast a playful smile. "I have to warn you, that drink—on top of the wine I had with dinner—knocked me for a loop. I might fall fast asleep."

"That's okay. As long as you're naked."

Six

Brenna lay in his bed, eyes falling shut. He stood over her, smiling. She'd been serious about that drink knocking her out.

"Are you awake?"

"Mmm," she murmured.

"Do you want to sleep in your clothes?" When she didn't answer, he added, "Or do you want me to undress you?"

"Mmm-hmm, that."

Damon much preferred undressing women who were awake and enjoying it, but having her sleep naked next to him still sounded good, and he'd undressed *enough* women that this wouldn't be a challenge.

He started with her boots, unzipping and slipping them off to reveal thin black knee socks underneath, the same as a Catholic schoolgirl might wear. The contrast between the socks and the rest of her outfit brought a smile to his lips. She was no schoolgirl, but even after what they'd shared in the closet, he sensed a certain innocence about her that drew him.

Dropping the boots gently to the carpet at the foot of the king-size bed, he next moved up to her blouse, reaching for the buttons between her breasts and proceeding downward. He'd barely had a chance to notice the sexy bra underneath—he'd seen it through the animal print and caught a glimpse when he was inside her, but now he took in the scalloped edges of the low-cut cups and the way they pushed her breasts upward, creating firm, round mounds.

Shit. He wanted to kiss them, massage them.

But she was asleep, or close enough to it, so all he could do was look—and suffer the hard-on growing behind his zipper.

Removing her blouse required her help. "Come on, babe, raise up for me," he whispered as he eased one arm beneath her. Letting out a slightly grumpy-sounding moan, she cooperated, and he soon got the blouse off. And, easing both his hands behind her back, he deftly unhooked the bra and removed it, as well.

Of course, then he had to look at her tits—because he couldn't undress a woman and not look at her tits.

Not quite as firm-looking without the bra, but still beautiful, ample, her pink nipples taut and elongated. Damn, he wanted to suck them, like he had in the closet. But he wanted to do everything slower this time, explore all these soft curves, her smooth, pale stomach, her silky shoulders, the length of her neck. He got harder with the wanting, especially when his gaze returned to her breasts. C-cups, he'd guess— then he remembered he held her bra in his hand. He checked the tag and, sure enough, found a 34C printed there.

She wore a sexy black beaded choker and long beaded earrings, but he decided to leave those on—out of pure selfishness. He liked the way she looked, mostly undressed but still wearing jewelry.

Laying her blouse and bra over the upholstered bench at the end of the bed, he returned for the last piece of clothing she wore. She was a study in erotic beauty, lying bare but for her skirt, her arms now flung sensually up over her head, that choker circling her slender neck, but he'd have been lying to himself if he denied not wanting to see her completely nude—even if she *was* asleep.

Gently, he eased the side zipper down, loosening the leather around her hips. "Lift up, honey," he urged, tugging gently downward on the fabric until her ass rose slightly.

He pulled the skirt to her knees and lower, soon dropping it on the bench, as well—all the while studying her pretty pussy. Shrouded with dark curls, he could still see her slit drawing a line down the center.

The beast in him wanted to spread her legs, watch her open, see the pink flesh where he had been not long ago.

Yet even *he* had his limits. He didn't bribe singers to have sex with him, and he didn't manipulate a woman who was asleep.

But he still thought about it—about parting her thighs, studying her cunt, about licking her, tasting her sweet juices—and had a feeling he was going to be awake for a while, fighting a raging erection.

Why the hell was he so turned on? He'd come less than an hour ago. And the sight of a naked woman in his bed wasn't exactly unusual.

She trusts you.

The words came out of nowhere, like an answer to his question. He barely knew Brenna, yet along with her genuineness, he felt a certain trust in her openness. A feeling now that maybe she *hadn't* ever fucked a guy in a closet before. After all, even suggestive billboards made her uncomfortable. So maybe what she'd been tonight, with him, she'd never been *before*.

And now, she'd trusted him to undress her and put her to bed. Of course, she was drunk—but still, when he'd offered to take her clothes off and she'd accepted, a sexily-content little smile had played about her lips, almost as if they had known each other for years.

Damon had never *been* with a woman for years, so he didn't often feel that sort of blind, open trust.

But wait, that was wrong. *Once* he had been with a girl for a long while, when he was young, still living in New York, trying to find his way in life. And she'd been sweet and pretty—and trusting, too—and he'd broken her heart.

He came from a family of people who were satisfied with average lives. His father had just retired after forty years as a Brooklyn insurance salesman. His mother had been a housewife, the kind who'd worn pearls and dresses every day when he was little, a holdover from a different era. His oldest sister taught school, another sister managed a Manhattan pet shop, and the last sister was a stay-at-home mom. Nothing wrong with any of that, but he'd known early on that such a simple, settled life held little appeal for him. And two weeks before his wedding to Angie, a good Greek girl from the neighborhood whom he'd dated from high school on, he'd gotten a job offer in L.A. and flown the coop.

His guilt hadn't outweighed the sense of freedom he'd felt stepping onto that airplane, leaving his existence in Brooklyn behind. And ever since, he'd known he just wasn't the settling-down type. He wouldn't have a wife, or kids—or a dog or a minivan or a picket fence. It had been hard for his parents to accept, but as years had passed, they'd finally made peace with it, come to understand that he was different from the rest of the Andros family, that he wanted a different sort of life.

And he'd always been happy with that life, where all the key elements meshed so well. Work and parties. Music and sex. He lived and breathed them.

And he was happy. Satisfied. A bone-deep satisfaction he couldn't have found at home, married to Angie.

But it had been a damn long time since he'd been around a woman who seemed so guileless and real as Brenna did. She seemed like a contradiction. One minute begging him to fuck her, the next sheepishly confiding that she'd never gone without panties before.

And then there was that trust he'd just sensed from her, as tangible as the clothes he'd just removed from her body.

Strangely, for perhaps the first real time since he'd hit the L.A. music scene and come to understand how ruthless the entertainment business could be, it kind of made him want to trust her, too.

THE THIRD NIGHT

"... to sin in secret is no sin at all."
—Molière

One

Brenna's first realization when she woke up was that she lay naked, a sheet pulled to her waist. She *never* slept naked, so it was a shock. And she didn't exactly remember *getting* naked, either. Damn drink.

But then she turned her head and saw the gorgeous man whose head rested on the pillow next to hers, and she remembered. It hadn't been a dream. Her second realization? She'd really had sex in a closet with Damon Andros.

Without the lull of intoxication clouding her head, it seemed all the more amazing. Who had she been last night? New Brenna, definitely. But apparently the new her was willing to go to extremes she'd never even imagined.

She suffered no regrets. Just a hint of sadness when she looked at him.

Because he was like a toy she couldn't keep. And so she would play with him as much as possible while she had him, but she knew every bit of the play would be tainted with the knowledge that she'd soon have to give him up.

Silly, she chided herself. She was acting like she really *knew* him, like there were *emotions* involved here.

But there weren't—there couldn't be, because she *didn't* know him. Not really. And because she had a feeling Damon Andros didn't *do* relationships. And even if he did, it wouldn't matter once he found out she'd been lying to him.

God, I can't ever let him know. Whatever happened, however this all came down, she had to keep her involvement in it quiet. Because maybe she didn't really know him, but she knew him well enough now that she'd die if he found out what an underhanded, conniving lowlife she was being—all to get a glamorous job.

From what she could tell, he was naked, too, wearing nothing but his earrings and the small cross she'd noticed on a chain around his neck last night. *Mmm,* he looked good.

Even better when he turned to face her, hair mussed, eyes slowly opening. "Hey," he said, a sleepy smile gracing his face, the lower half of which was covered with a dark, sexy stubble.

She smiled back. "Hey."

"Come here," he said, voice low and persuasive. She didn't hesitate to roll into his cozy embrace. Odd how easy it was, how normal it felt, to press her naked body against his, even though they'd never done that before. His warmth kindled in her a fresh desire as he kissed her good morning.

God, he was perfect—he didn't even have morning breath.

Which made her fear that she did. She backed slightly away, hoping she was wrong, and hoping he didn't see her distress. She was *so* not used to casual sex or waking up with a guy she didn't know well. "I have a confession to make," she announced.

He arched one sleepy brow. "Oh?"

"I, uh . . . don't exactly remember what happened after we got here last night. I'm . . . not very good with hard liquor."

He cast a naughty look. "Wrong, babe—you were *very* good." Then he winked. "But nothing happened after we came back here—unfortunately. We just crawled into bed and went to sleep."

She lowered her chin slightly, peering at him from her pillow. "Sorry about that."

His eyes shone as warm and sexual as always—but she'd not yet begun to get used to it. "Maybe you can make it up to me."

Suddenly remembering the closet, his hands, and the rough, welcome entry of his cock, her pussy tingled. "I'll do my best."

In response, his palm closed over her hip, heating her further—and she forgot all about the possibility of bad breath as she instinctively leaned nearer, nearer, until their mouths collided.

The kiss fueled her desire so much that she found herself wanting to touch his penis, wrap her fingers around it, make it hard. But she was feeling just a little more shy than last night, so instead she only splayed her hand across his muscular chest, liking how hard he felt *there*, too.

One hot kiss melted into another until Damon drifted downward, his mouth descending to her neck. And just like last night, the simple affection delivered a pleasure that stretched all through her, even as the stubble on his chin gently chafed her skin, adding still more sensation.

Soon, his tongue raked over one nipple as his hand closed over her other breast. Gasping, she instinctively thrust her chest deeper into his grasp—and his mouth. The swirl of his tongue around the wet tip of her breast made her crazy with lust, and she found herself looping one leg across his to draw him closer. What a few seconds before had been licking now turned to sucking, and he drew the sensitive peak deep, deeper into his mouth, shooting a blast of hot delight straight to her cunt.

Which is when her gaze landed on the digital clock on his side of the bed.

"Damon," she breathed, fingers threading through his thick hair. "Damon—what time is our meeting with Blush?"

He released her nipple from his mouth, his breath warming the pink bud when he said, "Eight. Why?"

Her lust deflated. "It's twenty 'til."

"Shit," he whispered, and they both went still—until he lowered one soft, gentle kiss to the flesh directly next to her nipple and said, "To be continued."

That quickly, he'd turned her just as feral and wild as she'd felt last night. "Definitely. I still have lots to make up for, and I expect you to hold me to it."

"Damn straight," he growled.

As she pulled away to roll out of bed, Brenna wanted to howl her frustration but held it in. Oh *God*, how she wanted him. Only more slowly this time. She wanted to explore his body, top to bottom. She wanted to kiss him more. Touch him. Let *him* touch *her*. She wanted more of those sumptuous treats at her breasts. She wanted him between her legs. She wanted *everything*.

Yet duty called, and they both knew it. Thus, moments later, she found herself back in her own room, shedding the white robe she'd grabbed from Damon's enormous bathroom, ready for the shower. Damon had offered *his* bathroom, but since they were late and all of her things were here, she'd declined.

Only when she passed by the wide bathroom mirror did she notice she still wore her jewelry from last night. The sight made her pause in place. Naked, with her hair mussed, she thought she looked . . . incredibly hot. Given that it remained a very new feeling for her, she relished it, so much that she almost wanted to stand there and study herself awhile and forget the shower.

Yet sense prevailed—along with the knowledge that the sooner she showered, the sooner she would see Damon again. In a hurry after the quick soap and rinse, she dressed simply—jeans and a fitted blouse— but still hoped she looked the part of an A&R rep.

When she knocked on the door of Damon's lavish suite a few minutes later, he greeted her with a kiss hello. Work like *this* she could get used to.

But she was glad she hadn't said that.

Because what happened in Vegas would stay in Vegas, she remembered.

And that was actually a *good* thing because of that nasty little deception taking place between herself and the object of her affection.

When the band showed up at Damon's suite at eight sharp, Brenna finally understood why he needed so much room. Despite the number of people at the meeting, the suite still felt large and comfortable, and it was easy to see the young women were impressed by it, and thus by Blue Night.

Over a large room service breakfast of eggs, bacon, muffins, and more, Brenna listened as Damon went over the terms they were offering. Until she got well-established in her job, she'd need to talk with him or Jenkins about deals before making them, but Jenkins had trusted Damon with the task for years now.

She paid close attention to the dealings, noting that, as Damon had promised was usually the case, the band seemed happy at the very notion of being paid to make a CD and, though they had lots of questions, were agreeable and easy to get along with, at least for now.

Of course, from time to time, Brenna's mind drifted, memories of last night flitting through her head: her hand around his amazing cock, his mouth suckling so hard and tight at her breast, the powerful way he'd thrust up into her. It was still hard to believe. Not only that Damon Andros wanted her. But that she'd fucked him in a closet! In a bar!

And as she tried to refocus on the business at hand, she kept her smile inside, thinking that Kelly would be so proud.

TWO

Recording contracts, Brenna learned, contained a lot of details and required a lot of explanation, at least with girls as smart as the members of Blush, who asked Damon probably a hundred questions before the deal was reached and the meeting ended just before noon.

When the band left, Brenna admitted that she could use some additional explanations on certain clauses herself, so Damon suggested they talk about it poolside as there was no more pressing work until this evening, when they would hit a few more clubs. As luck had it, Kelly had insisted Brenna add a sexy bikini to her new wardrobe, which Brenna had thought silly and frivolous—but she'd relented and now possessed a hot-pink two-piece with a short matching sarong.

Returning to her room to change, she felt thankful, too, that she went to the expense of hitting the tanning bed a couple of times a week. She wasn't much of a sun-worshipper, but a little color made her look and feel healthier—especially when she slipped into her new suit.

Taking a glimpse back into the bathroom mirror, she couldn't deny that she looked sexy. Like the new bras she'd bought, the pink underwire triangles lifted her breasts to make them look pretty and plump, and the scant bottoms showed off her slender tummy. Peering at her reflection, she made a mental note to fall to her knees thanking Kelly the next time she saw her. Apparently, she *did* need a man, she *did* need a penis, and she *did* need a fuchsia bikini—and from now on, she planned to follow any and every piece of advice Kelly doled out.

Slipping on the wedged, glittery flip-flops Kelly had insisted completed the look, she left her room to find Damon approaching her door. He wore stylish trunks of black with red slashes up the sides, along with his usual earrings and that silver cross she'd first noticed last night.

"*Damn,* babe," he said appreciatively, letting his gaze rake over her from head to toe. The warmth of a blush climbed her cheeks, but only because she wasn't used to such open praise of her body, let alone liking it.

When they walked onto the rooftop pool and out into the desert heat, Brenna felt overwhelmed by luxury. While the pool itself was large but simple, the surroundings were grand. Hundreds of elegant lounge chairs set amid huge stone pots cradling well-manicured trees and immense stone columns upholding wrought-iron arches strung with vines. Beyond the pool area, the Venetian's clock tower spired skyward between the Mirage and Caesars Palace in the distance.

As they settled in two chairs rimming the pool's edge, Brenna began to notice all the "beautiful people" lounging about. Oh, certainly there were people of *all* types—older folks on vacation, a few young families—but she immediately felt outnumbered and intimidated by all the glamour girls in barely-there bikinis and the hip, cool guys hiding their eyes behind sunglasses by Versace and Prada. One would think that after living in Los Angeles and working in the music business for three years she'd have grown used to such people, but this was different—because suddenly she was *among* them, with a guy who was *one of them,* and she supposed, in order to keep his affections, *she* wanted to be one of them today, too.

Not far from where they'd stretched out over towels spread across their chairs, a brunette wearing a narrow black cowboy hat and a black thong bikini lay on her stomach atop a large concrete pillar in the pool that rose just above the water's surface. She sported a sun tattoo at the small of her back and she rested propped on her elbows, showing so much cleavage that Brenna was surprised her nipples weren't exposed. Another scantily clad girl, this one a blonde in a gold-lamé bikini, her firm breasts bulging from too-small triangles, stood in the water next to her, smoothing sunscreen over her back.

The girl in black sipped a fruity-looking concoction from a plastic cup, and expensive sunglasses shaded her eyes as she looked up—toward *them*. "Why, if it isn't Damon Andros. Aren't you even going to say hello, baby?"

Oh hell. No wonder she'd been intimidated. Since Damon *was* one of the beautiful people, that meant he also *knew* beautiful people, and apparently he knew this one in particular, whose perfectly tan, round ass Brenna couldn't help but envy.

Damon turned toward the voice. "Tawny. What are *you* doing here?"

The brunette grinned. "Just catchin' some rays, baby. And you?"

Oh God, her name was *Tawny*. And now she was introducing her friend, whose name was *Honey*, and when Damon asked Tawny how things were at the club and she told him he should stop by, she got the distinct impression both girls were strippers. And that Damon knew Tawny via her work. Which meant, of course, that he'd seen her naked. And she'd probably given him a lap dance. Or twenty. And had quite possibly had sex with him, since any sane woman would if she could.

Swell.

But you can't let this get you down. After all, you know he has a lot of casual sex. Everyone knew that about Damon—and even if you didn't know it for sure, one look at him told you. And this wasn't going to matter at the end of the week anyway, because what happened here was going to stay here.

Although if what happened in Vegas had to stay in Vegas . . . well, Brenna was going to squeeze in as much pleasure as she possibly could before she left.

That's when she heard Damon introduce her and made sure to smile just as smugly as Tawny was smiling at her. Tawny offered a thin-lipped "Hi," which Brenna smoothly returned.

It wasn't that she wanted to lower herself to acting like a bitch just because Tawny and Honey were, but she also wasn't going to be Little Mary Sunshine and let them think they could steal her man. In fact, she was going to go one step further.

Rising from her chaise, she moved over to Damon's, parking her rear next to him, effectively blocking the view of the two bikini-wearing vultures, and handing him the bottle of sunscreen she'd packed with her bathing suit.

"Will you do my back, Damon?" she asked, giving him her best come-hither look. Although, realistically, she wasn't sure she even *had* a come-hither look, but she was trying, and Damon got her so hot with a mere glance that it inspired her.

"Of course," he said, taking the bottle and making her feel supremely victorious.

As the afternoon progressed, they ordered lunch from the grill— washing it down with a couple of fruity concoctions of their own—and went over the contract Blush had just signed, talking more about the particulars.

From time to time, other women who knew Damon approached— and Brenna struggled to keep her blood from boiling, instead just sticking out her chest, bending one knee, and trying to look as sexy and sophisticated as her competition. Still, with every sexy girl who talked to Damon, Brenna couldn't deny growing more jealous, feeling unduly possessive of her new man.

Which was bad, she knew. This could go nowhere, and even if it could, she had a feeling that *no one* possessed Damon Andros. The fact was—she was lucky just to be with him for this short time. It was like a gift, she thought. A karmic gift. The universe's hot little way of making up for her cheating husband.

But the more prickly pear mojitos she drank, the less she was able to reason and the more rank jealousy filled her veins. Until finally, just after a blonde bombshell in a slinky one-piece cut all the way to her navel departed, Brenna did what she was getting pretty good at doing the last day or so: following her urges.

Aware that Tawny and Honey were still observing from lounge chairs not far away, Brenna set her mojito cup on the ground and stood up, moving to Damon's chair. He was still talking sales and distribution when she stretched out alongside him.

He offered a soft but steamy grin, their faces close now. "What's this?"

"This is me thinking that all work and no play makes Damon a dull boy."

He arched a skeptical brow. "Dull? Me? Come on, babe."

He had a point. So she let her expression form into a sexy pout. "Okay, maybe not. But all work and no play definitely makes Brenna *want* to play." And with that, she slid one arm around his shoulders and eased the other onto that broad chest dusted with dark hair, then leaned in for a kiss.

Was it bad that knowing Tawny and Honey and probably half the women at the pool were watching made her feel even sexier? At the moment, she didn't care. And Damon didn't seem to mind her affections, since he kissed her back, his lush mouth moving on hers, making her cream her bikini bottoms.

"Let's get in the water," he said low, near her ear.

She would have preferred to make out some more, but so long as he was with her, paying attention to her and only her, she wouldn't argue.

Descending the nearby stairs into the pool, step by slow step, Brenna hissed in her breath upon meeting the cold water.

"Come on in, babe," he said, his gaze turning downright wicked. "Don't you want to get wet with me?"

The enticing words drew her straight down into the pool with only one gasp in response to the cold, after which her body quickly adjusted, heating up from mere anticipation.

Damon took her hands to pull her deeper, until the water came to chest level. Then he leaned in to press his mouth back to hers, his slow, lingering kisses reverberating all the way to her toes, his palms molding warmly to her hips beneath the water. As her breasts brushed his chest, sending a fresh spark of arousal all through her, he glanced down, so she did, too, to see her nipples erect and jutting at the hot-pink Lycra.

His voice came low and smoky. "Do you know what I want to do to you right now?"

She struggled not to let herself tremble with lust. "Tell me." She'd never gotten into dirty talk before. Well, before last night. And now she wanted more of it. "Tell me," she said again, throatier this time.

"I want to peel this sexy top off your pretty tits and lick those hard, pink nipples."

She swallowed, feeling the words in her cunt, and when he let his hand rise from the water just long enough to stroke the tip of his thumb across the peak of her breast, her pussy surged so hard she thought she would come.

Oh God, had he just done that—here? He had—and she loved it.

"What else?" she asked, eager for more.

His low rasp was downright intoxicating. "I want to take your skimpy little bottoms off, too, spread your legs wide, and taste your sweet pussy."

Instinctually, her arms looped loosely around his neck and she shimmied her breasts against his chest again, hungry for more sensation there. Despite all the people at the pool, no one was near them in the wide expanse of water, and she looked around, feeling at once alone yet crowded.

"I wish you could do it right here, right now," she told him softly. Her eyes stuck on another lavish spot at the pool—one of several beds situated along the water's perimeter, flanked by columns, covered by a vine-strung canopy of wrought iron. Though all were vacant, since they had to be rented, the beds struck her as a downright hedonistic and rather erotic decoration. "I wish you could lay me across that bed and lick me until I come."

The shudder that passed through him was more satisfying than any reaction she could have imagined. "Do you have any idea how hard you're making me?"

Her gaze stayed glued to his. "Let me feel it."

He didn't hesitate, gripping her ass and pulling her to him until his cock stretched long and hard up the front of her bikini bottoms. Even after the lust of last night, after the release of reaching that closet and being taken by him, hard, she didn't think she'd ever felt anything more deeply arousing.

"Your girlfriends would all be jealous," she told him in a saucy tone, "if they could see what's happening underwater right now."

He didn't balk at her calling them his girlfriends. "I think they're *already* jealous," he said instead, his voice teasing even as he began to grind gently against her, creating just a bit of blessed friction.

"You're right," she practically purred, still rubbing her breasts against him. "They want what I'm getting right now, but they can't have it."

He gave his head a sexy, playful tilt. "You don't like to share?"

She offered a smirking grin. "No way."

"Ah, I forgot." He tipped his head back. "You like it in private, too. Prim and proper little Brenna."

She let out a laugh, then a soft moan as his hardness rubbed against her in just the right way. "You still think I'm prim and proper?" Was he serious?

"Just around the edges," he conceded. Then he scanned the pool area. "But for your information, this *isn't* very private."

She swallowed, a little nervous—because he was right. It might feel like they were alone in a way, but in reality they were surrounded by lots of people, some of whom surely watched their little water ballet, especially the women who wanted Damon so bad. Even if they couldn't see them moving together under the water, surely they knew what was happening.

"Then maybe I'm becoming less prim and proper every time I'm with you," she boasted.

Pressing harder against her pussy beneath the pool's surface, the rigid column of his cock pushed perfectly at her clit—and at the same moment, one masculine hand snaked down behind her, quickly, gently, stroking between her legs. "Unh . . ." she heard herself moan.

"If it were up to me," he said, low, "and if I wouldn't get arrested . . . I would carry you over to that bed right now and fuck you 'til you screamed, private or not."

Her breath came shallow, her whole body going weak. "Believe it or not," she uttered, voice ragged, "if it were up to *me* and *I* wouldn't get arrested . . . I might just let you."

A lecherous smile unfurled on Damon's face. "Who knows?" he whispered near her ear. "Maybe before this trip is over you'll convince me you're not prim and proper at all."

Three

That night, Damon took Brenna to three small clubs, all of them on the southern outskirts of town. Two featured guys who played guitar and sang, and the third a duo—a guy on piano and his wife, who belted out pop songs. None of the acts had sent anything to Damon, but all had been recommended to him. "I meet people, I ask them to keep an eye out and let me know when they hear something they like," he'd explained on the cab ride to the first place. His leads for new music, he'd told her, came through everyone from club owners to bartenders and bouncers.

Although she didn't say it, she had to admit her surprise at what a socially intense job this was. She'd known Damon moved among jet-setters, but now she was finding out she was supposed to get friendly with club owners and bartenders, too? She liked meeting people, but she'd never been overly outgoing, so she feared this part of the job might be a challenge. Her stomach churned a little at the thought, yet like a lot of things over the past couple of days, she just pushed it aside for now.

As it turned out, none of the performers they went to see that evening particularly caught their attention or had a sound they felt worthy of pursuing. And in truth, she wasn't really into listening to music tonight. Oh, she still would have recognized something fabulous if she'd heard it, but she spent most of the evening just wanting to get back to the hotel with Damon.

After fooling around in the pool earlier, they'd been just about to head up to Damon's room to slake their lust—when his cell phone had rung and he'd ended up talking for a long while with Blue Night artist Jane Wyndham, an up-and-coming folk singer. And the afternoon had gotten away from them.

And now, just like at the pool, he continued to make her promises. Really alluring ones. Where he was going to touch her. Exactly how. He promised it was going to be slow, and thorough. "Last night was hot," he said as they found a table at the last club, "but it was like a meal eaten way too fast—just makes you want more. And today at the pool, that was a tease, an appetizer. Made me damn hungry, babe."

And then he slid easily into work mode, telling her what each of the acts they'd seen tonight had lacked.

At first, she found the way he was able to flow from sex to work and back again amusing—she could tell he loved both with equal passion. But as the night passed, she discovered it actually turned her on. It made clear to her that his whole life was a meshing of music and sex and sin. He didn't hold anything back, keep anything under wraps—he put his every thought and desire out there on the table, and she found his candor utterly arousing.

Although something in that made her wonder . . . If he could discuss music and sex almost simultaneously, could it have somehow created confusion and contributed to having women accuse him of sexual bribery?

"Can I ask you a question?" she said as they stepped into another cab, heading back to the Venetian.

"Sure, babe." He paused to give the cabbie their destination, then turned to her. "What's up?"

She hoped he wouldn't hate her for asking, but suddenly she burned to know. "What happened with Claire Starr?"

Damon failed to look surprised by the question, but his answer sounded a little intense. "Meaning did I fuck her? Yeah. And did she want it? Yeah. And did it have anything to do with giving her a deal? Nope."

"Are you mad at me for asking?"

He shook his head. "After all, I guess it's obvious that something *did* go on with her." Claire's accusations had been featured on *Entertainment Tonight* and *Access Hollywood*, not to mention the article in *People* magazine.

"I believed you when you told me it was all lies," Brenna felt eager to assure him, "but I guess I was just curious . . . if her story was strictly about getting money out of Blue Night—or something more. Like if it's possible she just somehow . . . misunderstood what happened between you."

He sighed. "There might have been a misunderstanding, but it had nothing to do with her record deal. We spent a week together in Seattle—I discovered her on a scouting trip like this one, and we hooked up. We had fun, but I considered it over after that—only she went a little *Fatal Attraction* on me. No boiled bunnies, but she didn't like taking no for an answer. I think *that*, combined with the label dropping her, turned her even more feral than usual. She's not a nice person, Brenna. I should have seen that sooner."

Brenna nodded in the dark confines of the cab. His voice had calmed now, and she spoke softly. "Thank you. For telling me."

He squeezed her thigh, bared by her denim miniskirt, then spoke more playfully. "Let that be a lesson to you, young Brenna. Don't screw the acts. It can come back to bite you in the ass."

"I don't plan on it. But then again . . . I didn't exactly plan on sleeping with *you*, either." Even if Kelly had been sure it was destiny. "So I guess you never know where things are going to lead."

His look bordered somewhere between teasing and arrogant. "The difference between me and all the other guys you might sleep with in this business is . . . I'm the nice one."

She tilted her head. "So every other man in the music industry is pure evil and out to get me?"

His gaze dropped to her breasts, concealed in a clingy halter top. "Pure evil? Likely. Out to get you, babe? *Definitely*."

Four

As they strolled into the Venetian's lavish lobby with Damon's hand closed warmly around Brenna's, one of the porters—in his gondolier uniform—politely said, "Good evening, Mr. Andros," then nodded to Brenna, as well.

As they traversed the tile floor beneath a huge and divinely frescoed ceiling, people stared—whether because they knew who he was or because he was just so beautiful, she didn't know.

Either way, she couldn't help wondering what people saw when they spotted her on the arm of a devastatingly attractive man. Even if they didn't know his reputation, he still emanated sex. Did they realize she was about to get laid? And did they disdain her in some way? Were they jealous?

The beauteous part of her musings, though, was that she honestly didn't care very much. This was Vegas, after all. And being with Damon felt almost as if she'd been suddenly promoted from mild-mannered office worker to jet-set celebrity girlfriend. She felt different on the inside, too. Freer. More confident. Like she was living, really living, maybe for the first time in her life.

When they entered Damon's oversize suite, he released her hand to approach the fax machine situated on the wide ledge between the dining area and living room. "Damn," he said softly.

"What?"

"Nothing big. Just tried to fax the Blush contract to Jenkins earlier but couldn't get it to go through. I'd like to have it on his desk by tomorrow morning, though, so I'd better try again."

"Let *me*," she offered. "I have a way with fax machines."

"If you insist," he replied, his look telling her he didn't mind ditching the mundane task. Then he moved to the stereo to tune in some soft rock.

"Once an administrative assistant, always an administrative assistant," she said cavalierly over her shoulder as Damon disappeared into the bedroom. Which was when it hit her. "I wonder if he's interviewing people for my position yet." She'd been so caught up in her new world that she hadn't even thought about what would become of her old one.

"Yeah, he is," Damon's voice echoed through the doorway. "He mentioned in an e-mail that he had three lined up for tomorrow."

"Oh. Good." Although she wasn't sure why the news made her feel a little proprietary about her old job. *Someone* would have to do all the work she usually did, after all.

It was as the pages were sifting through the fax machine, one by one, that she heard the sound of running water in addition to the music that wafted through the air—currently Norah Jones' seductive "Turn Me On."

"What are you doing in there?" she called.

"Running a bath."

Oh. The small of her back ached with possibility. What kind of bath? For one or for two?

"Join me when you're done with the fax."

Okay, *that* kind of bath. Her body resumed feeling warm and ready, and she willed the contract to move faster through the fax machine. The moment the fax was completed, she walked briskly through the large bedroom and into the bathroom—yet she hadn't been remotely prepared for what she would see.

Mirrors covered the gargantuan tiled space, stretching across the lengthy double vanity and spanning the walls around the large enclosed tub. Where Damon sat amid a bounty of white, frothy bubbles, holding a glass of white wine, casting a come-hither expression, and looking delectable enough to eat. She sucked in her breath at the sight.

"Take your clothes off." His voice came deep, quietly commanding.

She let the breath back out but felt far from relaxed.

Because she'd never actually stood and undressed for a man before. And this was a lot different from their frantic coupling in the closet, or even fooling around in the pool. She'd thought those acts were *wild, decadent*—because of where they'd taken place. But somehow, this, standing before him in a well-lit room and beginning to shed her clothes while he watched her every move—*this* felt decadent. Extreme. Intimate.

Reaching behind her neck, she slowly untied her slinky black halter top and found that letting it drop to her waist wasn't so hard—because she wore a black strapless bra underneath. "Pretty," he said, his expression fully sexual, devoid of all amusement. "Now more."

Brenna pushed the halter over her denim mini and felt it drop around her red strappy heels. Then she reached behind her back and smoothly unhooked the lacy bra, letting it fall, as well.

Damon's eyes locked on her breasts, making her already taut nipples tingle under his perusal. He'd seen them before, of course, in the closet, and after, as they'd slept together naked last night, but again, this felt more intense—to strip for him, to bare herself. It felt like baring her soul.

"Fucking beautiful," he said.

And as a slow heat began to pervade her, as nervousness gave way to pure lust, Brenna found herself grazing her palms up over her bare stomach and onto the two mounds of flesh. She'd never touched herself this way in front of a man before, but instinct had driven her. To do what felt good. To do what she'd known he would like.

She first cupped the undersides of her breasts, letting their weight settle in her hands. Then she let her palms close fully over them, sensually squeezing as she met Damon's gaze, as she saw the fire there and felt the result in her already-damp-for-him panties.

"That's so nice, babe," he said, his voice a low growl.

She licked her upper lip, feeling the full power now, and the full longing that was taking her over. Still gently molding her breasts, she tweaked her nipples between thumbs and forefingers, feeling how hard they were and as if they elongated even more at her touch.

"Keep going," he instructed.

And his wish was her command, she discovered—to her surprise, she actually liked him instructing her, telling her what to do. She liked the idea of being his play thing, his sex toy—the woman he wanted to fuck.

Lifting one foot to the tile step leading to the tub, she bent to undo the small buckle on her shoe.

"Not yet," Damon said.

She looked up at him.

"Take those off last."

A fresh *whoosh* of dirty pleasure rushed up her thighs and into her nether region. He wanted to see her naked but for the shoes. She *was* his sex toy. And she liked it more than she could easily understand.

Putting her foot back on the floor, Brenna undid the button on her skirt, which rested beneath her navel. Then she lowered the zipper and eased the denim over her hips until it hit the tile, leaving her in a black thong complete with embroidery and lace. She stepped free of the skirt and stood before him, drinking in his gaze, predatory and all male.

She had been careful not to drink much tonight—a total of two wine spritzers spread over the whole evening—but she felt drunk anyway, intoxicated by what she could only describe as animal desire. It grew from within, a raging force that defied logic or emotion.

She skimmed her palms up her thighs, then let them glide over her hips and back onto her ass, arching it into her hands as she thrust her breasts forward. Any remnants of nervousness were gone now—she was into this, into *him.*

Drawing her hands back around, she raked one middle finger teasingly over the front of her panties, then let it dip down inside. Her fingertip brushed briefly over her damp, swollen clit before she extracted it.

"Jesus God," Damon uttered, eyes glassy with want.

She bit her lip, feeling wholly seductive, like someone she'd never been before, someone entirely new. "Who's prim and proper now?" she asked. She hadn't realized their discussion at the pool had made her feel she had something to prove to him, but maybe she did.

Damon gave his head a slow shake. "Not you, honey. Not anymore."

She let a naughty smile unfurl across her face.

And he offered a nasty little grin of his own in reply. "You're a dirty girl, aren't you?"

Was she? Or was this partly an act? "When I want to be," she said. But the real answer, she decided, was: *When I'm with you.*

"Is your pussy wet?"

She nodded.

"Did it get your finger wet?"

She nodded again—then took a few steps forward, her heels clicking across the tile, and leaned down to slip her fingertip into his mouth.

They both moaned as his lips closed around it, and she felt his tongue, then the slight, suckling pull—felt him really tasting her. The sensation spiraled straight to the spot that was getting more drenched with each passing second.

When finally he released her finger, he said, "Now take off your panties. Show me that pretty little cunt."

No longer shy about the raw unveiling of her body in the bright glow of the bathroom's lights, Brenna faced away from him, eased her thumbs into the elastic at her hips, and smoothly peeled the thong down until it dropped to her ankles. Stepping free of it, she turned back around, naked.

Just as from the start of this little striptease, Damon wasn't shy about planting his gaze right where his interest lay—and at the moment, he studied her crotch. His eyes seemed to physically burn into her flesh, and just like every time she'd seen him since arriving in Las Vegas, he had a way of making her pussy feel like the greatest part of her, the part that dominated every action, every thought. And as much as she liked letting him look at her, she also wanted him inside her.

"Shoes now?" she asked. She wanted to get in the tub with him. She wanted to ride him, hard.

He gave a slight nod—yet when she bent to remove one, he said, "But not like that."

She looked up, confused.

"Sit on the edge of the tub." He pointed toward the opposite end, by the faucet.

When she followed the instruction, unsure of his plan, he said, "Give me your right foot."

Mmm. *He* was going to take off her shoes. Why was that sexy as hell?

Careful not to lose her balance, Brenna held her foot out to him. Damon set his wineglass aside and, for the first time, she noticed a second one on the tile enclosure for her. With one masculine hand, he cupped the back of her ankle; with the other, he grazed his knuckles lightly down her inner calf. She shuddered at the pleasure darting upward but kept watching him, not wanting to miss a thing.

Studying her foot, he ran cool fingertips over the thin red leather strap at her ankle, then overtop more criss-crossing leather before skimming his touch onto her toes, where the nails were painted to match her heels.

Then, oh-so-slowly, he undid the ankle strap and smoothly removed the shoe. She pulled her foot back as he set the sandal next to the wineglasses and prepared to offer him the other foot—but the angle would make the position more difficult to achieve without falling.

Damon tuned in to her quandary. "Bend your right knee and rest your right foot on the back edge of the tub."

She did so. And realized the move spread her legs and put her pussy fully on display. Their eyes met, acknowledging it, just before Damon's gaze dropped. "Do you know what my favorite color is?" he asked.

Huh? They were going to do the favorite-color, favorite-ice-cream-flavor thing *now*? "Uh, no. What?"

He studied the flesh between her thighs, unabashedly. "Pink."

Her own gaze dropped to see that, in this position, indeed her slit had parted and the pink creases of her cunt were clearly visible. Raw heat consumed her. "Oh."

"Other shoe," he said, and when she looked back to him, he wore a wicked little grin, having caught her looking at herself.

Carefully, she offered her left foot and absorbed the pleasure as Damon repeated the same motions as before, caressing her skin, gliding his fingertips over both shoe and skin, before finally removing the strappy, high-heeled sandal. This time, when the shoe was gone, he didn't release her foot until he'd kissed the top of it, creating a tingling sensation that scurried all through her.

"Can I come into the tub now?" she asked.

He arched one arrogant brow. "Why do you want in the tub so bad?"

The playful question, clearly designed to make her declare her lust, earned a coquettish response instead. "Maybe I just need a bath. After all, you said I was a dirty girl."

His gaze narrowed on her hotly. "Too bad." Then he scooted toward her in the tub. "Stay where you are. That sweet little taste of your pussy made me want more."

"Oh," she murmured, just as he leaned in to rake his tongue firmly up the center of her parted folds. Then, "Ohhh . . ."

The pleasure was almost overwhelming as he licked her again and again, from bottom to top, as if her cunt were an ice cream cone. "God, oh God," she heard herself breathe as she involuntarily began to move against his mouth. "God, yeah."

Soon, Damon lifted his hand from the water and eased two wet fingers into her already soaked opening, giving her the sense of having him inside her. It wasn't his cock, of course, but his fingers were nice, too, especially when he began sliding them in and out in time with her undulations.

She watched him, amazed at the rawness of what she saw—again, she usually did this in the dark, and she wasn't used to *looking at it*, looking at a man going down on her. She wasn't sure she'd ever witnessed such an erotic sight.

That's when a glance up from Damon, his face buried so sensually between her legs, reminded her of the mirrors lining the walls on two sides of the tub. They afforded her a view not only of her lover but of herself—with a man's head moving between her parted thighs, her hips lifting slightly to meet him. Witnessing the passion etched across her own face, she felt as if she were in a porn movie come to life.

Next, she looked across the room, into the larger mirror over the vanity. Yet another view. Damon's thick dark hair. Her legs spread wide. Her breasts bouncing slightly with her motions.

When Damon's attention narrowed, focusing more tightly on her clit, her breath came heavier, the pleasure building at her center. His skilled tongue swirled about the engorged nub, each move sending a fresh burst of heat exploding through her. The change drew her gaze from the mirrors back down to Damon, whose eyes were on her. He'd seen her watching them in the glass.

His mouth latched onto her clit then, pulling it inside, and his tongue thrust at it hard. Oh God, the rough ministrations made her clench her teeth, her arms and legs growing weak. She kept her eyes on his now, never wavering, and without planning it, she began to show him exactly how dirty she could be. "Suck me, baby," she whispered hotly. "Suck my clit. Suck it hard. Suck it. Suck it."

Her naughty demands were the last thing she remembered before the orgasm hit, hard and fast, coming on before she even expected it. Arching her neck in response to the intense waves of sensation, she cried out softly as she drove her pussy against his mouth—*yes, yes, yes*—soaking in every pulse of pleasure to be had.

When it finally ebbed, she went still and Damon eased back from her.

"You're fucking gorgeous when you come," he said from amid the bubbles, his eyes sparkling darkly.

Still breathing hard, she managed a smile. "Then you should make that happen often."

"I intend to."

In that moment, it struck her that their words were the kind that might be exchanged between people in an actual relationship, one that would last, go on—but she knew he only meant he intended to *while they were in Vegas,* and she brushed aside any hint of disappointment that might have produced to resume concentrating on the sexy, naked man in front of her.

"Can I come into the tub *now?*" she asked, allowing a teasing bit of sarcasm to color her voice.

He offered a slow, sexy grin, then reached for her hand. "Come on in, dirty girl, and let me clean you up."

Once she was in the tub, facing him, her legs crossing over his beneath the water, Damon reached for the two wineglasses next to her shoes, passing her one.

"Where'd you get this?" she asked.

"Minibar," he replied, then lifted his glass in a toast. "To my dirty little Brenna—who surprises me more every day."

She liked that, she thought, clinking her glass against his. Surprising him. And she wanted to keep doing it. So, without taking time to weigh it, she asked the question that had entered her mind a few minutes ago, watching him eat her. "What does it taste like?"

He looked confused and apparently decided she was talking about the wine. "Take a drink and see."

But she shook her head. "No. My pussy. How does it taste?"

Once more, his gaze darkened, and she knew she'd succeeded at shocking—and exciting—him yet again.

In reply, he simply held out his free hand—toward her mouth. "Like this." He touched two fingers to her lips, nudging—and after only a split second of doubt she parted them, letting him ease inside.

The taste on her tongue was strange—a bit salty, a bit sweet, somehow a little sour, and very pervasive. She didn't like it, but it still turned her on to share such extreme intimacy with him.

"Well?" he asked.

"Frankly . . . yuck." She made a face, then took a big drink of her wine.

He laughed easily. "I guess it's kinda like beer. An acquired taste."

"But you sincerely like it?" She'd grown curious, and a little fascinated.

His eyes told her the question was making him think about it in a way he never had before. "It definitely gets me hot," he said, "so yeah, I sincerely like it. But . . . if I didn't equate the taste with sex . . . well, let's just say I probably wouldn't spread it on my hamburger."

She let out a loud, quick laugh, then informed him, "You're getting a little gross here."

He leaned closer, still wearing a sexy grin. "You started the conversation."

Setting her wine aside, she twined her arms around his neck and said, "Well, now I'm finishing it," and kissed him.

Of course, she tasted herself on his mouth, too—but again, the rawness of it only added to her desire. She'd just come, but she still wanted much more of him, particularly the part underneath the bubbles. And she'd long since ceased feeling shy.

Reaching down into the suds, she wrapped her hand full around his hard cock and listened to his low moan, watched his eyes fall shut. She'd done the same thing in the closet, but again, this was different.

Now she had the time to run her fist up and down his length, to squeeze and caress, explore. Mmm, *God*, he was huge. She'd realized that last night, yet a penis the size of his wasn't the kind of thing a girl easily got used to.

"This is so much different than last time," she said, letting her thoughts out. "That was so rushed, so heated. And this is so much... slower. Better."

A lecherous expression made its way onto his face. "This is *still* heated, babe. *Very.*"

So true, so she only nodded—but this was ... so much easier. It felt less like sinning. Simply because they were in his private room, someplace where there was no danger of being discovered.

Of course, she was overthinking this—she knew that. This was no better or worse than fucking him in that closet had been. This was just as dirty, just as brazen—more so in ways. But it *felt* better. Just to have this private time with him. Time to be playful. Time to be sexy.

And now, she decided, was the time to ride him, ride that hot, hard erection, take her fill of him, show him all the wanton lust that had been building inside her.

Letting her tongue slide sensually along her upper lip, she locked her gaze on his and moved to straddle him.

"Find something you like down there, my dirty girl?"

"Mmm," she purred, situating herself until she felt the head of his shaft right where she wanted it.

"Then I'm gonna let you have it." With that, he clamped his hands over her hips and pushed her down to sheathe him.

They both groaned at the impact and Brenna knew she'd never been fuller—this position making him feel even larger than he had last night. "So big," she murmured.

"Tell me you like it."

"I love it," she sighed, then began to move on him.

Letting his palms close over her ass beneath the bubbles, Damon leaned in to deliver a sensuous tongue kiss that nearly turned her inside out. One kiss became two, and then more, more, as Brenna followed her body's instincts, undulating on him in rhythmic circles that stimulated her clit with every hot revolution.

Soon, she moved harder, harder.

Peering up into her eyes, Damon whispered the same words she'd said to him last night. "Fuck me, babe. Oh yeah. Fuck me. Just like that."

It supercharged every sensation already pulsing through her body, turning her still more ravenous and wild. As Damon's mouth closed over one sensitive nipple, she bucked against him, crying out. He suckled her hard, tight, and she thrust her breast deeper into his mouth, somehow wishing to have part of herself inside him just like he was inside her.

As she rocked on him, she grew aware that the water in the tub moved with them now, that she was making rough waves, some splashing out, bubbles flowing over the tub's edge. But she was too lost in pleasure to care or stop or even slow down.

She dug her nails lightly into his chest, moaning her joy, loving the very decadence of this moment and how utterly free she felt—until she heard Damon say, "Brenna. Stop."

Stunned—and slightly devastated—she went still. "Are you about to come? Because if you are, it's okay. I already—"

"No, babe. You're drowning me."

Oh God. She'd totally missed the fact that he'd somehow gradually slipped down into the tub as she'd ridden him so vigorously, and now his face rested barely above the water, framed with bubbles. She gasped. "I'm sorry. I didn't even realize . . ." Then she eased off of his erection, since it seemed to be the only way he could sit up.

After which he grinned indulgently, water dripping from the ends of his long hair. "I didn't want to interrupt you, but I was afraid you might push me under and not notice."

Warmth stained her cheeks. "I'm an idiot."

He lifted a wet hand to her face. "No, you're a wild woman. Which

I totally dig. But . . . maybe this particular tub isn't the best place for that position."

All things considered, she couldn't help feeling a little deflated—and thoroughly frustrated. "I was . . . getting close."

His gaze turned sexier, determined. "Don't worry, babe—I'll get you there."

She bit her lip as his palms skimmed over her hips and higher, until he was cupping the sides of her breasts, stroking his wet thumbs across their tips—again, again.

"Oh . . . God . . . that's nice."

Letting his eyes fall half shut, he bent to flick his tongue across one turgid peak. Blowing on it lightly then—and sending yet another light rush of pleasure to her cunt—he leaned forward to speak low and deep in her ear. "Do you want my hard cock, Brenna?"

"Oh God, yes."

He still teased her nipples, his breath coming warm on her neck. "Do you want it hard? Deep?"

Oh my. True, this slower, more exploratory sex was extremely pleasant—but *hard* and *deep* were calling to her now, beckoning. She wanted to feel him like she had in the closet, pounding into her, making each stroke echo through every inch of her body. And she wasn't sure exactly how they were going to accomplish that in the bathtub, but she was willing to find out. "Yes, baby. Yes."

Damon lowered his hands to her waist and said, "Turn around."

Careful not to slip, Brenna let him guide her until she faced away, on her knees. Like before, she caught sight of them in the mirrored wall straight ahead of her—a glimpse of her bared breasts, his firm hands on her behind, his eyes filled with dark intent.

"Bend over the edge of the tub. Lift your ass."

Brenna did so, watching in the mirror to see Damon studying her rear—or more likely, what was between her thighs. Despite already being in a bathtub, her pussy grew wetter, and she wondered what she looked like from that angle. Instinctively, she gave her hips a playful wiggle, which drew him down to deliver a gentle kiss to her bottom. "Mmm," she said, the tiny affection rippling all through her.

"You like that?" he whispered.

"Uh-huh."

She heard more than saw his naughty smile. "This wasn't part of my plan, but I'll be nice and give you a little more."

"Okay." Her voice came soft, almost childlike, so taken was she by such tender touches from his mouth.

His kisses on her already-moist ass sent the sweetest pleasure she'd ever experienced echoing gently out through every limb. And then—oh!—came fingers, prodding her below, where she was so ready for him. A low cry escaped her when he pushed two inside her, and she moved against them instinctively. She'd quit watching in the mirror—her eyes had fallen shut and this was now all about feeling, absorbing, experiencing.

"More," she heard herself say. "Fuck me."

A gentle growl erupted from Damon's throat, the warmth of his breath wafting over her bottom as he delivered one last gentle kiss—before the water started gyrating violently.

"What . . . ?" she asked, opening her eyes.

She met Damon's brown gaze in the mirror. "Turned on the Jacuzzi," he said.

"Oh," she sighed in response, realizing that the hard rush of water around her thighs, some of it splashing up onto her pussy, was going to make this even better.

The next thing she knew, Damon's cock arced upward through the valley of her ass, deliciously hard as he slid it back and forth, making her thrust back against it, simply needing to *feel* that hot erection anywhere—everywhere.

Then, finally, he plunged his full length inside her. Just like before, they both cried out at the initial entry—but there was no rest, no adjustment period to having the stonelike column inside her before he began to drive, *hard, hard, hard,* exactly as he'd promised.

She heard her own mewling cries, felt the rough pleasure burst like skyrockets inside her, shimmering all the way out to her fingers and toes with every powerful thrust. Below, the water pulsated in tumultuous waves and the bubbles began to increase, growing like foamy white mountains around them.

"Yes! Yes!" she screamed, just barely able to form words but wanting desperately to let him know she loved his cock slamming into her, loved how rough and wild Damon made sex, how rough and wild he made *her*.

The suds in the tub continued going crazy, billowing still more until bubbles were almost all Brenna could see. It was like being fucked in a white, sparkling cloud, and she sensed the bubbles overflowing the tub on all sides.

"Are you a bad girl?" Damon asked, still ramming into her, slick and deep.

"Yes!" she cried.

"Do you need to be punished?"

"Yes! Oh yes!"

With that, he brought the flat of his hand down to slap her ass as he delivered the next hot thrust.

"Oh!" she shrieked, the sensation heightening all others.

His hand came again, again, spanking her as he fucked her, the whole act turning her weak as a baby even as she drank in every ounce of delight. Never in her life had she experienced such overwhelming physical reactions that blocked out every emotion, every thought, leaving her body only to revel in the pure carnal joy of it.

She heard herself crying out, felt her ass driving back against him, her body responding without her thought or consent. Not that she didn't consent. She'd never enjoyed anything more in her life.

Until the spanking stopped and his hand slid over her hip and down into her cunt.

A deep moan left her as his fingers sank into her folds, rubbing her so expertly that she didn't even care how many other women he'd had to touch to learn to do it so well. No man had ever caressed her with such skill, so much like she would touch herself, in hot little circles, applying the perfect pressure each time his fingertips passed over her clit.

His hot cock still drove into her from behind and, just like his fingers, delivered perfect strokes.

Music still echoed from the outer room, but all Brenna heard now were Damon's groans as he fucked her and the sound of her breath growing heavier, harder, as she lost herself in sensation.

"Oh God," she heard herself murmur. "Close, baby. Close."

She was going to come. It was so, so near.

His cock, his fingers, working together, almost as one, pushed her further, further.

"Oh!" she cried when the climax hit, rolling through her in warm, enveloping waves that shook her, made her want to collapse—and Damon must have known that because while one hand still stroked her slit, his other arm circled her waist, supporting her.

And it was just as the delicious pulses began to ebb that Damon— still thrusting deep—came, too. She felt it in the hot shudder of his body against hers, the deep groan of ultimate satisfaction, the whispered pleasure: "Ah . . . ah, fuck yes . . . yeah."

They stayed quiet and still for a moment afterward, and only then did it strike Brenna how semi-weird and kinky things had gotten there for a minute with the spanking stuff. After which she let a broad smile spread across her face at the realization that semi-weird and kinky could be so much fun.

And that it didn't even feel semi-weird *or* kinky . . . with Damon.

Talk about a week of training. She felt sure that when Jenkins had sent her off on this trip he'd had no idea she'd be getting a sexual education in addition to a professional one.

When finally she'd come back down to earth after her orgasm, enough to look around, she was—*oh dear God!*—horrified by the mess. "Look at this place!"

Mounds of white bubbles had spilled to the floor, some flowing all the way to the vanity. On the other side of the tub, in the tiled corners, the fluff had piled several feet high.

Behind her, Damon just laughed as he gently withdrew from her body and turned off the Jacuzzi. "Don't worry, babe," he said. "Bubbles eventually melt. And I'm sure the maids have seen worse."

Five

While Brenna extracted herself from the bubbles, Damon rescued her shoes—which, he announced, were damp but didn't look damaged. She found her clothes, also predictably damp, beneath a pile of suds on the floor. After they toweled each other off, she looked back toward the tile enclosure still covered in white and said, "What about the wine?"

"Forget the wine—I want to lie down with you."

She couldn't argue with that, especially when they crawled into the lavish king-size bed and Damon pulled her naked body close, kissing her forehead.

Then he fell asleep, but she didn't mind—in fact, she almost thought it was cute that even sex god Damon Andros fell prey to slumber after an orgasm.

Watching him doze, smelling the fresh but still masculine scent of his body, watching the way his longer locks began to dry in little curls from when she'd nearly drowned him with her enthusiasm ... she couldn't help reflecting on the myriad experiences this man had given her. And the myriad emotions he'd drawn from her. She'd realized in the tub that the sex was so overpowering as to *obscure* emotions, but even that in itself, an awareness that all you wanted or cared about was the cock ramming into you ... wasn't that an emotion in itself?

She found herself remembering their other encounters, too. Her desires today at the pool had been so utterly intense. As intense as at

Fetish, but somehow even more extreme. At the bar, she'd behaved brazenly, but had at least needed a closed door. Whereas at the pool, she'd meant what she'd said—she'd wanted him so badly that she'd stopped caring about spectators.

And maybe, just maybe, a really deviant part of her had even been turned on by the idea of being watched by women who wanted what she was getting. She'd acknowledged that in the pool, but the truth was, she'd been thinking about more than just having them watch her kiss him. She'd known the fleeting desire to have them watch her fuck him, watch her take in the cock they lusted for but couldn't have.

And still, despite all that, what they'd done tonight, in private, somehow made everything else pale in comparison.

She'd never thought much about *real, true* intimacy before. She supposed neither Wayne, nor the few other men she'd been with, had ever really inspired such feelings. Yet she knew that tonight she had experienced it with Damon.

Brenna was still watching him when, a little while later, his hand moved across her bare hip beneath the sheets and his eyes fluttered open. "Hey," he said with a sleepy smile.

"Hey."

"Sorry I drifted off."

She gave him a tolerant grin. "Orgasm can do that to a man."

"Fucking you that hard took a lot out of me," he admitted with a lecherous little smile of his own. Then mused, "Lights are still on. Music, too."

Truthfully, she hadn't noticed, too caught up in Damon and the overwhelming sexual awakening he'd given her over the past twenty-four hours. "I'm too cozy to get up right now." And besides, the bedroom lamps were off—only light from the bathroom and dining area filtered in through the doorways, keeping the room shadowy and romantic.

He nuzzled closer. "Me, too."

When her gaze fell on the cross at his throat, she reached out to gently slide her fingertip down the smooth silver. "Is this special? I never noticed you wearing it before last night, but you've had it on ever since."

"I wear it all the time. Just ends up under my T-shirts most days."

"So it *is* special."

He gave a light nod against his pillow. "My grandmother gave it to me on my confirmation, when I was twelve. She brought it with her from Greece as a young girl."

"Wow." His reply surprised her on many levels. It amazed her to find out the cross was so old. And that Damon Andros was the sort of guy who treasured his grandmother. And that Damon Andros had a religious side. "I hadn't guessed you for a good Catholic boy."

He cast a sideways glance. "Catholic, yeah. Not necessarily good."

She smiled in reply. "Is your grandma . . . still alive?"

His expression transformed into one of warmth—maybe a sort of comfort—she hadn't seen there before. "Eighty-five and still going strong. She's back in Brooklyn with the rest of my family."

"Wow," she said again. She'd just never thought about Damon even *having* a family. "I bet they're proud of you."

He let out a short, cynical laugh. "Yeah, it's every parent's dream to have a son accused of sexual misconduct on national TV."

She winced. "Sorry—I wasn't thinking about that. I was thinking about your job."

"They love me and accept what I do—but it wasn't exactly their first choice."

"What was?"

He sighed. "Until his retirement a few months ago, my father sold insurance out of the same little office on the same Brooklyn street since before I was born. I have three older sisters, but my parents kept on try-ing until they got a boy so there'd be somebody to take over the family business."

"Oh." She couldn't imagine the pressure that would put on a kid. "And one of your sisters didn't qualify?"

He grinned. "They're very traditional. And proud, too—proud as hell that my grandfather started the business fresh off the boat and that my dad kept it going. So I was groomed from an early age to be the next Andros Insurance guy.

"Problem was, I liked music a whole lot more than insurance. I got into a band in high school, but when I figured out I wasn't much of a musician, I got a job at CBGB instead. So by the time I was eighteen, I was working in the insurance office by day and the bar at night."

Brenna was duly impressed—she knew the small Manhattan underground club had been *the* place to launch punk and alternative bands in the seventies. Groups like Blondie, the Ramones, and the Talking Heads had made their way to fame from CBGB's stage. "That must have been fabulous."

"It was un-fucking-believable," he said. "I was there in the early nineties and worked my way up from busboy to sound mixer to events coordinator. I got to see bands like Soundgarden, Pearl Jam, and Smashing Pumpkins before anyone knew who they were.

"In fact," he said, casting her a this-will-surprise-you look, "I first met Jenkins there."

She drew her chin back. "No way."

"Yep. Blue Night was brand-new then, and he was doing his own scouting in those days. We started talking music, and he thought I had a good handle on it. We got to know each other and he offered me a job."

"Was it hard to pack up and move to L.A.? Tell your dad you were leaving the insurance biz?" Before a few minutes ago, she couldn't have imagined anything being difficult for Damon Andros, but hearing about his family, picturing him as a young boy in Brooklyn, changed that.

"Yes and no," he said, his voice softening. "I didn't like letting them down, but I was suffocating there. Leaving to pursue what I really wanted to do was very . . . freeing. In more ways than one."

"What do you mean?"

His gaze flicked from the ceiling to her, then back again. "I was engaged."

It was all she could do to keep her jaw from dropping. "Really?"

He gave a slight nod. "Her name was Angie, and she was a nice Greek girl from the block. We'd dated since we were sixteen and . . ."

"And what?" she asked when he trailed off.

"It was kind of like the insurance business. I didn't want to be there, but I felt stuck."

"Oh."

He looked back to her. "I *did* love her once—but I had to go. Smartest thing I ever did. And a lesson learned."

Brenna bit her lip. "What was the lesson?"

"That being tied down in any way makes me feel ... well, *tied down*. So since then, I just don't do it. I'm happier that way. And I don't risk hurting anybody."

"Sounds wise," she said, trying to ignore the slight churning of her stomach. And it *did* sound wise, so why was her gut twisting? It wasn't exactly a news flash that Damon didn't get into commitment or relationships. He was basically telling her what she already knew.

Only maybe hearing it out loud made it sound a little different.

Because maybe she really liked him.

Not just liked sex with him—but liked *him*. Being with him, talking with him, learning from him, laughing with him.

"Tell me about your ex," Damon said, catching her off guard with the request. When she didn't answer right away, he added, "Unless you'd rather not."

She shook her head. "No, I don't mind. I ... met Wayne five years ago, and he seemed like my dream come true. We married after a year—big, traditional wedding, all the trimmings—and then a year after that his company transferred him from Ohio to L.A. So we moved out here and all seemed well. I guess, over time, I felt us growing apart a little, but I chalked it up to both of us being busy—me with my job at Blue Night, him with his systems development job, and he'd joined a health club and was working out a lot.

"Then one night he went to the gym, but forgot his cell phone. I noticed a missed call, and thinking it might be something important, I listened to the message. I heard a woman saying she was running late, but that she'd be there soon and that she had on a new teddy under her jogging suit."

"Damn."

She nodded numbly, lost in the reverie. "Yeah—damn."

"What did you do?"

"I went to the gym. And I found them working out together and confronted him. He told me everything—that he'd met her there, that they'd hit it off, that one thing had led to another. She was married, too, and a mother of three."

Brenna appreciated Damon's grimace.

It allowed her to share her feelings on this particular subject. "I know sex is great and all, but there are a couple of things I hold sacred: marriage and family. I mean, why even bother with those things if they're not what you want?"

He nodded. "Exactly. Which is why I don't have 'em."

"So you can see why I couldn't forgive him."

He glanced over at her. "He expected you to?"

"That's what he wanted. But . . . once that trust was so totally breached, I knew I'd never feel the same way again."

"I don't blame you, babe," he said, then leaned over to give her a little kiss, which she really needed at the moment. "But I'll tell you a secret."

She moved closer, glad they were leaving the subject of her ex behind. Their breakup couldn't have contrasted more with new Brenna. "What's that?"

"His loss has definitely been my gain."

They kissed again, then Damon's eyes fell shut, leaving Brenna back with her own thoughts—and her own words: *Once that trust was so totally breached, I knew I'd never feel the same way again.* Wasn't that how Damon would feel if he found out about her deception, that she was stealing the job he loved and had done so well for so long? Somehow, she'd almost forgotten about it today—so much excitement had passed between them, making it easier and easier to brush anything negative aside.

She knew she was committing all manner of sins with Damon, but the lie was far worse than the others, and as she eased out of bed, walking naked to turn off the stereo and lamps, she suffered a more heartfelt sense of guilt than she had up to now. Because she knew him now. And because this was seeming like a little more than just sex now. At the very least, she knew they had become friends. Well, friends with benefits.

Yet as she strolled to the wide wall of windows in the spacious living area, peering out on the lights of the city, she forced herself, once again, to shove the guilt aside. After all, hadn't he said that what happened in Vegas stayed in Vegas?

So the sex would stay in Vegas.

And with any luck, maybe the guilt would, too.

THE FOURTH NIGHT

"A sin takes on a new and real terror when there seems a chance
that it is going to be found out."
—Mark Twain

One

She couldn't know how good she'd felt to him last night.

Damon was used to waking up with a woman next to him, but when he rolled on his pillow to see Brenna, their heated bathtub fuck came roaring back to his thoughts. She was the very first woman he'd had sex with sans condom since leaving Angie—a damn long time ago. A lifetime, it felt like.

He hadn't done it purposely. He'd just climbed into the bathtub, invited her in, and somewhere along the way it had occurred to him he didn't have a rubber anywhere handy.

And maybe it had been unfair not to point it out, not to remind her, since clearly she'd forgotten, too—but he hadn't. Because when she'd slid down onto him, so moist, so tight, when he'd felt that hot, slick cunt hugging his cock, flesh to flesh, he simply hadn't the strength to *stop* feeling it.

He knew he was safe, because he'd *always* been careful up to now. And he was pretty damn sure Brenna was safe, too—he was pretty sure he was the first guy she'd fucked since leaving her shithead husband. And he knew she was taking birth control pills because she'd mentioned it among the things she had to do yesterday morning upon heading back to her room to get ready for their breakfast meeting with Blush. He'd suggested she put them in her purse so she wouldn't have to go dashing back to her room in the future.

Just then, her eyes fluttered open.

And he looked away. He wasn't sure why, but he supposed he didn't want to be caught watching her sleep. Something in that sounded . . . well, like someone else, not him.

Only when she stretched, yawned, did he turn to say, "Hey, babe."

Her sleepy smile lit up the room. "Hey." She definitely had the look of a woman who'd been well-pleasured last night, an observation that made his dick perk to life under the covers.

"Do you need to take your pill?"

She gasped softly. "Oh, gosh—thanks for reminding me. I thought about stopping them after my divorce, but they keep my periods regular." And up she hopped, walking beautifully naked out into the dining area, where he guessed she'd left her purse last night. He watched her sweet round ass sashay away, then a moment later got to see the return view, her pretty tits—nipples already erect—swaying as she walked.

When she glanced at the clock, he did, too—and damn, it was almost noon! "Shit," he said. "Good thing we didn't have anything scheduled for today."

She perched on the foot of the bed. "So then, what *is* our plan?"

Damon turned the question over in his mind. "Tonight we've got to make stops at a few more clubs, but we could use the afternoon to check in with some of my contacts around the Strip—and maybe make some more in the process."

"Sounds good," she said, and he loved how free and easy she appeared lounging about in the nude—this wasn't at all the way he'd envisioned Brenna before this trip, or even after he'd first met with her at the French café that first night.

"And if you're a good little girl," he added, "maybe we can see some sights. Which, here, means touring some of the hotels. Doesn't sound that exciting, I know—but some of these places are pretty spectacular."

She gave her head a coquettish tilt. "There's only one problem with that plan."

"What's that?"

She shook her head, her bed-tousled hair falling around her face. "I'm not a good little girl."

Two

Riding the tram toward the southern end of the Strip, Damon first took Brenna back to the Paris. He remembered thinking she'd seemed to enjoy the atmosphere of Mon Ami Gabi—and there was much more there to see.

He led her through the casino, situated beneath the base of an imitation Eiffel Tower and flanked by faux Parisian streets complete with more cafés and patisseries. Since they'd missed breakfast, they stopped into one of the French bakeries for some fresh, flaky croissants.

"Mmm," she purred, taking the first bite at the little café table where they'd settled. "This is heavenly."

He couldn't help smiling because her soft little moan reminded him of when he was touching her, just starting to get her excited.

From the Paris, they ventured across the street to the grandeur of the Bellagio, another Italian-themed hotel, famous for its "dancing fountains" that lined Las Vegas Boulevard. Although the whole place was lavish—and he'd gathered that Brenna *enjoyed* lavish—he mainly took her there to see the glass ceiling by artist Dale Chihuly, composed of hundreds of handblown, brightly colored glass discs suspended above the lobby.

"Oh my God," she said, leaning back to peer upward. "You could look at this all day and still find new parts of it. Amazing. I wish I could just lie on the floor and stare up at it a while."

Damon grinned at her girlish enthusiasm, then glanced around.

"I've got a better idea." Taking her hand, he led her to one of the plush sofas situated beneath the hanging sculpture and took a seat. "Lie down here beside me and rest your head on my lap. That way, we don't have to worry about anybody stepping on you."

She giggled, then did as he'd suggested, her auburn locks fanning across his thigh. He watched her vibrant green eyes as she explored the colors and shapes above, until finally she concluded, "I could get lost in this. It's like . . . something you'd see in a dream."

From there, he led her a bit farther up the Strip, crossing Tropicana Avenue to the Excalibur, where she seemed wholly entertained by the medieval theme, then onto the pyramid-shaped Luxor and classy Mandalay Bay, where they visited the shark tank and stopped to play a little roulette. He'd never seen anyone so amused by winning ten dollars on a spin as Brenna.

Of course, at each stop, he took the opportunity to pop into a bar or lounge where he knew someone—asking if they'd seen any good bands lately—and got a couple of leads. He also introduced Brenna, explaining she was joining him in A&R duties at Blue Night. He always saved an evening or two on trips like this for checking out acts he learned about along the way, and he started making notes as they hopped the tram from Mandalay back to the Excalibur, then took the elevated walkway across Tropicana Avenue to New York, New York.

As they meandered the winding streets laid out inside the resort, Brenna asked, "So, does this place do New York justice?"

He shrugged. "It's . . . an entertaining facsimile. It doesn't exactly feel like home, but I guess it's as close as you can come on this side of the country."

After a few hours of hotel tours and networking, Brenna announced she was hungry, so they stopped into a deli on one of the faux New York thoroughfares for sandwiches, and as he sat across from her eating, it hit him much fun he was having. Just eating a freaking sandwich with her. Walking around with her and showing her things she'd never seen before. Watching the way her eyes lit up with wonder at every turn.

He supposed he'd just gotten so accustomed to plastic women that Brenna was a pleasant departure. He hadn't ever actually thought of them that way before now—as plastic—but that pretty much described the women he usually hung out with. It wasn't that there was anything wrong with them—but Brenna was so different, so open, so willing to let her insecurities show. And the way she ran the gamut from eager, dirty sex nymph to wide-eyed innocent—hell, she just made them look so . . . two-dimensional. Flat. Unreal.

In fact, when was the last time he'd really enjoyed socializing with a woman when it didn't involve sex?

Shit—it was a sobering question.

Because he wasn't quite sure he . . . *ever* had.

Unless he thought back to Angie. But again, that was a lifetime ago. In another world. He was a far different person now than he'd been then.

"What's wrong?" Brenna asked.

He jerked to attention. "What? Nothing. Why?"

"You just have a weird look on your face."

Hell. People seldom accused him of wearing weird looks.

He considered just being honest—as honest and open and forthright as she would be if the situation were reversed—saying: *I just like you, that's all. I like you and I don't quite remember the last time I really, honestly* liked *someone I was fucking.* But instead he just smirked and said, "Thanks." And, on impulse, threw a potato chip at her.

At which she laughed, then threw a small handful of them back.

Which, for some reason, made him like her even more. He pointed a scolding finger at her and said, "Knock it off," unable to hide a slight smile. "You're supposed to be a hip, cool A&R rep. We don't have food fights."

Her expression went from amused to confused. "Didn't you throw the first chip? About ten seconds ago? I thought maybe this was part of my training."

He tilted his head, crossed his arms, and at least *tried* to get honest. "Let's just say . . . there are moments you make me forget we're working here."

Across the table, she lowered her chin. "It so happens you're more skilled at combining work and play than anyone I've ever met."

He shrugged. "It's a gift." And wondered what the fuck he was doing saying shit like that, about her making him forget things. Crazy talk. And it was time to change the subject. "Are you gonna eat those chips or throw them? We should take off—we've got a big night ahead of us."

Three

After heading back to the Venetian, Brenna and Damon went their separate ways, to their separate rooms, to get ready for the evening. She'd had a wonderful afternoon with him, but given that it was around a hundred degrees outside, she definitely needed a shower before they set out for a night of scouting new talent.

Of course, as she ran the soap over her body, letting the warm spray rush down, she remembered getting so wet and sudsy with him last night. She remembered the best, most powerful sex of her life.

And she thought of what a fun time she'd had with him today and how, somewhere along the way, a most amazing thing had happened: new Brenna had faded. Into some combination of new Brenna and old Brenna that, together, equaled what she could only now think of as *real* Brenna. Because nothing she said or did with him was pretend anymore. It was no longer calculated or planned or practiced—somehow she'd just started being herself with him, a self that was sometimes silly, sometimes sultry, and everything in between.

She couldn't help thinking that Damon had uncovered this *new, real* her. And that without the past few days she never would have found it, never would have felt so . . . fully realized and whole as she suddenly did now.

Stop thinking that way, she reprimanded herself as she slipped on a beaded tank top and miniskirt. Because thinking that way made her feel all warm and connected to him. Not only physically, either. Emotionally, too. And there was no place for emotion here—was there?

Shit. Stop this.

Standing before the vanity to apply makeup, she decided to make some mental rules for the rest of this week:

1. Learn your new job.

2. Concentrate on the physical aspects of the relationship.

3. Ban any and all emotions that equate to romance or attachment.

4. Keep right on pushing aside any thoughts of how you're deceiving him.

5. And fuck his brains out every chance you get.

She decided to especially concentrate on number five, and given that the night was coming on, the lights of Sin City beginning to glow in the dusk outside her wall of windows, she figured she wouldn't have to wait very long.

Four

They'd decided to return to Mon Ami Gabi for dinner, and all through the meal, Brenna tried not to let him affect her. She tried to ignore the way his eyes sparkled when he smiled at her; she tried not to feel the way he'd grown slightly more open and playful with her over the past days.

Of course, beneath her skirt, her pussy wept with wanting him, so the physical part of her quest remained right on target. But damn it—he just kept making her feel so . . . so girlish, almost even romantic. So some of her rules seemed almost impossible to follow.

The heart wants what the heart wants. Her mother used to say that to her. This wasn't the first time in her life she'd liked a guy she shouldn't—starting with her friend Lana's boyfriend in high school. That's when her mom had first imparted those words, and they came back to her now.

The truth was—she knew what her heart wanted.

But that still didn't mean she could have it. Just like she couldn't have Lana's boyfriend, either—she'd never gotten him, in fact had never even tried, and Lana had never known. She'd done the right thing back then, and no one had gotten hurt. She only hoped she could be so smart and in control this time around.

"Dinner was quick," Damon said, checking his watch after he slipped a credit card in the leather binder the waitress had just left. "Too early yet to hit the clubs—we've got an hour or so to kill."

"*I* can think of a good way to kill an hour," she flirtatiously replied, unable to resist running the edge of her shoe up his leg under the table.

As usual, those beautiful brown eyes twinkled as he tilted his head and sent her a naughty little grin. "Too bad you like it in private so much, because we don't have time to go back to the hotel. We'll have to come up with something more boring."

After flashing a teasing smirk, she looked around them—at the cars and limos rushing up and down the Strip, at the Bellagio's fountains across the boulevard, at the Las Vegas night beginning to hum with excitement—and her eyes landed on the Eiffel Tower just a stone's throw away.

"Let's go to the top," she said, pointing.

"I've never done that."

"Oooh—so finally *I* get to give *you* a new experience."

Ten minutes later, Damon had purchased the tickets and they were riding the elevator with an elderly couple and a young family—all 460 feet up, according to the guide, who also pointed out some of the more noticeable landmarks such as Caesars Palace and the Mirage visible from the elevator window.

Stepping onto the viewing platform a moment later, the warm night air hit Brenna like a brick—but somehow she found it more invigorating than oppressive as it came with a hot breeze that, combined with the view, reminded her she'd probably done more real living in the past few days than ever in her life.

"Wow," she said, stepping up to the railing. Like many tall structures, the platform was surrounded by small bars of crisscrossing steel, a sort of netting to keep people from falling—but every so often, there was a break in it to allow visitors a clear view. In addition to the hotels and casinos lining Las Vegas Boulevard, the tower's panoramic view afforded a look at the desert valley and, to the west, the last remnants of the sunset shone behind a silhouette of mountains.

Damon stepped up next to her. "The view isn't nearly as good as from the real one in Paris, but I have to admit, it's not bad."

She turned to look at him. "You've been to Paris?"

He nodded easily. "A few times."

What was she thinking? *Of course* he'd been to Paris. He was Damon-freaking-Andros, after all. At moments, she almost forgot that—she'd finally quit being as starstruck as in the beginning, she supposed. But then, at other moments, it came back to her with startling clarity.

"Why do you suddenly look sad?" he asked.

She felt like a total baby but answered honestly. "Envy, I suppose. I've always dreamed of going to Paris. And other than a few beach trips back in college, and then moving to L.A., I've hardly been *anywhere*. I guess seeing the hotel today and now this—even if it's just an amusement park sort of reproduction—brought my wish back."

He covered her hand with his. "You'll get there."

She tilted her head. "What makes you think so?"

"You're going brand-new places right now, Brenna—both figuratively and literally. A whole new world is opening up for you. You'll get to where you want to go."

He spoke with such confidence that it did something to renew *hers*. Having reflected earlier—even just briefly—on her deception had begun to make her doubt she was doing the right thing, just a little. Now that she knew him. And liked him so much. And the truth was, watching him walk so self-assuredly up to bartenders and club managers to talk music and business left her feeling a little . . . intimidated. Like no matter how good an ear she had for music, she'd never be able to do certain parts of this job well, or with comfort. But now, with Damon reminding her of the far-reaching rewards such a job held—travel, luxury—she felt a refreshed energy and determination about it all.

"I suppose you've been to Venice, too," she asked, casting him a sideways glance.

He nodded. "Only once."

"*Only once*," she mimicked, unduly pleased when it made him laugh even as he eased a warm arm around her shoulder. "You've ridden in a gondola, too, I'm guessing."

He shrugged. "No other real way to see the place."

She rolled her eyes at him, and he kissed her—which pretty much killed her jealousy and reawakened the lust she'd been feeling at dinner.

"Forgive me?" he asked softly, leaning his forehead to touch hers.

"For?"

"Going all the places you want to go."

She teased and flirted. "Another kiss might help."

This time, though, the kiss wasn't the short, quick kind—his warm mouth pressed firm to hers, his tongue snaking moistly between her lips. When her own tongue met his, she gushed with moisture in her panties, and like it or not, the romance of the moment, the night, the warm breeze, took hold of her, and there was little to do but surrender to it.

Which is when he moved behind her, wrapping around her, his arms circling her waist, his solid body pressing against her back, ass, thighs. Having sex with Damon Andros was an experience beyond her wildest dreams, but *this*—being held by him in the dark, looking down on the Las Vegas Strip, feeling at once as if they were in the center of the universe and at the same time blissfully alone—*this* held an undeniable magic of its own.

"This is nice," she whispered over her shoulder.

"You feel pretty damn nice yourself." His breath came warm on her ear.

Then one of his hands shifted upward to caress the underside of her breast as his other palm slid low on her belly, resting on the flat of her stomach just above her cunt—and "nice" no longer described what was taking place. Biting her lip, she leaned back against him, realizing his cock was getting stiff against her bottom.

That's when the hand on her belly grazed lower, lower, cupping her through her skirt, and her pussy literally pulsed at the possessive touch.

"Damon," she whispered.

"Yeah, babe?" His voice had gone shadowy, sexy.

"What are you doing?"

"Touching you."

"But..." They were situated at the very corner of the tower's railing, and she glanced to either side. No one was looking at them, and the crowd atop the tower was small, yet despite the sense of solitude, they were hardly alone. "There are people here."

"They can't see where my hands are," he assured her, low and persuasive. "No one is paying any attention to us."

"Well, they might pay attention if I start *moving* against your hand." Her voice went lower now, too, breathy with the passion stealing through her. He molded her breast more fully now, and his erection grew harder and harder at her ass. Her body burned to thrust against his fingers.

She more heard than saw his heated expression in the dark. "That's what I want, Brenna. I want you to fuck my hand."

Jesus, was he serious? "Right here? With people here?"

"Mmm-hmm."

She didn't state the obvious. That she liked it in private. She knew they were both thinking that. And that this was him urging her to step away from her safety zone a little further than she already had. This was him urging her to take a chance, the chance of getting caught.

She'd heard that could really excite some people, the fear of being caught doing something bad—but it truly *didn't* excite her. Moreover, it made her nervous. It brought the notion of sin alive in a whole new way. She'd been a good girl all her life, never doing anything too wild, too left of center—and the idea of being caught fooling around, even by strangers, mortified her.

But Damon's rigid cock stretching up the center of her ass felt too good to ignore. And now his hand was under her skirt, stroking her through her panties, rubbing her clit in just the right way and reminding her what an expert touch he possessed. Pleasure echoed through her, but at the same time, more beckoned—that overwhelming urge to grind against his fingers, to press back against his erection.

She looked again to the right, to the left. She saw people in shadow but not nearby. And it was dark—getting darker each minute now as the last glimmer of light in the western sky faded to deep purple and then black.

And as Damon pushed aside the bit of silk covering her cunt and sank his fingers into her wet folds, her lust overcame her fear. She gave in and let herself gyrate against his touch.

Oh God, yes. *Yes.* Relief tore through her at simply *responding*, meeting his warm fingers in front, his thick cock in back. Up above, he gently, rhythmically pinched her nipple through her top and bra with each hot undulation.

"That's right, babe," he whispered in her ear. "Fuck my fingers. Fuck my fingers with that sweet, hot little pussy."

The words spurred her on, and she prayed he was right, that no one would notice, that no one cared, because she was in too deep now to stop, moving against his hand, feeling how wet she was for him and knowing he felt it, too.

She bit her lip and did what he asked, even more vigorously, wanting to feel everything she could feel, wanting to drink in Damon and the night and all of Sin City. She leaned her head back into his chest, arched her breast deeper into his hand, took in all the pleasure he delivered—her only acquiescence to where they were being that she held in her moans and the *Yes, yes, yes!* she wanted to scream when her orgasm struck.

It rolled through her in delicious waves of heat, her breath coming harder, Damon's arm anchoring her to keep her from collapsing, and only when it faded did she remember all over again that they were on top of the Las Vegas Eiffel Tower—with other people!

Letting out one last ragged breath, she rested against him and said, "Please tell me no one is staring at us."

She sensed the turn of his head to check. "No, babe—we're fine. And you're fucking beautiful."

He dropped a kiss atop her head, and the reprieve of knowing they'd not been seen compelled her to turn in his embrace, lock her arms around his neck, and pull him into a passionate kiss.

"Mmm, your hands," she sighed, still a bit breathless.

"What about them?" he asked.

She smiled accusingly. "You already know. I know you do. They're . . . incredible."

He shrugged. "Okay, maybe I've heard that before."

She lowered her chin and cast her sexiest grin. "Well, you're hearing it again now, and . . . I'm going to reward you."

Damon arched one brow, looking almost as if he were daring her. "How?"

Brenna could barely understand what had just come over her. But the fact that she'd managed to climax without being noticed, and that the night seemed to grow darker still, and that the elevator had just departed, taking some people away but from the quiet around them apparently not delivering any—it all made her bolder than she'd ever been in her life.

They weren't *totally* alone—she could hear the soft echo of two people's voices from the opposite side of the tower. But she decided they were alone *enough*. And like before with Damon, she found herself wanting to be wild for him, naughty for him, wanting to be what *he* wanted her to be—that dirty, dirty girl he'd brought out in her.

The elevator sat on the side of the tower far opposite them, and she prayed the other people would stay there, as well, and that it would take the elevator awhile to arrive again.

She pushed him back against one of the tower's inner walls—then she dropped to her knees.

When she reached for his belt buckle, Damon gasped, "Jesus God."

The thrill in his voice was all the encouragement she needed to deftly undo his buckle, unzip his jeans. Spreading them wide, she pressed her palm flat against his sturdy erection.

Mmm, *yes*—nothing had ever felt better in her hand. Then she lifted the black cotton briefs over his enormous, jutting cock. God, it looked even bigger from this angle. And though she'd never thought she cared about size, that suddenly made her want it more.

She'd never been this up-close with his penis, and despite the darkness, she was able to see the roundness of the head and the straight, bulletlike shape. On impulse, she leaned in to kiss the front of his length. A shuddering breath escaped him, and—oh God, he was *so* hard . . . and yet incredibly silky against her lips.

But she had no time for a leisurely perusal, so, grabbing back onto his shaft as the breeze lifted the hair from her neck, she lowered her mouth over the tip, then farther, letting it fill her mouth.

Above, he let out a shaky sigh that told her he was trying his damnedest to stay quiet as she adjusted to the fullness—and then began to move up and down.

She'd never been one to instigate a blow job with a guy—she'd always sort of considered it a duty, an obligation, when she was in a relationship with someone, and it often felt like an intrusion she didn't particularly enjoy.

But somehow, after Damon had made her come, she'd *needed* to do this, *needed* to take him into her in whatever way she could, right here, right now. She'd yearned to pleasure him, deeply.

Accepting as much of his majestic cock as she could handle, she took delight in every move, every sensation. She looked up at him and hoped he could see her well enough in the dimness—even if she looked obscene right now, she wanted to, for him.

And yes, last night in the tub had been wonderful: a leisurely, expansive pleasure with no pressures or worries—she'd told him she liked it in private, and she'd meant it. But clearly he'd opened her to this new, forbidden sort of excitement, this hot thrill of taking sex out of the bedroom, out of any room at all at the moment.

Because the longer she worked over him, the more his large erection stretched her lips, the deeper he gently drove into the recesses of her mouth . . . the more ensconced in pure joy she became.

She wanted to do this right now more than she wanted to exist.

She didn't care if they got caught, if anyone saw.

She wanted what she wanted, and nothing else mattered.

The heart wants what the heart wants, but the same was true of the body, and at this moment her body wanted to suck Damon's cock, hard and deep and thorough, until he came.

That's when she heard the elevator doors open on the other side of the tower. And then light laughter, voices—more people.

She sucked him, felt his thrust, silently willed him: *come, come.*

She could tell from his ragged sighs that he was getting close, and he pumped harder between her lips, but she also sensed the new visitors growing nearer, working their way around the tower.

So she released his cock from her mouth, stood up, grabbed onto it, and—in one determined move—yanked her thong aside and mounted him, for once holding in her groan, and being thankful she wore heels high enough to make the angle feasible. "If someone comes," she breathed, her mouth swollen and stretched, close to his, "we can be still. But this way, it'll maybe look like we're just kissing, not fucking."

He simply nodded, but his eyes blazed with lust as he began to vigorously plunge up into her welcoming moisture. "Jesus, won't take long," he murmured against her lips. Then thrust again, and again, until a soft groan escaped him and he pulled her to him tight, driving his shaft in to the hilt—and a young couple holding hands appeared at the corner nearest them.

Brenna and Damon both instinctively went still, but he was *coming*, and she could *feel it*—she could actually feel his cock throb inside her, his semen spewing onto her inner walls in three astounding little bursts.

"Oh God," she whispered, their faces still close.

He said nothing, only angled his mouth over hers and kissed her hard.

She'd thought last night had been intimate. Hell, she'd thought everything they'd *done* together had been intimate. But nothing compared to *this*—looking into his eyes in the dark, knowing he was inside her even as other people stood near, knowing he'd just filled her with his hot fluids.

"You never cease to amaze me," he said softly.

"I guess you just . . . inspire me."

He kissed her again, and she reminded herself she wasn't supposed to be feeling anything emotional here, so she forced herself to move onto an issue of practicality. "I'm afraid we're . . . gonna have a problem. A, uh . . . *wet* problem."

Damon, however, didn't look worried. "*Not* a problem," he corrected her.

She scrunched up her nose. "How do you figure?"

His voice dropped even lower. "When those two leave, I'm going to pull out of you. Then I'm gonna rub my come into your pussy and your thighs, and you're going to feel a little bit sticky all night, in a way that's gonna make you hot and ready to fuck me again later."

"Oh." She felt a little breathless. And like she was becoming a dirtier girl by the minute because his plan sounded so brazenly good to her. "Oh God."

When finally the couple meandered out of view, Damon eased his cock from her, leaving her to sigh at the loss—then swiftly turned her so that *she* leaned back against the wall, and knelt before her.

As promised, he used his hands to spread his warm juices over her skin, massaging the wetness into her inner thighs, onto the already soaking wet flesh and curls of her cunt. Despite her recent orgasm, his touch made it impossible to hold in her sighs of pleasure as she gently thrust her pelvis against his palm, tingles of fresh longing trickling all through her.

He concluded the task by delivering a gentle kiss to her clit, extracting a hot gasp from her.

And when he drew the fabric of her skirt back down and rose to kiss her mouth, she was no longer sure if she tasted her pussy or his semen or just plain sex—hot, crazy sex—but she didn't even care. It all just felt good, *tasted* good, mixing and melding together.

"By the way," he whispered, "you may as well lose the panties. They're pretty messy."

God, she'd forgotten she was *wearing* panties—the silk that was meant to stretch between her thighs had obediently stayed shoved to the side throughout their naughty encounter.

She pressed on his shoulders. "Back down you go then. Take them off me." Given that no one else had ventured to their side of the tower, she felt bolder now than was probably sane.

But Damon didn't hesitate, dropping back to his knees and reaching smoothly up under her mini to slip his thumbs into the elastic at both her hips. Slowly, sensuously, he peeled the panties all the way to her ankles. Lifting one shoe for him, then the other, she watched as he drew them completely off, aroused still more when the warm night breeze wafted over her pussy, making it feel fluttery and ready for more fun.

When he got back to his feet, she pressed her palms to his chest and spoke low, conspiratorially. "I can't believe I'm going to walk around all night in a skirt this short with no undies and sticky thighs."

His naughty grin ignited still more lust in her soul. "Your second outing with no panties, and this time even starting the evening that way. I'm getting another hard-on just thinking about it."

Her gaze dropped to the red thong dangling from his fingertips. "What'll we do with those?"

"Were they expensive?"

"Yes, actually." Kelly had insisted they shop at her favorite over-priced lingerie boutique.

"Well then, I'll buy you some new ones—because I think we need to leave these behind."

They *did* look pretty ruined. But . . . "Up here?"

"Sure," he said, and she could only describe his expression as a laid-back version of wicked. "Think how it'll turn people on when they realize somebody fucked up here. Hell, maybe it'll inspire somebody else to do it, too." Only then he glanced toward the railing behind them. "Or better yet . . ."

Taking Brenna's hand, he drew her to the Eiffel Tower's edge where a break occurred in the steel net, then without hesitation let the scrap of red fabric drop, sending it wafting down toward Las Vegas Boulevard.

Shocked, Brenna gasped and smacked his chest. "You're so bad!"

To which he replied by pulling her into his arms, leaning his fore-head against hers. "Maybe *you* inspire *me*."

Five

The night was just like the other nights she'd spent with Damon this week—an inexorable blending of work and play, music and sex. By taxi, they headed to the first of a few out-of-the-way bars on Damon's list tonight—but even as they discussed the initial band, called Playground Bully, Damon slid his hand high onto her thigh beneath the table where they sat and leaned over to whisper in her ear, "Are you wet?"

Her heart beat harder at the question. "*So* wet," she told him. And it was true. Even as she tried to concentrate on listening to the rock band, she stayed aware of that stickiness between her legs, just as he'd promised she would. She felt wired for action, her breasts heavy and sensitive within her bra, her cunt tingling.

"Good," he said with a dominant smile that made her know she belonged to him, at least for tonight, for this week—and though she'd never liked the idea of that before, of being a guy's possession, with Damon it was just one more sexual nuance added to all the rest.

"Are you hard?" she asked then, wanting to take part in his naughty, teasing game.

He cast a wicked grin. "Find out for yourself."

She pulled in her breath. The room was dark, and they sat close to a small round table, side by side, so touching him without being seen wouldn't be difficult.

Biting her lip, she reached out, sliding her palm directly over the bulge in his jeans. Which was more than a bulge. It felt more like a concrete column, rock-hard against her hand. She pressed down, pleasure from the touch stretching all through her, tightening her chest with desire, and surely making her damper where her panties were supposed to be.

"How do you stand it?" she whispered. To be that hard, she meant. And it was fairly early in the evening yet.

His answer came with a sexy smile. "It's the price of mixing work and fun."

"You manage to do that more than anyone I've ever met."

His eyes sparkled with pure lechery. "So you've mentioned. I guess it means one is as important to me as the other."

It was all she could do not to throw herself on him and forget Playgound Bully altogether, but just then the waitress came, bringing two fresh drinks—wine for her; Damon was drinking rum and Coke tonight.

So they drank and they flirted even as they talked business, ultimately deciding Playground Bully didn't have a unique enough sound to build upon, and moved on.

The next bar was a bit more upscale, just off the Strip, with an outdoor patio featuring a young woman who played the guitar and sang. As they watched, a waitress recognized Damon and asked if she could get a picture of them together on her cell phone camera. Brenna thought he looked sheepish—and was likely remembering exactly why his face was becoming known outside L.A., due to bad press and stinging accusations—but he agreed, after which people began to look at them, clearly trying to figure out who he was, and Brenna once again felt like the girlfriend of a celebrity.

"What do you think?" he asked her about the singer.

She pondered it for a minute and concluded, "I like her. She's like . . . a Juliana Hatfield of another era."

Next to her, Damon looked impressed, yet then said, "Good comparison, but that's just the problem—the other era. Even when she sings more recent songs, there's something too nostalgic in her voice. Nothing about her says *new* or *now*."

His response surprised Brenna, since until that moment, they'd pretty much agreed on everything they'd listened to together. "But she's so good, Damon. Don't you think so?"

Instead of answering the question, he said, "Who's her audience? Who would you market her to?"

The crowd around them consisted strictly of mature adults with an upwardly mobile feel—in their thirties and up; in fact, Brenna felt a bit young among them in her miniskirt. "The same people who are listening to Michael Bublé and Jason Mraz," she said.

Only Damon gently shook his head. "Bublé and Mraz *do* say new and now. They put a fresh twist on their music that brings it up to date, even if a little left of current pop sounds. I don't think this girl is in their league."

Brenna couldn't help feeling a little deflated—as if maybe she really *wasn't* a good judge of what would sell.

She found Damon flashing a slightly scolding expression. "Don't look so depressed. Music is subjective. Even people in the biz don't agree on *everything*."

She heard the honesty leave her even before she could temper it. "Up to now, I've felt like I'm really getting this. But if you weren't here, if I were on my own, I'd probably approach this girl and tell her I was very interested. And if you're right, if she doesn't have what it takes, then that means I'd be making a big mistake."

Damon tilted his head. "Everybody makes a wrong decision every now and then. It wouldn't be the end of the world—or even the end of your job."

"Have *you* ever made a mistake?"

"Claire Starr," he reminded her frankly. "A mistake for different reasons—she turned out to be demanding and unreasonable to work with—but I still messed up. And I'm paying for it in a big way."

Even bigger than you know, Brenna couldn't help thinking.

Before they left the club, Damon introduced himself and Brenna to the singer and told her that if she wanted to send him something more edgy and up-to-date, he'd love to hear it.

The girl, who hadn't had a clue she was being scouted by Blue Night, had seemed appreciative, even if a little embarrassed by Damon's unspoken criticism. And as they left, he explained to Brenna that when someone showed promise, he'd rather risk hurting their feelings than not give them some guidance that could help them succeed. "And as much as you liked her, I'm willing to give her a chance to show me more."

But as they climbed into a cab, setting off for their next destination, Brenna wasn't sure she could do that—just walk up to someone and, effectively, tell them what they were doing wasn't quite good enough, even though they'd never asked to be courted by a recording label.

Yet given other bits of growing confusion about exactly how she would pull off the one-on-one parts of this job, the parts that weren't just about giving someone good news, Brenna decided to do what she'd gotten far too skilled at this week—she pushed her doubts aside and concentrated on the good parts of the evening: being on Damon's arm, knowing later she would be in his bed.

Their last stop of the evening was at one of the older hotels on the north end of the Strip, in a lounge where a red-haired female singer belted out alternative hits at a piano. After about fifteen minutes, Damon leaned over to Brenna and said, "Please tell me you're not digging this chick."

Fortunately, she could. "She's got a good enough voice, but . . . no. I'm not sure why. Because she's trying too hard? Her stage presence is a little too harsh? Something about her feels like . . . it's already been done?"

It restored Brenna's confidence when he nodded. "All of that. She's a Tori Amos wannabe. And you can't duplicate Tori. You're right—this girl's got a decent voice, but she's the epitome of a Las Vegas lounge act, and she'll be stuck in places like this forever."

"That's . . . kind of sad," she couldn't help adding.

"That's the biz," he said, then lifted her chin with one bent finger. "But you're sweet as hell, you know that?"

His eyes were sparkling on her again, melting her as usual, and she found herself amazed that he could still think her sweet after some of the things she'd done with him and how dirty they'd been together. It touched her heart—because even if she'd really, truly become new Brenna now, maybe that didn't mean *all* of old Brenna was gone, and maybe he'd just honed in on the part that remained. The part that was softhearted, the part that worried about hurting people's feelings, the part that . . . hated lying so very much.

Yet as they stepped out into the neon-lit Las Vegas night, sin of a different kind recommenced. "Tell me something," Damon said as he opened the cab door.

She met his gaze beneath the bright lights. "What's that?"

"Are your thighs still sticky?"

A fresh wave of lust washed through her as she boldly replied, "Very. And I hope you'll make them even stickier soon."

Six

When they exited the cab outside the front doors of the Venetian—where the numerous lanes buzzed with cars, people coming and going, the whole world seeming to congregate in this desert oasis—all Brenna could think of was getting inside, and back into Damon's pants.

So it surprised the hell out of her when he took her hand and led her away from the lavish entry area, away from the crowds, along a winding sidewalk.

"Um, where are we going?"

Mystery tainted his grin. "It's a surprise."

She blinked. "What kind of surprise?"

"You'll see. Just walk with me."

Without quite planning it, Brenna locked her arm through Damon's, and his free hand rose to cover hers. And as they strolled the grounds, finally reaching an expansive white staircase that welcomed pedestrians coming off the Strip, Brenna felt . . . close to him. *Romantically* close.

Which she knew was terrible, bordering on tragic.

But Damon's body next to hers was so snug and cozy, and the night felt too good for her to do anything but bask in it. And see what her surprise was.

The sprawling piazza at the top of the stairs was quiet but for the echo of music wafting from a dance club high above. The hotel's arched gothic windows and columns rose majestically around them, lit from within. And just like so many times over the past few days, she felt amazingly alone with Damon despite being right in the middle of Sin City.

Still arm in arm, he led her to the gondola landing where all lay dark and still, as well, but for one lone gondolier manning one of the long, ornate vessels.

"I thought you might enjoy a gondola ride," Damon said.

She swung her gaze from the gathering of narrow boats to his face. The idea was unbelievably sweet, but . . . "I think they're closed for the night."

Yet he gave his head a confident tilt. "For most people."

She raised her eyebrows. "Most people?"

"I made a call earlier—while you were in the ladies' room."

"And . . ."

His eyes twinkled in the darkness. "I stay here a lot and they seem to like me—in spite of all my bad publicity. They agreed to open the canal for one last ride tonight."

Just then, the gondolier called up to them. "Mr. Andros?"

"Yeah, that's me. Thanks for being so accommodating."

"It's my pleasure, sir . . . and miss," the young man said, nodding to them as Damon led her toward the boat where he stood, pole in hand.

This particular gondola, she noticed, was even more grand than its counterparts, gleaming black with lavish gilt ornamentation framing the plush, black seats. Damon discreetly passed what looked like a sizable wad of money into the gondolier's fist as Brenna settled into the velvet upholstery.

"Sit back and enjoy," the gondolier told them, and she'd just noticed his Italian accent when he broke into an elegant operatic serenade that blocked out all other sound—and the rest of the world beyond the canal.

Damon sat close and, as the boat departed the landing, she leaned over to whisper in his ear. "This is so wonderful, Damon—thank you. But . . . you didn't have to go to so much trouble. I would have been thrilled with a normal ride tomorrow—one that didn't cost you an arm and a leg, I'm betting."

"But I *wouldn't* have been," he said deeply.

"Why not?"

"Because sometimes even *I* like certain things in private. I wanted to be able to make out with you if I felt like it—and I didn't think you'd let me in broad daylight."

Brenna laughed, reminding him, "I just went down on you on top of the freaking Eiffel Tower."

His eyes locked on her possessively. "Yes, you definitely did. But during the day, people stand around the canal to see the gondolas go by. I didn't think it was a good idea—unless I want us to show up on the cover of the *National Enquirer* next to the latest alien baby."

"Ah," she said. "Well, I suppose that's a valid worry. But just to be clear, if you started kissing me while a thousand people watched, I *still* don't think I could resist."

He gave his head a speculative tilt. "I can't get over you. You're the last girl I would have expected to be so damn much fun."

"And what exactly made you think I was so prim and proper in the first place?"

"Well, don't take this the wrong way, but I saw you in the office every week for the last few years and my impression was of a . . . nice, dependable woman who . . . probably thought I was someone to be-ware of."

Some bold, new-Brenna part of her wanted to convince him he was off the mark, that he'd had her pegged all wrong, but she never *had* been good at lying—honesty just came so much more naturally. "Well, maybe I *was* a little more prim when I was with Wayne. But now there's no reason to be. And as for what I thought of *you* . . ."

"Yeah?"

She sort of hated telling him what he already knew but . . . again, she had a hard time not being truthful. In fact, the more she got to know him, the easier it was to simply speak from the heart. "I . . . thought you were the hottest thing poured into a pair of ripped jeans I'd ever seen."

He lowered his chin, looking utterly provocative. "Is that so?"

She hoped her nod came out more sexy than sheepish.

Either way, he slid his arm around her shoulder, pulling her close as he reached out his free hand to lift her legs across his lap. And he leaned near, his whisper echoing as sultry as the night. "You're pretty fucking hot yourself."

Being so close to him, but not kissing, got her hotter still. Just looking into his eyes and feeling that sense of possession again—of belonging to him, being at his sexual mercy. "Still want to make out?" she asked.

"*Oh* yeah," he replied, then leaned in for a long, slow kiss.

The gondolier's Italian song permeated the night air, his voice strong and deep, as the private boat glided along the canal's smooth surface. He stood behind them, guiding the boat, but a large awning shaded the seat from his view—and thank God, since Damon's kisses grew more passionate. Soon, her breath turned labored as an intense heat climbed her thighs. She wasn't sure she'd ever gotten so turned on from mere kisses in her whole life.

As usual, when his mouth trailed down onto her neck, she thought she'd implode. Tendrils of pleasure curled through her arms, her breasts—the small of her back ached with hard, sensual need.

When the gondolier's song ended, Brenna and Damon both paused and looked over their shoulders, in case he were to speak to them—but when he simply began another tune behind them, they resumed kissing.

Until Damon eased his hand between her thighs.

Sensation pulsed through her, creating a maddening need. "Please," she heard herself whisper in a shaky voice, "more."

She parted her legs just slightly and felt his fingers ascend, slowly, so slowly, until they met her damp slit.

"*Mmm,*" she sighed, unable to hold it in—and thankful the gondolier sang so blissfully loud as their ride continued through virtually dark, private waters.

"Still hot and sticky for me," Damon breathed low in her ear.

She nodded. "Mmm, *yes.*"

His tongue invaded her mouth once more, kissing deeply, possessively, again taking ownership of her, just like she wanted—until she said, "God, I need you, baby."

"You'll have me soon—deep inside your perfect little pussy."

The body part he mentioned involuntarily convulsed around his fingertips, and they both let out a heavy breath. "Jesus," he whispered. "You're *so* ready, babe." She'd never heard him sound so intensely aroused.

Or felt that way herself, her whole body burning with a reckless, feral hunger. "I . . . I almost can't control myself. I almost want to fuck you right here."

Unparalleled heat filled his dark eyes. "Just a little longer," he promised.

"You . . . you should quit touching me now. Or . . . or I don't know what I'll do."

He pulled his hand away, and they both let out low groans of frustration even though she'd insisted. Yet he couldn't seem to stop touching her *entirely*, since he slid his hand upward to the side of her breast to stroke his thumb over her almost painfully hard nipple.

A gasp of unrestrained pleasure escaped her as he leaned in to ask, in the dirtiest voice she'd ever heard from him, "Does it get you hot to imagine it? Fucking me right here, right now, in front of the gondolier, in front of the people walking around in the dark? Does it get you off to imagine the whole canal lined with people, but you can't stop yourself, so you lift up your skirt and climb onto my cock and fuck my brains out while they all watch?"

Oh God—the pictures he sent darting through her head made her pussy pulse with raw, hard need. He still stroked her breast, making her crazier with each touch, and she heard herself speaking still more unbridled truth. "Yes. Oh, *yes*."

"Tell me," he urged her, low, demanding. "Tell me how hot it gets you."

"It's . . . like at the pool," she tried to explain, breathless, every fiber of her being growing more ravenous with each passing second. "How I said I would do it with you on the bed there if I could, even in front of all those people. And right now—I would straddle you and ride your big, beautiful cock so hard. I would fuck you so hot, baby, until I came all over you."

He was kissing her again, harder now, their mouths struggling, trying to take more of each other in somehow.

And then the gondolier stopped singing again.

And they both went still, looked up over their shoulders again.

And this time he *did* glance down. "I hope you both enjoyed our gondola ride here at the Venetian. Have a wonderful evening."

God, they were back at the landing already. She hadn't even realized—she'd lost track of space and time and everything else. She couldn't speak, her breath trembling too much, but Damon managed to sit up a little straighter and say, "It was great. Thanks again for the favor," as Brenna worked to calm down and act normal until they could depart.

As they walked away a moment later, hands clutched tightly, Damon said, "You okay, babe?"

"No," she told him. "I'm going crazy. I think I could come just from kissing you right now."

They walked briskly toward a line of doors that led inside. "Just hold on, honey, a little longer, and I promise I'll make it all better."

His voice was soothing, but when he squeezed her hand, her pussy surged with still more moisture, and she began to worry—insanely, she hoped—wondering if she could emit so much wetness that, without panties, it would begin to run down her legs. Was such a thing even possible? She feared she might soon find out.

"Hurry," she said, then pulled him onward even faster, breaking into a light jog.

Seven

Damon had been with eager women before. He himself had been eager before. But not since his youth did he remember ever *running* to reach someplace to have sex.

And it wasn't just Brenna who was eager. He was just as anxious—so he let her pull him through the Venetian's doors and then through the casino toward the elevators, feeling like he would explode in his pants if they didn't reach the room soon.

Damn, he wanted her. And he *liked* her. So fucking much. *Too* much. And he'd spent the last few days doing exactly what he'd told himself he *couldn't* afford to do anymore, especially right now—he'd indulged his lusts, he'd let himself be seen in public with a woman right when he was being accused of *taking advantage* of women, and he'd been taking too many chances with her. But something about Brenna made it impossible to stop.

She might try to act casual about having been "a little more prim" before now—but he still suspected that she'd been a *lot* more prim until very recently, and he had a strong hunch he'd changed her into the sexual animal she was now. He knew that made him an arrogant bastard, but he felt it in his bones. And God help him, he *loved* it. It made him feel like . . . a god. *Her* god. But also like . . . he wanted to take care of her. *Needed* to. He felt almost as if he'd saved her from something—and had to *keep* saving her.

Normally, he didn't enjoy feeling any sort of responsibility toward a woman, but this was different—*she* was different. She didn't demand it, she didn't even ask for it, she was just her open, genuine self and it made him want more. He wanted to keep saving her, keep fucking her, keep laughing with her, just keep on *being* with her.

Of course, *this* moment, as they stepped to the rear of a rapidly filling elevator, was all about fucking. The urgency was palpable.

Standing behind her, he let his arms fold gently around her waist, pulling her back against him, knowing how hard his dick was and that she could feel it pressing insistently into her soft, sweet ass.

As the elevator climbed, she trembled in his arms, fueling his lust still more. And shit—the damn thing stopped on floor after floor. People getting off, more people getting on. He rubbed against her. He couldn't help it. She covered his arms with her own, squeezing, caressing—and soon gently digging her fingernails in.

When finally the elevator stopped on *their* floor, they practically tumbled out into the hallway and he grabbed her hand, pulling her down the quiet corridor toward the suite.

"My God," she uttered, sounding frantic, breathless. "I can't believe this."

"What?"

"I can feel it . . . actually rolling down my legs."

He was confused. "What? What's on your legs?"

"My . . . wetness."

He stopped, pulling her up short, then his gaze dropped to her miniskirt—and below. She'd clearly been holding her legs together in the elevator, but he could see the moisture there, on her inner thighs, below the hem of her skirt. "Jesus God."

Unable not to, he followed his instincts, pushing her back against one of the lavishly decorated walls, dropping to his knees, parting her legs, and fervently licking her inner thigh.

The salty-sweet taste of her come met his tongue, making his heart beat faster, making every muscle in his body tense with pure, hard want. His cock felt like it would burst from behind his zipper—so stiff now that it actually hurt.

He licked one thigh, then the other, listening to her low, uncontrolled moans, aware she was still trembling and now clutching helplessly at the wall behind her, splaying her fingers over the wallpaper, curling them inward as if she could grab on to it. And he hadn't even come anywhere near her pussy yet.

"God, Damon. In the room. Now. Please. Or I'll die."

He almost believed her. He'd never felt quite this tortured with lust, either.

They made it the rest of the way up the hall, but it was all he could do to get out his wallet and key card to get them inside.

She headed through the large foyer and dining area straight to the bedroom, Damon hot on her heels. And then, just when he thought she couldn't surprise him anymore than she already had—she did. When he stepped into the room, she turned, grabbed his forearms, and shoved him hard onto the bed. He fell back easily, not having expected it, then watched as hot, hungry little Brenna straddled his thighs and started working ravenously at his belt buckle, just as she already had once tonight—but with more fervor now.

A few seconds later, his hungry cock jutted free, and he helped her, pushing his jeans farther open, his briefs down. And then she mounted him, lowering her wet, warm, tight little cunt down over him so fast and hard that they both cried out.

Ah, God—just like before, the sensation of being flesh to flesh almost overwhelmed him. She rode him like a wild cowgirl, at the same time ripping her tank top off over her head. Underneath she wore a sexy red bra, cut low, the round curves of her breasts arcing upward. Hot pleasure filled him—the pure pleasure of sex, but also the unexpected delight of Brenna having her way with him, so rough and nasty.

"Need more of these gorgeous tits," he said through clenched teeth, then reached to yank down the lace-rimmed cups of her bra so that they merely outlined the two pretty mounds of flesh. She gasped hotly, then moaned when he took them in his hands, squeezing, molding their lush softness, feeling those hard, beaded nipples point into his palms.

And then her movements slowed, just a little, turning more rhythmic, and her eyes fell shut, and he knew, that fast, she would come.

"Oh God, baby," she purred—then, softer, "yes. Now. *Yes.*"

Her head dropped back and he sensed the orgasm pounding through her as he watched her breasts bounce, her whole body jolting slightly—again, again. Damn, she was beautiful when she came.

Of course, most women were, but when Brenna climaxed, he couldn't help seeing that staid office girl in his mind, and the contrast between that vision and this one made it all the more incredible.

"Oh, wow," she sighed, her body dipping slightly forward, a sexy smile of relief taking over her face as she met his gaze.

"That was fast," he said with a grin, going still now, just for a minute, to let her recover.

"I told you how close I was."

"I love that you stayed aroused all damn night long."

She nodded, smiled, and lazily licked her lips, confirming that—indeed—she had.

And for some reason he remembered her trying this position in the tub last night, and nearly pushing him under, which he'd thought was cute as hell. "This is a much better place for you to be on top," he said, gritting his teeth again as he began to drive upward again into her hot, drenched flesh.

As she began to meet his thrusts, her answer came on labored breath, between strokes. "This is . . . the first time . . . we've done it . . . in a bed."

His breathing turned just as ragged. "Don't . . . get too attached . . . to the bed, babe."

"Why?"

"It's . . . a surprise." Something that had occurred to him on the gondola, when they'd been talking dirty, when he'd been making her fantasize about fucking him in the boat.

"Another one?"

"For tomorrow night. And I promise . . . you'll like it. Now let me . . . suck your tits." He needed them in his mouth more than he needed air to breathe.

Biting her lip, she leaned over, bracing her arms on both sides of his head, letting those beautiful breasts dangle over his face. He captured one erect nipple between his lips, letting the hardness on his tongue drive him mad as he licked, French-kissed, then sucked.

Above him, her moans flooded the room and he understood that

Brenna's tits were even more sensitive than he'd realized. Moving to the other breast, he drew the beautifully beaded peak into his mouth, still plunging his cock up into her welcoming pussy. "Oh *baby*," she breathed as he suckled her still more roughly, and when she arched deeper, he took in as much of the soft female flesh as he could.

Her breath grew thready again—quick, and her movements more sensual. Damon closed his hands over her ass, stretching his fingers to encompass as much of her rear as he could, massaging, matching the rhythm she used to fuck him now. He felt her desire gathering, tightening—and he was more than ready to erupt in her but held back, because he knew she was going to come again.

Her moans intensified, her breath growing still more shallow.

He sucked hard, pulling her nipple as far back in his mouth as he could, listening to her soft cry of pleasure.

He rammed his erection upward in hard, slow strokes.

And then it broke—he heard her sob, felt the slight collapse in her pelvis, then her cunt thrusting, thrusting, as she rode it out, her whole body moving and sliding against his, creating perfect friction.

Finally, she sank to his chest, appearing thoroughly spent. "Oh my God," she finally whispered. "I can't believe I came twice—just like last night."

Running one hand through her silky hair, he smiled. "Why not?"

She sounded exhausted. "Well, I hear all the stories about multiple orgasms, but . . . I just never really had them—until you."

"How was this one?" he asked softly.

"Um . . . *intense*."

"In a good way?"

She nodded against his T-shirt.

And he instinctually rolled her to her back, without ever withdrawing, until he lay on top of her, peering down at her face, her cheeks flushed, her expression still impassioned.

He thought maybe he'd never looked so closely at her before this moment. Her green eyes possessed little flecks of gold and brown that made him think of a starburst. "Pretty eyes," he whispered without weighing it.

Her smile was utterly sweet, her voice tender. "Thank you."

And something in his chest tightened. He hardly ever had sex in the missionary position. Mainly because he generally found it boring, and confining in ways—but . . . it wasn't boring *now.* Now it was like . . . too much; he was too close to her, face-to-face, their eyes locked.

And he knew he'd been close to her *before,* during all the other times they'd fooled around or fucked, but somehow *this,* just now, felt dangerous, like something he needed to back away from.

So he pulled out and said, "Turn over. On your hands and knees."

She obeyed without argument, arching her pretty ass in the air, her skirt hugging her hips now and giving him a sumptuous view of her parted pussy before he molded his hands to her rear and rammed his cock back into her.

She cried out, and he said, "Tell me you like it. Tell me you like it hard."

"Unh," she moaned. Then, "Oh God, yes—I do! Give it to me hard."

That was all he wanted, all he needed. Good, mindless fucking. He forgot about her eyes and drove back into her still-wet passageway— *hard, hard, hard*—as hard as he fucking could, until he reached the edge of bliss and let himself tumble over, yelling, "Christ, babe, I'm coming in you! Now."

Ah, yeah—it was *so* damn good spilling his hot come in her, letting it loose, finally, after all these hours of building lust.

And when he'd emptied completely, that familiar exhaustion hit and he crumpled on top of her, felt them tumbling to the bed together— and as they lay there, silent and close, as he heard her breathing and took in the scent of her perfume combining with the rich aroma of sex, he realized turning her over hadn't really changed anything.

He still felt close to her and there was apparently nothing he could do about it.

Shit.

So he simply kissed her on the cheek and let himself drift into post-orgasmic slumber.

Eight

A little while later, Brenna dragged herself from the bed, heading to the bathroom to wash up a bit. She took off her shoes, then shed her skirt on the way, exhausted but bubbling with a happiness she'd never quite experienced before. She felt downright giddy. And dreamy. About sex. About Damon. She'd just never known it could be this good. She'd never known being so naughty could feel so invigorating. It felt as if Damon had opened a whole part of life to her that she couldn't have experienced without him, and her entire body hummed with an unsurpassed satisfaction.

Peering into the mirror, she sighed happily. She'd quickly grown used to her new hair color and cut. And now ... she was even getting used to being a highly sexed woman, using her body in exactly the way it had been built to use.

And it suddenly hit her once more, with new force ... that new Brenna didn't really exist anymore—because this wasn't an act anymore, someone she was pretending to be, or even *trying* to be. She really *was* new Brenna now, totally at home with Damon and totally at ease with all the outrageous sex they enjoyed together.

And this was probably stupid, probably dangerous as hell to even let herself ponder, but what if ... what if this all somehow worked out and Damon wasn't fired and they *did* keep working together? What if what happened in Vegas *didn't* stay in Vegas, after all? What if they spent so much time together that he realized he was crazy about her, more than just physically, and that maybe a relationship wasn't really such a horrible thing?

Letting out another sigh, this one girlishly hopeful, she withdrew her gaze from her reflection and reemerged into the bedroom, where she found that Damon, too, had kicked off his clothes and made his way under the covers. God, he looked good lying there, all sleepy and sexy and rumpled—and spent, because of her.

"Cell phone's blinking, babe," he told her, eyes shut.

She swung her gaze to the dressing table at one side of the room, where she'd dropped her purse and phone earlier. She'd left them at the hotel every night they'd gone out, having decided the purse would be a hindrance she didn't need, especially since Damon's Blue Night credit card covered all her travel expenses. And that was before she'd even understood that so much sex would be involved, so it had turned out to be an excellent decision.

Padding naked to the table, she picked up the phone, flipped it open, and retrieved the message.

Then she heard Jenkins' voice. "Just checking in with you, Brenna. Damon mentioned in e-mail that you're learning fast and have a real ear for music, so good job. Especially since things aren't looking promising with Claire. I wouldn't be surprised if she files suit very soon, and if that happens, you know what it means—Damon's out and you're in."

Oh hell.

She flipped the phone shut, hoping Damon was asleep.

No such luck. "Anything important?"

"No."

"Then why do you look upset?"

She glanced over to find his gorgeous brown eyes now open and studying her with clear concern.

"It was Kelly," she fudged. "She's having man trouble, that's all."

"Ah," he said, tipping his head back lightly into the pillow, then letting his eyes close again. "Turn out the lights and come to bed. I want to wrap around you."

So now she'd lied to him. Up to this moment, it had only been deceit, keeping something from him that affected him greatly, and that had been awful enough. But now she had pointedly, purposefully, *lied* to keep her dirty little secret.

And like she'd told Kelly when all this had started, she *hated* lying.

She did her best to swallow back the stinging guilt as she flipped off the bedside lamp and crawled beneath the covers with her lover—the man she was misleading in order to steal his job.

THE FIFTH NIGHT

"Pleasure is the bait of sin."
—Plato

One

The next day, Damon informed Brenna that he needed to make a few phone calls to some of the acts he managed at Blue Night, and he was going to put them on speaker phone so she could hear how he dealt with "the talent."

Thus she listened as he assuaged the fears of an alternative band whose first CD wasn't getting as much attention as they'd hoped. And as he explained to an R&B singer why the release of his next long-awaited CD was being pushed back another two months. And as Blue Night's biggest star, British rocker Malcolm Barstow, bitched Damon out over everything from song selection on his upcoming CD to not liking the photographer who'd done the cover shoot.

Damon dealt with each person differently, she noticed, playing into his or her personality and particular issues, until each seemed adequately appeased—although with Barstow, "appeased" was probably too optimistic a term.

After pushing the disconnect button the final time, he looked up from the sofa where he lounged in his usual jeans and tee to face Brenna, who rested on a satin-upholstered chaise. "There you have it," he said. "The dark side of A&R. Think you can handle it?"

Not on my best day, she was tempted to say.

She knew how to deal with Jenkins when he was overworked and stressed out. And she knew that when Kelly was having a rotten day, the best thing to do was just agree with everything she said and it would all work out in the end. She knew how to fix copy machines and finesse Microsoft Word and efficiently run a small office with one hand tied behind her back. Yet despite Jenkins' and Damon's belief in her, she had no idea how to take care of people who probably had good reasons to be upset about problems that likely couldn't be solved.

And sure, she'd talked to most of these people on the phone before herself, but only to patch them through to Jenkins or assure them their check was in the mail—and this was different. Old Brenna was a hand-holder, but not to angry, hysterical rock stars.

"I'll admit I'm intimidated by everything I just heard," she replied, trying not to sound as freaked out as she was.

"And *I'll* admit that I usually don't have to make three phone calls like that in a row. But being on the road allows things to stack up a little, and part of why they were all so mad is because I didn't get back to them five minutes after they called. Artists are temperamental—that's a fact of this business. You just have to address their needs the best you can."

She nodded and hoped she didn't look too worried. As she'd acknowledged to herself when he'd been networking with club personnel, Damon was a natural people person—and she just wasn't sure she could see herself being that skilled at initiating relationships, or dealing with ones that were difficult, as Damon had just done.

"You know what you need to cheer you up?" he asked.

Okay, so clearly her fears were still written all over her face. "What?"

"Some new panties."

She cast a flirtatious smile, having grown much more comfortable with her current *social* life than her *professional* one. "That's right—you owe me a pair, don't you? Or two," she added, thinking back to their encounter at Fetish.

"Lucky for you, the Fashion Show Mall is close enough to walk."

"Lucky for me, I happen to be sleeping with a guy who actually *knows* things like this," she replied on a laugh.

"Well, I hope this won't shock you too much, little miss Brenna," he said with a wink, "but it won't be my first time in a lingerie store."

She let out a mock gasp, splaying her hand across her chest.

"And not only that—I'm not the kind of guy who stands at the door with his arms crossed, looking at his feet. I'll be helping you pick these panties out."

She laughed softly. "I can't wait to see your choices. And just so you know, I'm not into crotchless. I require both practicality and sexiness in my undies."

In reply, he snapped his fingers and muttered, "Damn."

Two hours later, they'd crossed Las Vegas Boulevard and made the short trek to the stylish, upscale mall. In addition to replacing the red thong they'd ruined last night, Damon had picked out a black thong, a leopard-print thong with a black lace inlay on front, and an embroidered demi-bra and panty set of lavender silk and lace.

They'd held hands, kissed as they'd walked and shopped, and kissed some more as they'd stopped to grab a couple of sandwiches in the food court for lunch. Then they made their way back to the Venetian, Damon toting the little pink shopping bag with a natural confidence that made Brenna see how truly masculine he was.

"Not all guys would be happy about carrying a pink bag," she pointed out, impressed.

He simply replied, "I'm not all guys."

You can say that again. He was easily the sexiest, most confident, most seductive man she'd ever met. And he'd been giving her kisses over top of panty displays and around turkey clubs and—oh God—it was getting really easy to start thinking of him like . . . a boyfriend.

Which was emotional suicide—she knew that still.

He'd told her this was a temporary thing.

And she was lying to him anyway, so it was *good* it was only a temporary thing.

So quit thinking of him like a boyfriend, *like someone you're getting* attached *to.*

If only it were that easy.

The fact was—she'd never been that kind of woman, the kind like Kelly, who could get physical with someone without starting to care. And she'd deluded herself there for a few days, thinking that maybe new Brenna *was* that kind of woman. But now that new Brenna was the real her . . . well, she *was* getting attached to Damon. And she was going to be hurt and lonely and empty when this ended, no doubt about it.

The only answer for now was the same she'd relied upon all week. *Push it aside. Don't think. Just feel.*

He kissed her at the door to her room—since he had more phone calls to make and some e-mails to send, and she'd decided she could use a nap—and when his tongue twined around hers and made her body tingle from head to toe, just like *everything* she did with him, she definitely *felt*. She felt it all. The pleasure. The emotion. The need to be with him.

The sad truth was that she didn't even really like parting ways with him for the afternoon. She'd grown so used to being with him almost around the clock these past few days, and *that*'s what had made her into the *real* new Brenna. Damon's presence, his influence—the things he made her think, feel.

"Dress up tonight," he said, still holding her hand.

"Dress up . . . how?"

He shrugged. "A sexy dress, if you have one."

"Why?"

"You'll see."

Ah, her surprise. She'd almost forgotten. And she couldn't imagine exactly where Damon planned to fuck her tonight that required her being dressed up, but she also couldn't wait to find out.

Two

"Whoa," Damon said when she answered the door that night at six sharp. His long once-over made her breasts tingle and her cunt pulse.

She bit her lip, feeling both sexy and sophisticated. "You like?"

"Babe," he said, as if it were a ridiculous question. "That dress is . . . amazing. The way you look, I'll be damn lucky if I can do our business before our pleasure."

The black satin dress hugged her curves perfectly and revealed more of her body than anything she'd ever worn, with molded underwire cups that held her breasts in place of a bra, leaving much of them exposed. The hem dropped to mid-thigh, but a slit on one side made the short length even racier.

Kelly had insisted Brenna buy the dress, but she'd left the tags on, thinking she might return it—until Damon's wardrobe instructions earlier, after which she'd known it was perfect for a night out in Vegas on the arm of the hottest guy alive.

She'd completed the outfit with strappy black heels featuring a bit of rhinestone bling across the toes and the dangly diamond earrings she'd worn at her wedding. In retrospect, this seemed like a better use for them.

Damon had dressed up, too—more than she'd ever seen him before—wearing a crisp white shirt, untucked, under a carmel-colored leather jacket, with his usual jeans below. As always, his grandma's cross rested near his throat, visible between open buttons. "You look good, too," she told him, offering the same bold perusal he'd used on her and not hesitating to let her gaze linger on his crotch, where—even without an erection—a very pleasant bulge appeared.

An enormous gilt-framed mirror hung on the wall next to the elevator and as they waited, Brenna couldn't help checking them both out and thinking that tonight, more than ever before, she looked like she belonged with him, like she was someone fabulous heading out for a night of glamorous fun—and the best part was, at the moment, it was all true.

Damon took her to Bouchon, a French restaurant at the Venetian, where they were seated on a beautiful tiled patio near the pool. After dinner, they shared a chocolate mousse in an atmosphere of soft music, clinking glasses, and elegant stone columns and archways. And Brenna tried very hard not to feel the romance of it all, but it was difficult to ignore.

On one hand, she knew Damon was a man of the world, and a lover of women, so that, for him, taking someone to a terribly romantic restaurant was surely no more than a respectful measure of affection, a good meal with someone whose company he enjoyed.

But when she looked into his eyes . . . did she see more?

Or was she just imagining that?

At times, she could have sworn Damon was falling for her, too. But then . . . a guy like Damon was just so naturally personable, so skilled at making someone feel special, that she knew it probably meant nothing.

And that's okay, she reminded herself. *This is only an affair, and that's exactly what you wanted it to be. No-strings-attached sex.*

From dinner, it was out for an evening on the Strip. Tonight, Damon explained, they were going to see performers who all happened to work in the mega-resorts that lined Las Vegas Boulevard.

And it hit her—*oh, that's why he told me to dress up.* This promised to be more of a real "night on the town" than any they'd shared thus far, and it made her don't-get-too-attached-to-the-bed surprise all the more a mystery.

Their first stop: one of the few traditional Vegas shows still remaining, complete with topless showgirls sporting tons of feathers and sequins. It was a variety mix of entertainment, and Damon pointed out the singer they'd come to see, recommended by a bartender he'd spoken to earlier in the week. But Damon quickly declared that the guy had "more of a Broadway sound," with which Brenna agreed, and after that, she simply sat back and enjoyed the gaudy spectacle of it all, marveling at the number of bared breasts on the stage.

Afterward, as they were filing out with other theater-goers, Damon said, "Sorry if that was kind of cheesy, but the guy I talked to made that vocalist sound spectacular, so I thought it was worth checking out."

Brenna let her eyes go wide. "Are you kidding? I loved it! It's so totally classic Vegas. I had a great time." And she had. Given that most of the "showgirl shows" were dead and gone now, it pleased her to have seen a little slice of the old Sin City.

Damon just smiled, then wrapped an arm around her waist and drew her to him for a kiss. "Do you know how cute you are?"

She lowered her chin and cast a playful grin. "I thought I was *hot*."

"You're cute *and* hot," he assured her. "And if you haven't noticed, every guy we've passed tonight has had his eyes all over you."

Actually, she *had* noticed. And she'd been caught between feeling sexy and exciting and carefree . . . and wondering if they sized her up as a slut, wearing a dress so revealing. Surely, if all those men could see the things she'd done the past few days, they'd believe the latter, but only *she* knew that she could only have indulged in such behavior with Damon— nobody else.

And as he led her by the hand back out through the casino and onto the street, the hot night air filling her senses, she knew, undeniably, that she was falling in love with him.

But also, of course, that the whole situation remained impossible, no matter how she viewed it.

And that meant she had to get as much of him as she could now, tonight, and in the nights to come. She had to soak him up, absorb him, his body, his mind, those beautiful, beautiful eyes—all of him.

So as they climbed into a cab and Damon instructed the driver to take them to Caesars Palace, she lifted her hand to his face and kissed him, bold, passionate, and unapologetic, without a care if the driver watched in his rearview mirror. Now that it was accompanied with love, her lust for him took on a fresh new urgency that she feared knew no bounds or limits.

"Nice," he said when the kiss ended.

In reply, she boldly lowered her hand to his thigh, then inward, onto his cock, which grew stiff for her within mere seconds.

His gaze was half amused, half aroused. "You must be looking forward to your surprise."

"Very much," she admitted.

At Caesars Palace, they made their way through the casino to a stylish theme bar called Cleopatra's Barge, crossing a small wooden bridge to step into the floating, boat-shaped club. Darkness had fallen, and it was prime dance time—lights swirled across the floor where twenty- and thirty-somethings moved to a band playing Top 40 hits.

"This is who we're here to see," Damon told her as they squeezed through the crowd to reach the bar. "They're called Razor's Edge."

The band was fronted by a pretty blonde, the only female in the group. Over glasses of wine, they watched and listened, and Brenna stayed aware of all the male attention she garnered—and if she wasn't mistaken, even a few *females* cast admiring glances. She was starting to think she should wear such daring clothes more often and reminded herself to thank Kelly for making her buy the dress.

Actually, it reminded her again that she had a *lot* to thank Kelly for—not just shopping help and a hair appointment but the whole concept of seducing Damon. Maybe it would have happened anyway, but somehow she felt as if Kelly's various forms of prodding had helped bring all this into being.

After half an hour, Brenna set her empty glass on the bar and leaned up to tell Damon over the sound of the music, "I don't know—they seem like a good bar band, but there's nothing fresh about them. I know we haven't heard their original music, but something about them feels very . . . nineties to me. Am I off the mark?"

Damon drained his own glass and shook his head. "Right *on* the mark, in fact. I've been standing here waiting for them to wow me, but it's not happening. Good ear, babe."

After leaving Cleopatra's Barge hand in hand, they took a cab up the

Strip to another of the large mega-hotels—Brenna didn't even know which. Given all their whirlwind stops on this and previous nights, she forgot to pay attention.

Wandering through yet another casino where slot machines whirred and jingled and roulette wheels spun, Damon led her to a dark, quiet club where her eyes were drawn instantly to the young man on the stage, who sat on a stool, singing and playing a simple wood guitar. With slightly shaggy hair and a smooth, olive complexion, he couldn't have been more than seventeen, but his voice and instrument proclaimed otherwise, sounding as if they belonged to an old soul. The sound was pop alternative—catchy but hip, clever but stroked with meaning—and after only a few seconds, Damon and Brenna gave each other a look that silently said: *This guy's good.*

"I'm blown away," Damon said.

In response, Brenna fell into her new habit of making comparisons with an eye toward marketing. "He's like . . . a young John Mayer, but with major teen idol appeal. Every high school girl is going to swoon for him."

"The CD cover will be a close-up of his face," Damon mused, eyes on the stage, clearly thinking ahead. "With only his name above it. Austin Cole."

"Back in the days of albums," Brenna said, "we could have put a poster of him inside."

Damon wasn't dissuaded. "We can still work with that idea. That's what websites are for. We could offer a free poster to the first thousand people to send in their CD receipt, something like that."

"How old is he?" Brenna asked.

"Not old enough to get *in* here—just old enough to *perform* here," he explained. "He sent me a CD a few months ago, and I knew he was good, but I didn't know he was *this* good, or I would have dropped everything and gotten my ass over here faster."

From there, they found a table, ordered a bottle of wine, and simply sat back and enjoyed Austin Cole's soulful, heartfelt music. Until he took a break. After which Brenna got to see, once again, the fun side of this job—watching the boy's face light up when Damon introduced himself and told him how impressed he was.

They set up a meeting with Austin and his mother for the next day, but Damon made it a lunch meeting instead of breakfast, "because," he explained to Brenna with a wink as they left the club, "we're gonna be out late tonight."

She grinned. "This involves my surprise, of course."

He gave a succinct nod.

"And just when do I get this surprise?"

"Our next stop."

Despite herself, Brenna's pussy trembled with anticipation. Of course, having so many lustful eyes on her as the night had progressed had kept her in a fairly aroused state all evening, as had the provocative topless show, and merely just being with Damon. So it wasn't only the promise of what was to come that had her excited. It was *everything*—everything Damon and Sin City had to offer.

And she was more than ready for whatever the night held.

Three

The next cab sped them up busy Las Vegas Boulevard, where all around them Brenna saw limos and trolleys and more of those moving billboards offering up lingerie-clad women for sale. Out the windows, she noticed the neon signs marking the MGM Grand, the Paris, the Monte Carlo, and others zipping past and making her feel—along with the wine she'd drank—totally consumed by the dizzying lights and fast pace of the Strip. The next thing she knew, the cab turned off the boulevard onto a shrubbery-lined drive that led to another brightly lit mega resort and casino, but again, she'd failed to catch the name.

As Damon led her through the sprawling front doors into yet another grand lobby, she felt still more eyes upon her, felt her man's hand in hers, felt her heart beating with the excitement of wondering what was to come and how she would please him tonight.

After they stepped into an elevator, Damon waited until most of the other people inside had exited onto their floors, then punched the very top button, marked simply with an R.

"What does that stand for?" she asked. "Roof?"

Damon's mouth curved into a mischievous smile. "No. It's a club. Called Rendezvous."

So they were going to another club, this one high atop a hotel on the Las Vegas Strip. "That's my surprise?" she asked unguardedly. "Another club?" She didn't mean to sound disappointed, but she'd already been to plenty of clubs with Damon, so she'd been expecting some-thing . . . more unique.

As the last two people with them on the elevator stepped off, the doors closing behind them, Damon cast a dark, seductive look. "Don't worry, babe. You haven't been to a club like *this* before."

"What do you mean?"

At that moment, the elevator doors opened and the aura of glamor-ous nightlife assaulted her senses. Before them stretched a dimly lit room, swirling with red and purple lights that flashed across scantily clad bodies on a dance floor. The scents of alcohol and expensive per-fume wafted past. Every face she saw was . . . beautiful, no other way to say it. This was clearly where the beautiful people came to party.

But before reaching the club's interior, they had to be admitted by a doorman, and she'd just noticed the line of people waiting to get in when Damon led her past them, right up to the guy manning a red vel-vet rope. "Mr. Andros," he said easily, then unhooked the rope, motion-ing them through. Damon discreetly passed the man some folded bills as he entered.

Inside, she saw the beautiful people closer up. The women were confident and gorgeous, most wearing cocktail dresses that rivaled her own for sexiness, and the men were like Damon—clearly hip, stylish, comfortable in their surroundings.

The lighted dance floor was dotted with platforms and even a few barred cages. On the platforms, more beautiful people danced—mostly girls who seemed unafraid to rub their bodies up against one another as they moved. The cages, however, held what she thought of as "go-go girls," all dressed in black sequined bustiers and miniscule black skirts—below the skirts stretched garters that led to black fishnet stockings and high platform "stripper heels." All she could think was—*yikes*. Damon was right—she'd never been to a club like this before.

Just then, a thin blonde breezed past her and she turned to look, saying to Damon, "Am I crazy, or was that Paris Hilton?"

"You aren't crazy."

"Wow."

The sexual aura in the air was downright palpable. People on the dance floor moved in liquid undulations, clearly more interested in sex than dancing. Shirtless bartenders served up drinks at the bar as waitresses rushed past carrying trays of glasses and bottles, wearing the same bustier and stockings as the cage dancers. Everywhere she looked, Brenna saw people kissing, and those who *weren't* kissing someone looked like they wanted to be.

"Damon," yet another dazzling blonde said then, coming up to curl killer red nails around his arm. She wore a slinky white dress with a V-shaped bodice cut all the way to her navel, the swell of her breasts protruding prominently. "What are you doing in town, baby?"

"Hi, Cherise," he said with an easy smile. "Just here looking for fresh talent, as usual."

"*I* can be fresh, and I *definitely* possess certain talents." She was downright predatory, and Brenna tried to keep her blood from boiling with jealousy—but at the same time, she found herself clutching onto Damon's other arm more possessively than she'd intended.

"This is my date, Brenna—new A&R rep for Blue Night," he said, pulling his Cherise-held arm free to motion toward Brenna.

"Lucky girl," Cherise said coyly, by way of greeting.

"Yes, I am," Brenna replied, noting that it seemed to be the universal consensus: any woman with Damon Andros, even for a night, was to be envied.

"Good to see you, honey," he said to Cherise in parting, and Brenna couldn't have been happier to leave Miss White Dress behind as he pulled her away through the shadowy room.

Still, she couldn't help noticing more sexy girls feasting their eyes on her man—but when she also noted guys giving *her* the same look, it helped even things out in her mind. Was it all the eyes on her, the sexuality floating in the air here, that had her breasts aching and her cunt swelling? Or was it just because she'd been wanting Damon all night?

Despite the sex just dripping from this place, she was on the verge of asking him how exactly Rendezvous was her surprise—when they emerged into a whole new area of the establishment. The dance floor remained visible behind them, but the atmosphere had just changed—dipping even deeper into a slower-paced, more sultry sensuality.

The large room around her was filled with . . . beds. Well, not *actual* beds, but big, plush, jewel-toned ottomans and divans that did a good imitation. Patrons lay across them in sophisticated cocktail wear, drinking, talking, some kissing. Like at Fetish, she spied two girls making out, but *unlike* at Fetish, here no one seemed particularly interested—other than the guy lying with them on the emerald divan, caressing one of the girls' legs.

The music, too, was different—though the dance floor was still in sight, the fast, pounding beat could no longer be heard and instead slower, steamier songs echoed from hidden speakers. The lighting was soft, inviting, sensuous.

And around the perimeter of the room—*oh my!* At first, she hadn't noticed, seeing only dark, sapphire-colored curtains circling the area, but now she realized some of the curtains were drawn back, each open drape revealing a large U-shaped compartment containing a bed custom-made to fit against the curved walls. They were like half-round booths in a restaurant, but instead of booths, she saw more plush places to lie down.

Those that were visible allowed her to spy the people lounging there. In some, she saw couples, while other beds held three or four or even five people. Like on the beds in the room's large open area, people on the boothlike beds drank, laughed, and some made out.

The mere presence of so many ornate beds, with so many people reclining on them, turned her warmer inside, made her pussy a little wetter. Did people actually have sex here? Is that why some of the curtains were closed?

While she was still trying to adjust to the seductive atmosphere, an attractive slightly older woman in another dress as revealing as her own—this one a pretty coral color—approached, placing a hand on the arm of Brenna's lover. "Damon."

"Cynthia, hi." He covered her hand lightly as he leaned to kiss her cheek.

This woman seemed more friendly than flirtatious, so Brenna didn't burn with jealousy like before, but she was beginning to think Damon knew everyone on the planet.

"I saw your name on the reservation list," Cynthia said, "so I put aside my favorite bed for you."

Oh, she worked here.

And she'd . . . *put aside a special bed for him.* Brenna's stomach curled with strange anticipation, still caught in shock and wonderment over this whole place.

Cynthia led them past several closed curtains and a couple of open ones, then pulled a blue velvet drape aside to reveal . . . the most seductive bed Brenna had ever seen. Thick red velvet covered the U-shaped bed, while plush pillows of black and purple, in all shapes and sizes, lined the rounded edge. The U-shaped wall was upholstered in still more red velvet and, higher up, covered with plush red wallpaper. The private compartment came complete with ledges for placing drinks, and gilt-framed mirrors hung at various angles, clearly designed to fit the curved walls.

"This is great, Cynthia," Damon said as casually as if she were a waitress bringing him a meal.

"Can I get you drinks?"

He looked to Brenna. "More wine?"

"Sure." She felt so out of her element that she feared her voice had come out sounding mouselike. Even if she looked the part tonight, she wasn't used to being surrounded by so much glitz.

Damon asked Cynthia to bring a bottle of her best Pinot Grigio and, when she departed, took Brenna's hand and led her onto the red velvet.

It felt undeniably odd to lean back into the comfy pillows in her satin dress, bared legs stretched out before her with knees bent, especially in a roomful of people—yet at the same time, it made her suddenly feel much more a part of the open sensuality of the setting. Damon lay next to her, propping on one elbow to face her.

"So, this is my surprise?" she asked.

He gave a short nod.

"It's . . . pretty wild. I'm still trying to adjust."

"Adjust?"

"I'm used to clubs that have tables—not beds."

Just then, a low moan echoed from somewhere nearby—one of the other beds, she supposed. She pointed vaguely toward the sound. "Are people really having sex here? *Right* here? In the club?"

Lechery laced his grin. "That's kind of the point of the beds."

She rolled her eyes at him, offering a contrite smile. "I get that part. But . . . why go *out* to have sex when you can have it at home or your hotel? Especially since I'm guessing you have to pay for one of these beds."

Damon reached out to touch her knee, using his thumb to caress. "Some people come here hoping to meet somebody they want to fuck. And people like us, who already *know* who they want to fuck . . . we come for the thrill."

Suddenly, she got it. "It's . . . forbidden."

His eyes sparkled. "Right."

"Like doing it on the Eiffel Tower," she went on. "Or in a gondola."

His hand slid warm up her thigh. "Remember what you said on the gondola last night? You said if you could, you would fuck me right there, and you wouldn't care if anyone was watching."

A thin ribbon of embarrassment combined with arousal twined through her. Indeed, she had said that. Hard to believe, but true. Even harder to believe was that she'd *meant* it. Damon had transformed her into a shameless sex addict, it seemed.

And just a little while ago, she'd been ready for whatever he wanted her to do, wherever he wanted her to do it. And maybe she'd been taken aback by the bluntness of this place, where the sex was so "in your face," but as Damon's warm touch slid gently higher, his fingertips flirting just beneath the hem of her dress now, maybe her shock was starting to fade. It faded even more when he kissed her, his tongue flirting gently with hers—a soft, sensual meeting of mouths.

Just then, one of the bustier-clad waitresses appeared at the edge of their bed, bearing two stemmed glasses and an ice bucket with an open bottle of wine inside. "Your Pinot Grigio," she said when they both looked up.

And it occurred to Brenna that she should feel uncomfortable—but she didn't.

Because this was normal here—to be lying down, making out, in front of other people.

"Thanks," Damon said, then raised to pull out his wallet and pass the girl a tip.

When the waitress had gone and Damon began pouring the wine, Brenna said, "I have some questions."

He paused to flash an amused look. "I can't wait."

She smiled, knowing he found her naïveté entertaining. "Okay, how do you pay for the bed? I mean when? I didn't see you give Cynthia any money."

"You give your credit card number when you call to make a reservation."

"Ah." Made sense, she supposed. Her next question, though, wasn't quite as pleasant. "And if people have sex on these beds, are they, um . . . clean?"

"Yes, babe, they're clean. The velvet cover is removable. Each time a bed is vacated, the whole compartment is sanitized."

"Good," she said, then tilted her head. "But how do you know that?"

"Because the brochures say so."

Brenna felt her eyes go wide. "They have brochures? That talk about cleaning the beds after people fuck on them?"

Damon let out a throaty laugh. "It's worded a little more delicately than that, but yeah. They're at the door and probably on the bar. And . . ."

"What?"

"If you're wondering about people hearing you, the compartments were designed to keep noise inside. I know you heard that moan a few minutes ago, so yeah, some leaks out, but mostly it's contained."

"I suppose that's delicately described in the brochure, too?"

He gave a concise, playful nod.

And she couldn't help teasing him as he passed her a glass of wine. "Sounds like you're an expert on this place."

"It's not my first time," he said with a wink. Then lifted his glass in a toast. "To new experiences."

She bit her lip, feeling at once shy but adventurous—and adventurous was quickly taking over. She gently clinked her glass against his. "To new experiences."

Four

They drank their wine and talked a little more, and Damon shed his jacket, laying it aside on the edge of the bed. They kissed, cuddled, listened to the music, and did some people watching through their open curtain.

When Damon drained his glass, he moved closer to her, resting his palm full across her stomach, his thumb barely grazing the underside of her breast—and making her yearn for more. She'd grown pleasantly intoxicated throughout the night, and now she was getting pleasantly drunk on this *place*—the bold colors, the lush fabrics, the flirtatious people all around them.

"I want you," she whispered.

He leaned his forehead over to touch hers, his look deliberate and pointed. "You're gonna have me."

Just then, Brenna caught a glimpse of a sexy leopard-print dress drifting past the edge of their bed—but then it stopped. Both she and Damon looked up.

"Damon Andros," the girl in the dress said with a smile.

Hell. Yet another female fan. And this one was even more beautiful than most—her long, straight hair a stunning coppery color, her olive complexion flawless, her lips pouty and moist, the curves of her pert breasts peeking from inside the dress's halter top.

"Jenelle," Damon said, sitting up to greet her with a smile more sincere than when other women had approached him. "How the hell *are* you?"

The striking girl leaned her head back and gave a playful eye roll that—to Brenna's surprise—made her instantly warm to her. That quickly, she seemed more likable and less affected than most of the women in Damon's "fan club."

"I'm okay," she said, but she didn't *sound* okay. "Broke up with Danny."

Damon tilted his head, his look slightly scolding. "I warned you about him."

"Yeah, and I should have listened. Rat bastard cheated on me. With Darla."

"Shit," Damon said, sounding truly shocked.

At which point Jenelle shifted her focus to Brenna. "Darla's my best friend," she informed her as if they were pals. "Well, my *ex*-best friend." Then she held out her hand across the bed. "I'm Jenelle."

"Brenna," she introduced herself, briefly taking the girl's soft hand. "And . . . sorry about your boyfriend."

Jenelle tossed her head in the other direction, clearly trying to play it off as no big deal, though it clearly was. "He didn't deserve me," she said, trying for a smile. "Which Damon told me the last time I saw him, like six months ago, but did I listen? No. Though you know how it is with some guys—how they're just so hot and they just get under your skin somehow and make you crazy?"

Brenna didn't *used* to know about that—but as of this week, yeah, she did. So she cast a smile that said she could relate. "Yeah, I do."

"Brenna's ex-husband was the same kind of rat bastard," Damon said to Jenelle, then turned to Brenna. "I hope you don't mind me sharing that."

She shook her head. "Not at all." Wayne was *such* old news—yet she liked that Damon understood how awful cheating was, and she *knew* Jenelle agreed.

"Your husband cheated on you?" Jenelle's face twisted into an expression of true revulsion, as if she'd never heard such a terrible thing.

Brenna nodded, then summed it up simply. "He was an ass."

Sitting down on the edge of the bed, Jenelle leaned closer. "My

God—you poor girl. I mean, it was horrible enough with Danny, but I can't *imagine* how awful it would be with someone you're *married* to."

Brenna sighed. "Well, it definitely sucked. But the good news is—he's history."

"And now you're hanging out at Rendezvous with yummy Damon." Jenelle grinned.

"Indeed I am," Brenna replied, and at the moment she couldn't be sorry Wayne had driven her to end her marriage—given that Damon was an indisputable upgrade. She reached out to gently squeeze his knee through his blue jeans, and he covered her hand with his larger one.

"So you're out and about enjoying the single life again, huh?" Damon asked Jenelle.

Like before, the gorgeous girl sighed but attempted to play if off lightly, smiling as she spoke. "Trying to get back on the horse is more like it. But I kind of messed up." She scrunched her nose. "I came out alone tonight, thinking I'd see people I knew, or maybe meet someone nice, but I've basically just wandered around feeling lonely."

Damon gave his head a doubtful tilt. "Don't tell me no guys have put the moves on you in that dress, honey, or I'll know you're lying."

She gave another light eye roll. "Oh, they have. But they were just . . . bleh. Too pushy. Or presumptuous. Or gross. That's the problem when you go out looking to get laid. I can enjoy casual sex as much as the next girl, but it's only fun if it happens naturally. Know what I mean?"

She looked to Brenna for that last part, so even though the only casual sex she'd ever had in her life was with Damon, and even though sex with Damon was starting to feel way more than casual, she said, "Absolutely."

"So I think I'll just go home and drown my sorrows in a bottle of wine, then sleep it off and start again tomorrow." With that, she pushed to her feet. "It was nice meeting you," she said to Brenna, "and great running into you, Damon. Call me the next time you're in town and we'll do lunch or something. I'm kind of hard up for friends right now because all of mine are hanging with Darla and Danny, the shitheads."

Despite wanting to be alone with Damon—well, as alone as one could be at Rendezvous—Brenna truly felt bad for Jenelle. It was one thing to lose your man, but another entirely to lose your friends at the same time. "If you're just gonna go home and drink, we have wine *here*." She motioned to the ice bucket, the bottle jutting from it. "Hang out a while."

Jenelle tilted her head and flashed a knowing smile. "That's sweet, but I don't think you two came here to socialize—except maybe with each other." She winked.

"We've got all night," Brenna told her, not even embarrassed anymore that it was assumed she and Damon were going to have sex. And though it was already late, she'd learned that Las Vegas nights lasted longer—even for her—than nights most other places. She went so far as to pat the red velvet next to her. "Come on in and have a drink."

Jenelle bit her lower lip, looking tempted, and Brenna was struck again by her beauty. "Are you sure you don't mind? I won't stay long."

"Yes, I'm sure." And even if it was a bit hard to believe she was inviting such a stunning girl into "their bed," Brenna kept insisting because Jenelle was so much nicer than most women that attractive—and because hearing about her evening made Brenna realize that maybe life wasn't *always* beautiful for the beautiful people. In fact, maybe it even sucked sometimes.

"Well then," Jenelle said, "I'm headed to the bar for another glass— and I'll grab another bottle of wine while I'm there. What kind?"

"Pinot," Damon replied, then eased the bottle from the bucket to flash the label.

"Be right back," Jenelle tossed over her shoulder with a smile just before the leopard-print dress disappeared.

After which Damon turned to Brenna, his eyes brimming with surprise.

"Are you bummed?" she asked. "That I asked her to stay?"

He smiled softly. "No—you're right, we have all night. But it sure as hell caught me off guard."

Brenna shrugged. "She seemed nice. And kind of adrift. Maybe I'm just thinking back to when my marriage broke up. It really sucks, especially when your friends in common have to choose sides."

He nodded. "She *is* nice."

"How do you know her?"

"She's a showgirl—a dancer at the MGM now, but I originally met her when she danced at the Tropicana, at an after-show party. I've known her for years."

"Have you had sex with her?"

"A long time ago. Just once."

"Does she dance topless, like in the show we saw tonight?"

"Used to. But the last time I saw her, she'd just gotten promoted to a more prominent role where the costumes aren't quite as revealing. In fact, I'm betting that has something to do with her troubles. Darla's in the same show, and I don't think she was happy when Jenelle rose to the feature spot."

Brenna grimaced. "So you think Darla got together with Jenelle's boyfriend for revenge?"

Damon shrugged. "Who knows, but it seems likely."

Brenna couldn't help thinking how ugly that was. And what a racy and competitive world Jenelle lived in. "What makes someone want to be a showgirl here?" she wondered aloud.

"Jenelle once told me she'd tried her damnedest to make it on Broadway, but couldn't—her voice wasn't strong enough. All she wanted to do in life was dance, so this seemed like the next best place."

Just then, Jenelle reappeared, an uncorked bottle of wine in one hand and a glass in the other. "I'm back."

"Come on in," Brenna said, motioning her inside.

Jenelle lounged on the other side of Brenna, holding out her glass for Damon to fill. With Jenelle suddenly so much closer, Brenna's attention was drawn unwittingly back to the other woman's breasts, her cleavage looking tan and perfect. And for the first time, she also saw Jenelle's feet—wrapped in red, strappy, fuck-me heels. Though Brenna would never have matched them with the leopard print, Jenelle had enough style to pull it off.

"This dress is gorgeous," Jenelle said, reaching out to run one hand softly over the satin at Brenna's hip.

Unbidden, Brenna's pussy flinched at the touch—to leave her utterly unnerved. She took a long swallow of wine and tried to act normal. "Thanks."

"Your boobs look great in it," Jenelle added, her hand still on Brenna's dress.

"Mmm—they do, don't they?" Damon chimed in, leaning over to drop a small kiss on the ridge of Brenna's breast. A shiver echoed through the small of her back—not only from the kiss but the fact that the curtain was still open, and Jenelle was still touching her, so casually, easily, as if such contact were commonplace. Maybe it *was* in her world.

"Yours look pretty fabulous, too," Brenna then heard herself say to Jenelle.

God, what was she doing? Why had she said that? They *did* look fabulous, but since when did she hand out compliments on other women's breasts?

Yet neither Jenelle or Damon seemed taken aback. Instead, Jenelle playfully jiggled her chest in the leopard print and replied, "That's why I bought the dress."

At which point Brenna recalled what Jenelle did for a living and decided it was probably completely normal in her circle of acquaintances for women to discuss their breasts.

But the crux of her thighs still felt heavy, and her mind spun, confused. Now she sort of wished she hadn't invited Jenelle to stay. Because she just wanted to roll over into Damon's arms and kiss him, touch him, have her way with him. The need had been building all night, and now, with an alarming suddenness, it was growing fierce, like it had last night in the gondola.

"So how do you two know each other?" Jenelle asked.

Damon answered, explaining about Brenna's job change and why they were in Vegas.

"Wow—that's so cool," Jenelle said, finally moving her hand away as casually as she'd first placed it. "Congratulations."

Brenna struggled to pretend she wasn't burning up with lust. "Thanks. I'm really excited about it, and Damon's been a great teacher." Meeting his gaze, she—once again—couldn't quite stop herself from spewing out her next thought. "In more ways than one."

"Is that so?" Jenelle lowered her voice and cast a grin that said, *Spill.*

"Well," Brenna began, trying to think how to answer—because she wasn't going to admit to either one of them that she'd never had a casual affair before—"I hadn't been with anyone since my divorce. And Damon . . . helped get me out of that rut."

Next to her, Jenelle sighed. "I'm *so* jealous. I need somebody to get me out of *my* rut. I haven't had sex in a month." She said it like it had been a five-year drought.

But Brenna was beginning to understand something. Maybe you didn't miss sex so much if what you had was average or even just good. Now that she'd had Damon, though, she knew she was going to miss it like crazy when it was over. Once you'd had mind-blowing sex, it would be harder to live without it—and she was guessing Jenelle had had plenty of mind-blowing sex.

Jenelle wanted to hear more about what they'd been doing since they'd arrived—what bars they'd hit, how many acts they'd signed, what restaurants they'd eaten at. They both supplied answers, and Brenna drained what was probably her fifth glass of wine tonight— thankful she'd stretched it out over so many hours or she'd have surely passed out by now.

"Today," Damon went on, "I didn't have much business to take care of, just a few phone calls, so I took Brenna shopping."

"Oooh, what'd you buy?" Jenelle asked, her perfectly coiffed eyebrows raising.

Brenna couldn't hold in her light grin. "Panties."

Jenelle gave her head a conspiratorial tilt. "And I bet you're wearing them right now."

"I am," Brenna confirmed, feeling drunker by the second.

"Which pair?" Damon asked.

"It's . . . a surprise," she said, teasing *him* the same way he'd teased *her* about surprises.

"I bet you went with . . . classic black," Jenelle offered, "to go with that killer dress."

"We did get a black pair, but *I* think she went with the red," Damon decided. "Since I ruined her *last* red ones."

Brenna let out another short laugh, since they were both wrong— but said nothing.

Until finally Jenelle reached across Brenna, slipping her red, polished nails into the side slit of Brenna's dress and pushing it toward her hip to reveal a swatch of fabric—the front of her leopard-print thong.

"Oh my God, you totally match my dress," Jenelle exclaimed, and Brenna was trying to fight the surge of moisture between her thighs even as Damon laughed and Jenelle went on. "Mine match *your* dress, too—so maybe we should trade," she said on a giggle. "See?" Then rose to her knees and lifted her dress to show off her own thong, this one of pretty black lace.

Damon shifted, too—moving to shut the curtain.

"What are you doing?" Brenna asked.

Damon arched one eyebrow. "Well, if we're gonna start showing each other our panties, it's probably time to close it. Unless you want me to leave it open."

"No," Brenna said. Because it only made sense. Because both she and Jenelle's dresses *were* pulled up high enough to show their thongs. Even though she wasn't sure exactly how that had happened.

When Damon adjusted the curtain at the foot of the bed, the space seemed to grow smaller, more intimate. And even though they could still hear the music beyond, people laughing, and the occasional moan or groan from another bed, it still felt very much as if the three of them were alone.

Which is when Jenelle, still upright on her knees, leaned across Brenna to reach for the wine bottle, already needing a refill—but lost her balance and fell forward, across Brenna's lap.

All three of them laughed, but Brenna felt more aroused than amused. She'd never been attracted to another woman before, but Jenelle's slender body stretching across hers made her pussy tingle still more maddeningly. And hadn't she also felt unwittingly aroused each time she saw those billboards with barely dressed women? Hadn't she gotten aroused watching all those topless showgirls with Damon earlier, thinking once more about how on display sex was here? When you were so surrounded by beautiful people, men *and* women, didn't it all somehow mix and gel together? Wasn't it *all* arousing? Hell, like it or not, even Kelly's touch on the day she'd hoisted Brenna's breasts upward had gotten her a little hot.

"Sorry," Jenelle said, still giggling, bracing her hands on the red velvet in order to raise up.

But when she did, something strange happened. She stopped midsway, hovering directly over Brenna, and let her gaze drop to Brenna's chest. And when Jenelle spoke, her voice had dropped an octave. "Are those . . . as pretty as I think they are?"

Brenna could smell the fragrance of Jenelle's shampoo as a lock of the other girl's long, voluminous hair brushed the ridge of her breast. She could barely breathe at the question, finally saying, "You'd . . . have to ask Damon about that."

They both shifted their eyes to find that pure animal heat had invaded his gaze. "Yes, they are," he said definitively. And as Jenelle eased back down onto the bed, her tan shapely legs stretched out beside her, Damon reclined next to Brenna, sliding his palm onto her torso. "Why don't I show you," he suggested.

Brenna thought about protesting, but the truth was, she didn't want to. She'd told herself she was ready for whatever the night held, and she couldn't deny being curious, intrigued, to see where this most forbidden encounter would lead. So she simply watched as Damon used both hands to slip her dress off her shoulders, then dipped his fingers into the molded black satin that held her breasts, easing it down until they were fully bared, her nipples pink and erect.

Her gaze slid to Jenelle's, but their eyes didn't meet. Jenelle already studied her naked breasts, the tip of her tongue slipping out to touch her upper lip. Brenna's heart beat madly, passionately.

Only after a long, tantalizing moment did Jenelle's eyes finally lift to her face. "Can I kiss them?"

Brenna felt lost in a sea of confusing lust. She didn't know how far to take this or what she wanted or how she would feel afterward.

Helpless, she looked to Damon—but *he* didn't appear confused at all. He met her gaze darkly, and he moved his lips to say one word: *yes.*

Damon wanted this. Wanted to see her with another girl.

And what *Damon* wanted, *she* wanted.

Because she loved to please him, loved to excite him, and right now—this night, this minute—nothing else mattered.

"Yes," she said and listened to the low groan of satisfaction from Damon as Jenelle bent toward her.

Jenelle's tongue raked gently across one turgid nipple, light and airy—and *hot*.

Brenna gasped with pleasure—the lick had felt just like when Damon did it, only softer somehow, and it was strangely thrilling to know it had come from another woman.

Then Jenelle did as she'd promised, bestowing a simple, gentle kiss to the peak of the same breast—before closing her mouth over it to tenderly suckle. The pull of her feminine lips shot straight to Brenna's cunt, and when she shifted her gaze from Jenelle to Damon and their eyes met, his pinning her in place with more fire than she'd ever witnessed there before—God, it felt like entering a forbidden heaven.

Moving to the other nipple, Jenelle closed both soft hands around the outer curves of Brenna's breasts, warmly massaging—and still Brenna looked to Damon, even as she sighed, even as she moaned, her eyes dropping shut at the sheer pleasure Jenelle delivered.

Damon reached to hold Jenelle's hair back, clearly wanting to see her lick and suckle Brenna. And Brenna wanted . . . everything. She wanted every sensation, every touch—she wanted to feel all a person could feel. She wanted Damon, she wanted Jenelle. She wanted to quit thinking and lose herself in pleasure.

And that's exactly what she did.

Damon leaned in to kiss her other breast, so that both were being suckled simultaneously. Oh God, she'd never experienced such a barrage of pure physical joy as when she arched her breasts upward, deeper into their mouths, attempting to pull the hot sensations inward.

Damon's ministrations were harder, more masculine, the stubble on his chin gently chafing her tender flesh, while Jenelle's lips worked soft and sweet, her every move more feminine. Brenna heard her breath growing more ragged as the physical delights assailed her, radiating down through her torso into her panties.

When Damon finally released her breast from his mouth, his lush lips shone wet, his eyes falling half shut in passion. He raised, kissing her lips, and . . . *mmm, yes*—as well tended as her breasts currently were, she needed to feel *more*, in other places.

Next Jenelle rose, too—bending to kiss Brenna's welcoming mouth while Damon watched. Just like on her breast, Jenelle's kiss was inexorably softer as she slanted her lips across Brenna's lips first one way, then another.

Which is when Damon moved back in to initiate a scintillating three-way that Brenna felt all the way to her toes. Their tongues all met, licking delicately at one another, until Brenna felt hands pushing their way up beneath her dress's hem. Damon's or Jenelle's? It was thrilling not to know for sure, but she concluded they belonged to her man since she soon realized they felt larger, slightly rougher.

Both her companions pulled back then, rising onto their knees, and Jenelle bent to push Brenna's dress up, biting her lip as she studied Brenna's panties, now fully displayed. "So sexy," she breathed, grazing her fingertips across the front, just above Brenna's mound. Brenna sucked in her breath at the skitter of sensation and heard herself whisper, "Please."

Please hurry. Please don't stop. Please keep making me feel good.

"You can have whatever you want, babe," Damon said, his voice soft, deep—adding, "Lift your ass for me."

Planting her heels on the bed, she raised, letting Damon peel her new panties down while Jenelle studied her freshly revealed cunt, audibly sighing at the sight. "Mmm, so pretty."

Brenna wasn't sure she'd ever really thought of her pussy that way before, but Damon had used the same word for it, too, and she decided that—yes, it *was* pretty. In its own special way.

Tossing the leopard-print thong aside, Damon gently parted her legs wide, making her feel her own wetness as he put her wantonly on display.

"Pretty and pink," Jenelle cooed, her voice thick with flirtation.

"Pretty and pink and *delicious*," Damon added, his gaze on Brenna's— and then he glanced to Jenelle. "Hold her open for me."

Brenna's heart pounded harder at the command, especially when Jenelle used both hands to tenderly part the lips of Brenna's cunt wider than they already were.

And when Damon sank his mouth there—oh God, it was almost more pleasure than she could bear. She found herself clutching at the velvet at either side of her, clawing her fingernails into it as she lifted her pussy to meet Damon's thorough licks.

Soon, Jenelle left Damon on his own and returned to Brenna's breasts, running her soft hands over them, teasing the sensitive pink peaks between her fingertips, and again dropping down to lick and suck her.

She heard her own cries of joy and vaguely wondered if they echoed beyond the compartment but didn't care enough to stop. Being pleasured by two people truly delivered twice as many hot delights and took her passions to incredible new heights. Her whole body undulated with desire, her breasts rising to meet Jenelle's hands and mouth, her pussy driving upward to meet Damon's skilled tongue. She'd lost control and felt as if she were being tossed about on a sea of pure pleasure, as if it battered her from all directions.

"Oh God, oh God," she heard herself breathe. Now Damon sucked on her clit and even plunged two fingers inside her moisture. "Oh!" she sobbed at their hot entry, and then she fucked them, along with his mouth, still absorbing Jenelle's hot licks across her nipples.

"Oh . . . oh God, baby—yes, yes." She was so close to coming, and she almost didn't even *want* to, because she wanted to keep feeling like this forever. But at the same time, as she looked past the fall of Jenelle's coppery hair to where her lips closed over Brenna's engorged nipple, her feminine hand cupping Brenna's other breast, and down to Damon, whose gaze met hers even as his mouth was buried between her legs— she knew she couldn't hold back. "Oh baby," she purred, looking into those dark, sexy eyes.

She said nothing more. But at the same time, she thought she'd just said everything. *I love this. I love you. I need you. Make me come. Make me come.*

And then the climax ripped through her at the speed of light, pulsing wildly through her whole body, forcing her eyes shut, making her cry out even louder than before as the hot waves of pleasure carried her to someplace new—before finally lowering her back to the red velvet bed where she'd just indulged in the most scandalous encounter of her existence.

Jenelle was sweetly kissing her mouth, smiling sensually into her eyes, while Damon rained tiny kisses just above the dark curls covering her pussy, up to her navel.

"Mmm, was it nice?" Jenelle asked.

There were simply no words to describe what she'd just experienced. And now that the orgasm had let her come back down to earth, the whole thing felt . . . surreal. Her, with another girl? *And* Damon? At the *same time*?

But the return of sanity didn't make it any easier to deny that she'd enjoyed the naughty indulgence more than she could easily understand. "God, yes," she finally managed.

Jenelle caressed Brenna's breasts some more and looked sincerely pleased. "Mmm, I'm glad."

And Brenna still liked her so very much, thought her so very sweet, even if they lived in entirely different worlds—because, after all, Brenna's world seemed to be edging closer to Jenelle's with each passing day. So it seemed only fair to say to her new friend, "Now it's your turn."

Jenelle bit her lip, cast a sexy smile, and kissed Brenna one more time.

Of course, Brenna didn't have the faintest idea how to proceed—she only knew she wanted to bring Jenelle the pleasure she'd come out tonight seeking, and that Damon would help her.

Reaching gingerly up behind Jenelle's neck, Brenna located a fabric tie and pulled, causing the top of Jenelle's dress to drop gently to her waist.

"Oh my," Brenna whispered at the sight of Jenelle's perfect breasts. Large and round, they possessed no tan lines and stood pertly on their own. Probably enhanced, she figured, but if so, Jenelle had gotten her money's worth.

Still, it was more curiosity than desire that led her hands upward to gently curve around the outer sides of both breasts. Soft and firm in her palms, the touch sent a fresh new lust careening through Brenna. Whether she really desired another woman or not, she couldn't say— she thought much of her excitement might be from simply daring to do something so wild or from sensing how much Damon was enjoying it.

A thought that drew her gaze to his.

"Kiss them," he told her.

And she obeyed, her natural response now being always to please him, whatever it took.

Lifting her head from the black and purple pillows, she gently kissed the tip of Jenelle's mauve nipple, listened to her new friend's pretty sigh and Damon's soft groan, and let the sounds flow all through her. The sensation of the small, hard bead of flesh against her lips sent a fresh current of electricity crackling across her skin.

Be bolder, a little voice inside her said. *For Damon. Thrill him. Thrill him more than he thinks you're even* capable *of thrilling him.*

Biting her lip, Brenna sat upright, curled her hands around Jenelle's shoulders, and pushed her gently to her back on the bed, reversing their positions. Then she paused, only for a second, struck by how beautiful Jenelle looked lying topless with her hair fanning across the velvet.

Brenna drew in her breath, then dove headlong into being the hot, aggressive creature she wanted to become for her man. On her knees now, her dress still gathered at her hips, her own tits still exposed, she bent toward Jenelle, closing her mouth over the turgid pink peak of the lovely girl's breast. Satisfaction roared through her when Jenelle gasped, then moaned, deeply. Brenna's whole body tingled as she began to suck, gently at first, testing the feel of the rigid nipple on the flat of her tongue, the flesh surrounding it filling her mouth.

As she suckled, she let her hand close over Jenelle's other breast, exploring, massaging. How strange and heady to be with another woman this way, she thought, still pulling on the nipple deep, deep. Jenelle's breast in her hand was smooth and flawless, like a perfectly round little mountain topped with a hard pearl that grazed Brenna's palm as she kneaded the flesh around it.

Behind her, Damon watched. She knew because of the low, heated groans that left him, even as his hands molded over her ass, his thumbs stretching inward, inward, toward the center, building in her a whole new sort of desire, something deep and strange and wanton.

And in that moment, she knew she *did* desire another woman. Yes, this was about pleasing Damon—but even independent of that yearning, the pleasure she took from Jenelle's body was more than merely peripheral. Jenelle's breasts were so lovely, creating in her a fever she'd only ever before experienced with a guy. And she wanted more of them somehow, needed to reap more hot pleasure for herself, and so she ceased her sucking, ceased her caresses—and instead shifted slightly upward, to lower her own breasts atop Jenelle's and rub their tits together.

Jenelle's impassioned sigh filled their lavish compartment, soon to be joined by Brenna's. So much softness—hers, melding with Jenelle's. But punctuated by tiny bits of hardness—their nipples, raking over each other, creating tiny pinpricks of sensation that shot straight to Brenna's pussy.

Behind her, Damon rained kisses across her ass, and the tumult of sensation from both sides made her crazed with lust. They moved together, her hot friction with Jenelle in front setting the rhythm with which she arched her ass toward Damon in back, Brenna losing herself in it all... until Damon reached around them both, gently stroking both women's breasts, and whispering in Brenna's ear, "Take off her panties."

Brenna's stomach contracted. It was one thing to have her own pussy pleasured by both of them, but another entirely to bring Jenelle's into the fray.

Still, she didn't hesitate. The passion was too powerful, driving her forward, along with Damon's desire. What Damon wanted, she would give him. She'd never meant to turn into some sort of submissive—but the longing to please him was simply too great to want to fight. It had become a part of their sex, a part of what they shared.

Drawing his palms back to Brenna's bare hips, Damon gently eased her off of Jenelle, imposing his will even as she submitted to it, eager to let him guide her.

Just as he and Jenelle had hovered over Brenna's body a little while ago, now he and Brenna hovered over Jenelle's. Slowly, Damon slid his hands up Jenelle's outer thighs, leisurely raising her animal print dress. Jenelle watched just as intently as Brenna, unabashedly massaging her own breasts now that Brenna was gone.

Beneath the hem, they found a thong of black lace that curved beneath Jenelle's pierced navel and a tattoo of a red heart turned on its side. Just like Jenelle's breasts, Brenna thought this part of her appeared perfect, too—so much that it was hard not to be envious, especially with Damon spying it, as well. And for a split second it made her self-conscious, worrisome, as if she could never measure up to a girl so model-perfect with her dance-toned body—until Damon's gaze rose to hers. "Take them off for me," he said.

And then it hit her. He didn't care. Or maybe he didn't see. But either way, it was still Brenna he desired. If he only wanted to get to Jenelle, he could have taken her thong off himself. Yet he wanted Brenna to do it. He wanted to keep guiding her through the intense sexual education he'd been giving her this week. This was still about *her*.

Swallowing back her nervousness and hoping Damon didn't see it, she reached down to hook her thumbs through the lace at Jenelle's hips. When Jenelle lifted her ass from the bed, allowing Brenna to pull the panties gently to her knees, her gaze naturally gravitated to Jenelle's pussy. The sight of which made her suck in her breath, hard—because all of Jenelle's pubic hair had been removed!

She supposed she'd caught sight of such things before—in a *Playboy* magazine Wayne had once bought, or when she had accidentally opened spam e-mail containing obscene photos—but it had never occurred to her that any other sort of woman would do that.

And now, as she studied the silky, bare slit between Jenelle's slender legs, she couldn't help being both taken aback and . . . amazed. At how much more on display it seemed—like everything in Sin City—and how much more *exciting*.

She'd never thought she could have an interest in another woman's cunt, but suddenly, more curiosity tugged at her—prodding her to reach down and gingerly stroke her middle finger through, making Jenelle moan and leaving her fingertip wet.

Oh God, had she just done that? Just touched a girl's pussy? Without Damon even asking her to?

She peered across Jenelle's body at Damon, knowing she must look shocked. But Damon's gaze was all heat, all hunger. She didn't even realize she was holding her hand up, fingers separated, the moistened middle one protruding slightly, until Damon closed his warm hand around hers and drew her wet finger into his mouth.

Her own pussy surged with the knowledge that he was sucking another girl's juices from her hand. And though a bit of jealousy could have entered the mix, too, there *was* none—there was simply the strange sense that bringing another woman into their sex had somehow drawn them closer. She didn't quite understand how that had happened, but as she peered into Damon's eyes, she felt it in her bones—and in the hot pulse of her cunt.

She felt it so strongly that she reached across Jenelle, cupped his face in her hands, and kissed him hard. She closed her eyes and thrust her tongue in his mouth and lost herself in the wetness there, the taste of him mixing with the taste of her, and even of Jenelle—and she followed the instinct suddenly gnawing at her, and said, raggedly, "Lick her. I want to watch you lick her. I want to see you doing that to someone else."

A low sound left his throat as his eyes went glassy with arousal. As she withdrew her hands from his face, he grabbed her wrists and this time kissed *her* just as feverishly before saying, "Spread her legs for me."

Brenna's pussy surged again, but she managed to break her gaze with Damon and peer back down to Jenelle's smooth cunt. The thong still rested around her knees, but Damon swiftly pulled the lace down and off.

Every nerve ending sizzled with awareness and anticipation as Brenna gently lowered her palms to the tops of Jenelle's tan, shapely thighs, listening to her sigh. She glanced up to see Jenelle sensually tweaking her nipples and licking her upper lip as she looked into Brenna's eyes.

Slowly, Brenna eased her touch inward, each subtle move drawing another tiny gasp of pleasure from Jenelle—until she pushed Jenelle's legs apart, wider, wider, until the flesh at their crux opened, revealing the pink folds inside.

Brenna's breasts ached with desire as her own cunt swelled—all from sharing something so strangely intimate with Damon. How was it possible that having another party in their sex made her feel so connected to him? She didn't know, but when their eyes met overtop Jenelle's pussy, she could have sworn he felt the same way.

"Lick her now," Brenna breathed, bewildered by how much she wanted that, needed to see it.

After bestowing another moist kiss on Brenna's lips, Damon knelt down and stroked his tongue through Jenelle's open slit. His eyes met Brenna's as he finished the long, thorough lick that made Jenelle sob, and the whole combination of sensations turned Brenna still crazier with lust. "Again," she said.

He obeyed, and the tide had turned—suddenly *she* was no longer the submissive one.

And somehow, by licking Jenelle on Brenna's command, their eyes meeting the whole time, it felt—inexplicably—almost as if he were doing it to *her*. She was still a part of it, still intimately involved in the act even without reaping the direct physical pleasure. She loved watching him so closely—closer than she could when he licked *her*. She loved how wet and open Jenelle's inner folds appeared each time his tongue ascended them. She loved hearing Jenelle's moans, watching her pelvis lift to meet his mouth—and knowing *she* had made it happen, by her whim, her wish, her desire, her command. She'd never felt such sexual power without touching or being touched.

But the more she watched her lover tongue another woman's cunt, the more she, too, needed physical interaction, friction, pleasure. So she turned her eyes from Damon and resumed her attentions to Jenelle's breasts. At first, she kissed them some more, licked them, delighting in the way Jenelle's erect nipple sprung back when she flicked her tongue across it. But soon she returned to the hot joy of simply rubbing her own breasts lightly, playfully across Jenelle's.

When Jenelle wrapped her arms around Brenna's neck, splaying her hand over the back of her head and pulling her down into a ravenous kiss, Brenna surrendered completely. To everything. Every sensation. Like before, when she'd been nearing orgasm, she ceased thinking—letting the physical pleasures consume her.

And soon Jenelle was sobbing into her mouth and thrusting madly at Damon's, and Brenna dropped to kiss and suckle her breasts some more, wanting to help deliver her there, make her come.

"Oh!" Jenelle finally cried. "Oh, fuck! Yes! Yes!" Her whole body undulated madly, fucking Damon's mouth as she screamed, and Brenna knew people beyond the curtain had to have heard *that*, but she still didn't care.

Until finally Jenelle ceased moving, going completely still and looking utterly beautiful—even spent, with her dress bunched at her torso, her arms flung back over her head. "Oh my God," she said, more softly now. "That was *so* damn good. You two have no idea how much I needed that."

Damon, his white shirt slightly rumpled now but otherwise looking hot as ever, rose to his knees between the two reclining girls, sensually running one hand up each of their thighs. "You two were fucking amazing," he said, heat sparkling in those dark eyes.

"Damon," Jenelle said, almost as if he were being silly, "your *tongue* was fucking amazing."

He only laughed, but Brenna bit her lip in wholehearted agreement, remembering exactly what it felt like to have it swirling over her clit. Yet then she realized they were tossing around the word "was" here, and she peered up at the man she'd fallen for. "We're not done, are we?"

He lowered his chin, arching a speculative brow. "You don't want to be done?"

She shook her head and, without weighing her words, said exactly what was on her mind. "I want your cock."

His expression darkened as he pointed toward the enormous bulge in his pants. "It's right here."

She bit her lip, needing desperately to give him as much pleasure as he'd given both her and Jenelle with his oh-so-skilled tongue. And as she reached for his belt, she peered up into his eyes and said, "Now it's *your* turn, baby. Get ready."

Five

Brenna wasted no time extracting Damon's cock. Because even if she had learned to enjoy fooling around with a women, she still needed a man to reach real, true fulfillment—*this* man.

She and Jenelle both sighed when they saw it, all strong and long and hard, the tip glistening with pre-come, the shaft pink and veined. She hadn't thought ahead to what she would *do* with Damon's majestic erection—she'd only known an abject yearning for it.

She ran her hands over his length, from bottom to top and back again, gently cupping his balls underneath, unduly pleased to hear his rough breath above her and feel his eyes boring through her.

But very soon, it seemed there was only one thing to do to make this night complete, and fair—so she looked over the head of his cock to Jenelle, who sat waiting patiently, and said, "Lick him with me."

Jenelle smiled, and Damon growled. And Brenna again knew the satisfaction of making the forbidden a reality.

While Brenna held the base of Damon's shaft, she and Jenelle both delicately, sensually licked their way up the sides, as if sharing a large Popsicle. It was at once shocking and arousing to see another woman, that close, at Damon's cock, but like before, arousal overrode jealousy, and soon she and Jenelle were exchanging light tongue kisses around his erection even as they pleasured him.

Although Brenna couldn't bear to wait long before taking him in her mouth—after licking the dot of fluid from the tip, she lowered her lips over the rock-hard column of flesh, relishing the groan that echoed from Damon above. Jenelle fondled his balls as Brenna moved up and down, making him wet, letting him fill her throat—energized by his small, slow thrusts and his hand in her hair.

"Ah, yeah," he said, his voice wafting down. "Suck me. Suck my cock."

When Brenna tired, she offered the shaft to Jenelle, who didn't hesitate to lick her lips and go down on him, as well. Jenelle worked quicker, more ravenous and less sensual—and Damon adjusted his thrusts, making them faster, harder. "Suck it," he said, low and demanding. "Suck it."

Brenna felt somehow as if she'd ascended to another plane—where all that mattered was pleasure, where no rules or taboos existed. And when Damon's eyes met hers, she knew she must look desperate, crazed, so filled with lust as she was. And she was *so* tempted to say what she was thinking—*I love you, I love you, I love you*—but she managed not to somehow.

Still, he must have read the wild need in her eyes, because just then he pulled gently away from Jenelle, carefully lifting her head, then looked to Brenna, his eyes wrought with emotion. "I need to fuck you bad, babe—*now.*"

"Oh God, I know—me, too. I need your cock deep inside me." She was clutching at his muscular thigh and felt like she was begging him, but she couldn't stop.

Damon lay down behind her on the red velvet, wrapping one arm around to cup her breast, massaging it, and she turned her head back toward him, pulling him down into a kiss.

"Lift your leg," Jenelle said, her hand closing over the leather strap at Brenna's ankle.

Oh God—Jenelle! She'd nearly forgotten—that quickly—that the other girl was even there. She'd just needed Damon so much!

But now she complied, letting Jenelle raise her leg high—and watched between her thighs as Jenelle wrapped her fist around Damon's thick erection, pulling it, positioning it, guiding him into her welcoming pussy.

All three of them groaned as Damon entered Brenna—and Jenelle's expression made Brenna hungry to see for herself what he looked like going into her, penetrating her softest flesh with his hardest.

As Damon began to pound into her from behind, Jenelle lay down in front of her to kiss her breasts. Damon even held the mound Jenelle suckled, as if offering it to her—reminding Brenna that she was experiencing the ultimate form of sharing.

Soon, both girls fondled each other's tits, and Brenna felt out of her head with pure reckless joy—and before she knew it, she and Jenelle were rubbing together below, too. One of Jenelle's legs slid between hers, connecting with her clit as Brenna instinctively pressed her thigh forward between Jenelle's.

It reminded her of high school, making out with a boy, feeling your legs interlock with his that way, grinding together, getting lost in that marvelous friction. Only this wasn't high school, and Jenelle wasn't a boy. No, Brenna's "boy" was behind her, plunging his stiff shaft into her moisture—again, again, again—making her cry out and thrust back against him, which also meant thrusting the other way, too, against Jenelle's smooth thigh, until . . . "Oh! Oh God! I'm coming!" she sobbed, the pleasure taking her from both sides, burying her, owning her.

"Oh, yeah—me, too." Jenelle moaned, undulating harder against Brenna, thrusting their breasts together wildly—just as Damon let out an enormous groan that meant he was climaxing, as well, emptying himself deep inside her. And the three of them moved together like tumultuous waves on a red velvet sea—until they all went still, collapsing from utter exhaustion.

Six

Brenna's whole body still tingled half an hour later as she and Damon walked hand in hand back out through the hotel's casino and lobby toward the front doors. As was often the case since she'd started fucking Damon, the experience had left her almost giddy. Giddy because she felt so *brazen*. And feeling so brazen was so *easy* here—here in Sin City, and here with Damon.

She couldn't believe what she'd just done with him, but she had no regrets. Damon and the hedonistic aura of this city were teaching her to *live*, really *live*, experience it, soak it all in.

As they exited through a brass revolving door to the taxi stand, a warm night breeze blew up under her dress and reminded her that, once again, she wasn't wearing panties—they were tucked in Damon's jacket pocket.

"Just so you know," he said with a wicked grin beneath the lights of the large awning above, "Jenelle wasn't part of your surprise. That part was pure serendipity."

Heat rose to her cheeks as she sighed and peered up at him. She wasn't remorseful, and not even exactly embarrassed, but she still felt a bit shy as she admitted, "I never thought I could . . . you know . . . want to be with a woman."

He flashed a knowing, confident look. "Sex isn't always logical. You just feel what you feel."

"Who would have believed it?" she said on a sigh. "And guess what? Apparently, I don't mind sharing, after all."

Damon let out a laugh as a porter held open a cab door for them.

"At least sometimes," she concluded softly, after climbing inside. She knew already that . . . well, even as astounding as the experience had been, she wouldn't want to do it all the time. That quickly, she ached for more of the kind of sex they'd had in the bathtub—slow, leisurely, and *alone*.

After instructing the driver to take them to the Venetian, he whispered, "You were astounding."

She bit her lip, wondering how much to say. "Somehow you . . . make me *want* to be. Astounding. And then . . . I am."

They exchanged soft smiles in the dark backseat of the car now turning onto Las Vegas Boulevard. "You really are, you know," he said. "I never would have dreamed you could be so . . ."

"Neither would I," she mused when his voice trailed off, and it earned her a kiss. After which she teasingly asked, "So, how are you going to top *this*? How else are you going to inspire me to new heights?"

He cast her a sideways glance. "You'll see."

Since she'd only been kidding, she said, "*Huh?* What are you planning *now*?"

He tilted his head, cast a mischievous look, and leaned near her ear—and she waited to hear just what he had in mind, but instead he only said, "Babe. It's a surprise."

THE SIXTH NIGHT

"Commit the oldest sins the newest kind of ways."
—William Shakespeare

One

Damon rolled over in bed and thanked the fates that he'd been smart enough not to schedule a breakfast meeting with Austin Cole. It was 10 A.M., which meant the Las Vegas Strip was just beginning to stir with tourists out seeing the sights before the temperatures became infernal—but inside his suite, heavy drapes blocked out the sun and let him and Brenna sleep in and recover from the night past. Once upon a time, he could stay out until four and function fine the next day. But at thirty-five, a guy needed some sleep.

He caught sight of Brenna in bed next to him—prettily naked. They had gone straight to bed after reaching the room, but not before she'd stripped off that sexy dress. He feared he was growing too accustomed to that—to bumping up against her bare body in the night, occasionally wrapping around her, soaking up her heat.

Damn, last night had been . . . beyond his wildest imaginings. At least where Brenna was concerned.

He'd been with two women at once before. But he'd never felt the things he had last night: pure awe and pure . . . *affection*. And when he'd awakened just now, curled loosely around her, he'd felt warmer and safer than he could understand.

Something in the emotion took him back in time . . . to Angie.

The two of them had had sex, of course—they'd lost their virginity together. And though they'd both lived at home, as they'd gotten older, they'd had occasional opportunities to spend the night together. And maybe . . . maybe he'd felt this way *then*—that warm comfort of waking up together.

But he'd always known he was cut out for something more than the life he was living in Brooklyn, so, even as much as he'd cared for Angie, with each passing day his aspirations had tainted their relationship with more doubt.

With Brenna, though, it felt almost as if he could have it all. The sweet, genuine girl who a guy could take home to Mom . . . and the wild sex kitten who was never afraid to experiment, never afraid to indulge in her pleasures.

Shit—why the hell was he thinking about taking her home of all things? He didn't *take* women home. Ever. Not since Angie.

Because he didn't get into relationships.

Because he didn't want that kind of life.

And you best damn well remember it, Andros.

After all, he and Brenna only had two more nights together before they headed back to L.A. At which point he'd planned for this to be over. And that still made sense.

Didn't it?

Two

"All right, we'll talk next week," Damon said, showing Austin Cole and his mom—who'd been wary and full of questions about the contract they offered—to the door of the suite. "And if you or your attorney have any questions I can address in the meantime, please give me a call."

Brenna watched him shut the double doors, leaving the two of them alone again. She'd stayed mostly quiet through the meeting, during which they'd had lunch delivered. She'd listened to the way Damon answered the woman so thoroughly, always respecting her inquiries, even when they got repetitive and confusing. Brenna herself had only chimed in to let Austin know how much she loved his music and how much she wanted him on board at Blue Night.

Turned out, though, that only three days ago Austin had been approached by a scout from one of the majors—who was offering more money, of course.

"The upside," Damon told Brenna now, crossing the tiled foyer, "is that we got to meet with them first." The other label's A&R rep had simply invited them to L.A. next week, rather than talking business here where Austin lived. "We got the opportunity to show Austin how much we want him, we got to let him know how much we're going to respect his music and that he's going to get the personal touch with us."

"And the downside?" Brenna asked, still sitting at the table.

Damon sighed. "We just don't have as much money as they do."

"Then what hope do we have? Why would he go with us?"

"For the reasons I just said. He likes us, I could tell. And he's a bright kid—I got the idea he's done his homework on the business and that he understands the perks of going with a smaller label. He knows he'll just be a little fish in a big pond with the other guy, but that if he goes with us, he'll have all our attention.

"And it's actually very smart of him and his mom not to rush into anything, to talk to a lawyer, to find out what both sides are offering before making a decision. Frankly, our job is to try to rush people into signing before somebody else discovers them, just like we did with Blush, but when a performer is wise enough not to leap on the first contract shoved under his nose, I have to respect that and work with him on it."

Brenna had never thought about that—that despite asking lots of questions about their contract, the girls in Blush had signed without seeking any legal counsel, asking friends or family, anything. And it had been Damon's goal—and was now hers—to make artists do that. It suddenly struck her as another part of this job she might not excel at—trying to push someone into doing something that might not be in his or her best interest.

"What's wrong?" Damon asked. Her feelings must have shown on her face—something she really needed to work on if she was going to be a good A&R rep.

"Nothing," she lied. She found it so easy to be honest with Damon when they were talking about sex or most other things—but the last few days, she'd found discussing her new job . . . *less* easy. The truth was—the more she learned about it, the more she began to wonder if she'd really be any good at it.

"Listen," he said, "if we get Austin—and I *plan* to get Austin, even if I have to get down on my hands and knees and beg the kid—I want you to take him."

"Huh?" She tilted her head.

"I want him to be your first official artist."

She felt her jaw drop in shock. "You're kidding."

Yet he misread her reaction as worry. "Don't panic, babe—I'll be there every step of the way to guide you. And I think the kid'll be big, and not *too* temperamental. He'll give you a nice head start in the biz—he'll be an act to hang your hat on, get your name out there."

Brenna let out a huge breath. Was he really offering her this? "Damon, you don't have to do that. I mean, it's hardly fair. You're the one who spent the time talking with him and his mom today, not me. You're the one he likes—and surely the one he wants to work with. And . . ." She sighed, letting her voice soften as she ran out of steam, her eyes dropping to the table's wood grain. "I really haven't done anything to earn a gift like that."

In response, Damon sat down in the chair next to her, turned her toward him, and took her hands in his. "Brenna, I have a lot of faith in you to make it in this business. But it's not easy to get people to trust you with something as big as a music career, and it can be tough to get that first successful act. Start out with a promising one already under your belt and that's half the battle. So I want to do this for you, okay? I'm not taking no for an answer."

Brenna could barely breathe around the lump in her throat. It had gotten pretty easy to forget about the terrible truth she was keeping from Damon when they were flirting or kissing, eating dinner or listening to music, hitting clubs or having sex. But now, in this moment, she *couldn't* forget. In fact, it was all she could think about.

She'd never been so stunned or touched—or so horribly guilt ridden—in her life.

"So that's the way it is. We sign him, he's yours. Okay?"

She still couldn't answer. So instead she threw her arms around his neck and kissed him—with all the love in her heart and all the admiration in her soul. She kissed him until he pulled her over onto his lap, his hands on her ass as she straddled him in the wide chair.

Finally the kisses ended, and they simply sat there, silent, Damon leaning his forehead against hers in that sweet way she loved. And a slow, proprietary grin unfurled across his face as he said, "Now that's the kind of answer I like."

Three

There was little Brenna could do to fix this. She couldn't refuse to take Austin, and she couldn't tell Damon the truth without losing her own job. And not just the A&R dream job—she'd surely lose even her administrative job, too, if she came clean. Hell, Jenkins might even have hired someone to take her place already. And as a recently divorced woman, she *needed* her job. To live. To pay rent. To eat. It was non-negotiable.

So she had no choice but to keep going with this insane charade for the next couple of days. And in the meantime, she could at least give Damon the things he wanted from her—heat, passion, sex. She could be his dirty girl.

And since Damon seemed so full of sexual surprises for her, she decided to give *him* a surprise, too. One he would never expect.

So as she stood naked before the wide vanity mirror in her room, ready to shower and change for another night of scouting—and fucking—she bit her lip and reached for her shaving cream.

But instead of smoothing the fluffy white foam over her legs, she instead spread it over the flesh between her thighs and reached for a pink disposable razor.

She'd never even thought about shaving away her pubic hair until last night, after seeing Jenelle's denuded pussy. She'd thought she'd immersed herself in bold, unabashed sexuality this week—but seeing Jenelle's cunt, so smooth and ready, had inspired her to be bolder still. Revealing her own to him, like this, seemed like the last little vestige of old Brenna that she could let go of—or shave off, as it were.

Four

That evening, they took a cab to Fremont Street, the "old Las Vegas," home to the few remaining casinos that had started the town. In recent years, the city had revived the area, turning the old new again by erecting an enormous arched ceiling over several city blocks, which also served as a screen. The street was cordoned off, allowing patrons to roam without traffic worries, and every night after dark, a light show seemed to flash across the night sky.

Fremont Street had also become the perfect venue for street performers—attracting mimes and artists and magicians, as well as musicians. Damon explained on the ride over that he always checked out Fremont Street when he came to Vegas. "Usually nothing noteworthy," he concluded, "but I found Graham Maxwell here, so I don't want to risk missing somebody great." Graham Maxwell was a jazz pianist whose CDs had been respectable earners for Blue Night for the last ten years.

Brenna had dressed down compared to last night, wearing white capri pants with a fuchsia halter top. Normally, she would have finagled a strapless bra under this particular piece of apparel, but the week's experiences had truly altered her way of looking at things—at least for as long as she was in Vegas—so she hadn't bothered and didn't mind if her nipples showed through a little. As usual, she felt a whole different kind of sexy being on Damon's arm—as if just being with a guy so hot gave her license to be racy.

They arrived early to have dinner in a steakhouse Damon knew, and afterward hit the street. After passing a truly amazing airbrush artist at work and a juggler on stilts, they reached a bandstand at one end of the street where a slightly overweight guy played a piano and sang hits by Billy Joel and Elton John. The crowd seemed entertained, but Damon and Brenna quickly decided there was nothing uniquely appealing about him.

Traversing back up the thoroughfare, they found a guy playing guitar, singing soft rock standards in a stark, gravelly voice that turned gentle at just the right times. Slowly, a crowd amassed and passersby dropped bills in his open guitar case. Between songs, he pointed out his wife and baby, who stood nearby watching. He looked like an aging hippie—in his forties, dull blond hair pulled back into a ponytail, and maybe even like a cradle robber, since his young wife couldn't have been a day over twenty-two. But when he dedicated his version of "I Love You," by the Climax Blues Band, to her, Brenna's heart melted.

"I like him," she said to Damon when the song ended.

"You like him because you think he's sensitive and romantic."

She turned to him, smiling, surprised. "And what makes you think I value those things?"

He grinned in return. "Maybe I'm wrong—maybe you don't. But I have a feeling that girl I used to see in the Blue Night office values them."

She blinked, still curious. "And why do you think *that*? Just because I once told you I liked my sex private and that I was a little more subdued when I was married?"

He shrugged. "Just a hunch."

"Haven't we gotten past the prim and proper thing *now*? I mean, if I value romance so much, how is it possible for me to have a wild, crazy affair with you all week and not even blink about the fact that we'll be going back to business as usual in a couple of days?"

His smile faded, just slightly—and she was almost sorry she'd said it, reminding them both that this would soon end. After all, what if he'd been planning to alter that decision somehow, to keep seeing her when they got back to L.A.?

"You want to know what I really think?" he finally asked.

She swallowed but knew her smile had disappeared, too. "Sure."

"I think I happened to come into your life at a time when you were hurting over your divorce. I've never been married, or divorced, but I know plenty of people who have, and I know divorce can really change a person, change what they want and how they view life. And even if you're wilder now, and more adventurous, I think deep down you'll always be a woman who swoons a little when a guy like that"—he pointed to the guitar player—"dedicates a sweet song to his wife."

Brenna barely knew what to say. Because she thought he was probably right. She had no intention of going back to her old "prim" Brenna ways when this was over, but . . . yeah, she'd probably always appreciate a sweet, loving man. God knew she'd appreciated Damon giving her control of Austin's career today, that it had touched her . . . probably too deeply. And even if she didn't *want* to resume being prim, she also couldn't quite imagine herself falling into bed with anyone else as easily as she had with him. "I guess . . . you have me pegged, Andros."

"Don't look so bummed about it," he said, his voice lightening. "It's not a crime."

As usual, when they discussed stuff like this, she was honest. "Maybe I don't *want* to feel that way. Maybe I just want to be a dirty girl and nothing more."

He peered down into her eyes, all amusement leaving his face. "But then you wouldn't be you, Brenna. And for your information, I like the whole package. I like the dirty girl. But I also like how sweet you are, how *real*. Hell, I like that I can have an intelligent conversation with you. It's not always that way with women I know."

Oh. So he was saying he liked her just the way she was. Or just the *new* way she was. And she wasn't sure how to respond to that, but *I love you* came to mind. And since that was definitely a bad idea, she instead took his hand in hers, then simply leaned up to kiss him.

"Thing is," he said then, "we're still not recording this guy."

Brenna scrunched her nose in disappointment. "But they look . . ."

"Like they need the money, I know," he said. "Only we're in the music business, not the charity business, babe. That's something you can't be soft on, okay?"

He was right, of course, so she nodded. "Except . . . he's good. *Really* good. Don't you think? And he even has a nice stage presence."

"But he hasn't played one original song."

"Doesn't mean he doesn't have them."

Damon grinned, probably at how argumentative she'd suddenly gotten. "Tell you what. When he takes a break, you can introduce yourself. Give him my card but write your name on the back. Tell him to send you a CD of original stuff if he has it. How's that?"

She smiled. "That sounds perfect."

And it did.

As the guy quit playing, saying he'd be back in a few minutes, Brenna took a deep breath and approached him, leaving Damon on the perimeter of the crowd. When she told him she was from Blue Night, his crinkled-at-the-edges eyes lit up, and he flashed a smile showing he needed some dental work. After expressing her interest, she requested he send her a CD of any original music, and he thanked her, shaking her hand so hard it nearly fell off—at which point she glanced up to see Damon smiling at her.

"Nice work," he said, sliding an arm around her shoulders as they turned to go.

"That was actually fun."

"See? I told you—this is the best job in the world when you can make someone's day—or, in some cases, *life*."

"So what's next tonight?"

"Well," he said teasingly as he glanced around them at the blend of artisans and tourists, "we could get your caricature done. Or we could taunt one of the mimes. Or we could . . . proceed to your surprise."

Going coy and confident at the very suggestion, she said, "This surprise—it's sexual in nature, right?"

He nodded. "Of course."

"Then give it to me, baby."

Five

They caught a cab back to the Strip, on the way talking more about the business—and dear God, there was so much to learn that, at moments, Brenna wondered if she would ever take it all in.

Of course, they also flirted and made out a little. Enough that by the time neon-lit casinos towered on both sides of the car, she was thinking a lot more about doing naughty things with Damon than about music. Each time he kissed her, the sensations seemed to dissolve through her, making her breasts tingle and her pussy swell. The clingy fabric of her halter top rubbed against her hardened nipples with every move she made, adding to their sensitivity.

So, again, she didn't quite notice where the cab turned off the boulevard—in fact, she was so busy twining her tongue around her lover's that it caught her off guard when the taxi stopped beneath another of the large, neon-lit awnings that fronted all the big resorts. As Damon paid the driver, then led her into one more busy, ornate lobby buzzing with people, she wondered if they were visiting another stylishly risqué club like Rendezvous. But she didn't bother asking, because she knew he would only cast her a chiding look and remind her it was a surprise.

They approached the concierge desk, where a handsome man in a dark suit looked up—then pushed to his feet. "Mr. Andros, welcome back." He reached out to shake Damon's hand, and as usual, Brenna stood amazed at how many people knew him—and clearly revered him.

Damon smiled easily. "Thanks, Richard."

Richard's gaze flicked quickly toward Brenna, then back to Damon. "Can I trust you'd like to visit our special club this evening?"

When Damon nodded, Richard smiled, then left the desk. "Right this way," he said, guiding them across a whirring, clanging casino floor, until they reached a back corner of the room and a rather nondescript door marked PRIVATE, which Brenna would have assumed was a supply closet or maintenance room—until Richard inserted a key in the door's lock. "Enjoy your evening," he said, showing them inside, then letting the door fall shut behind them.

Brenna found herself in a space about the size of a large closet, yet it was decorated in lavish Las Vegas decor—plush red carpet and wallpaper of tan and gold—and before them stood a shiny gold elevator door. Damon pushed the only button, an up arrow, and Brenna said, "Um, I know this is a surprise, but . . . why is this place behind a locked door?"

"It's a *very* private club," he said, his expression giving away nothing.

Beginning to get a little nervous, she swallowed. "Private how?"

Just then, the elevator door opened. Inside, the walls were mirrored from top to bottom, and each corner sported thick gilt molding from ceiling to floor. They stepped in, Damon's hand at the small of her back. "Not many people know about it," he replied, "and when we reach the top, we'll be asked to sign a statement saying we won't reveal anything about the club—its location, what we see, *who* we see—to anyone."

"Um, why?" Her skin prickled. "There's nothing illegal going on, is there?"

Damon ran his palms reassuringly up and down the tops of her arms. "Relax, babe. This is just a place where people come to indulge in activities they'd rather keep private, that's all."

"Oh." Not that he'd really answered her questions or assuaged her curiosities.

But before she could ask anything else, the ride ended, the elevator doors parting to reveal a small, dark area that automatically drew the eye to yet another shiny gold door. Above it, a rather old-world, Roman-looking script spelled out *Caligula's*.

Stepping from the elevator, she turned to Damon. "Caligula. Wasn't he the Roman emperor who had a lot of sick, kinky kinds of sex?"

Damon's eyes glimmered in reply. "Correct." And without another word, he opened the gold door.

Inside Brenna found a hallway lined with pristine white Roman arches draped with greenery and flowers. The walls on either side sported murals that gave the impression they stood on a Roman street and that the ancient city stretched in all directions around them. A man and woman, each attractive and wearing white togas trimmed in gold edging, greeted them.

"Welcome to Rome," the guy said, lifting a hand as if to motion to the city's splendor. Around his head rested a gold laurel wreath like those worn by Caesar and other men from that age.

"We're pleased you have arrived," the lady said, her voice warm, formal. Her short, toga-like frock draped over one shoulder and left her pointed nipples clearly visible through the white cloth. She held out two rolled pieces of what looked like weathered parchment tied with thin gold cord. "These are the terms you must agree to before entering our fair city." Then she motioned to two open archways on either side of the hall. "And there you shall find the garments of our citizens—choose one to your liking and prepare for an evening of sensual delights unlike you have ever known."

"My lady, you shall find your dressing room through the arch on the right," the guy said, "and sir, proceed to the left."

And before she knew what was happening, Brenna found herself ushered through the indicated arch, her roll of parchment clutched in her fist.

She wasn't sure whether she was happy or sad to find another "citizen of Rome" waiting inside. The lovely dark-haired girl wore another revealing white dress and smiled prettily as Brenna entered. "Welcome," she said. "I am your maid, Clodia. Once you've signed the document, I will help select your apparel for the evening."

Brenna stood dumbfounded, given that she still didn't know exactly what took place here. "Um, okay." Hurriedly, she unrolled the parchment and found, in historic-looking script, the same general message Damon had relayed. Signing with a pen fashioned to resemble a quill, she passed it to "Clodia," who then motioned toward various styles of women's togas displayed on mannequins around them.

"When you choose," the woman said, "bear in mind that everything you're wearing now must come off. All jewelry and undergarments included."

"I see," Brenna murmured, studying the scant apparel.

She selected the same dress Clodia wore—gold shoulder straps led down to silky white cups that held her breasts and a bodice wrapped with gold, crisscrossing cords. The varied hem flowed to mid-thigh on one side, higher on the other.

When she slipped it on in a private dressing room, she feared it might too easily allow her pussy to be seen, but decided not to worry, since *all* the togas were short, and they'd come here to have sex, after all. As also seemed to be the case with all of the outfits, her nipples showed clearly through the white cloth and the cut of the fabric created ample cleavage. She wasn't sure if she felt sheepish or sexy exiting back to where Clodia waited for her.

"Lovely," the young woman said, taking her in from head to toe, her slow perusal causing a frisson of anticipation to race up Brenna's spine.

Next, she was fitted with gold shoes—essentially strappy heels with cording that crisscrossed their way up her calves. Finally, they chose a headpiece from the many available—a circle of entwined gold links that rested around her head like a delicate crown.

"There," Clodia said, spinning her toward the mirror. "You are now a perfect Roman goddess."

And—oh God—she *was*. She felt as if she were going to a Halloween party, but . . . the kind *Damon* probably went to, where every woman was hot and sexy and every guy was ready. Though she'd never indulged in any sort of Roman fantasy, she suddenly thought maybe she could get into this—and for the first real time since stepping off the elevator, she found herself truly anxious to see exactly what awaited her.

"Go," Clodia said, still in character. "Meet with your lover. He is waiting to take you to a bacchanalia at the emperor's palace."

Exiting into the hallway, Brenna found Damon, sexily clad in his own white toga and laurel wreath. She wouldn't have guessed he could look so hot in what was technically a dress, but on the other hand, she wasn't sure how Damon could succeed in *not* being sexy. She also couldn't help noticing that despite the no jewelry rule, his cross still adorned his neck.

His eyes traveled appreciatively from her head to her feet, making her pussy pulse slightly. "Damn, babe—I should have brought you here sooner."

She fleetingly worried that she'd end up with the same problem she'd experienced the other night with no panties to absorb her moisture—but she had bigger things on her mind. She pressed her palms to his chest, letting her eyes widen, but spoke low since their original greeters stood nearby. "So what happens here exactly?"

He gently squeezed her elbows, his expression sultry. "You're about to find out."

She was on the verge of arguing when the white-clad woman from the entrance approached. "Proceed onward toward pleasure," she said with a smile, so Damon led Brenna farther down the hallway still lined with Roman murals as a patrician voice began to echo from hidden speakers.

"Welcome to the Holy Roman Empire. You have been invited to Caligula's palace for a grand bacchanal feast. Many of the emperor's guests have already arrived. While you are here, your wish is Caligula's desire. You may swim in his baths, eat his grapes, drink his wine, play with other visitors, indulge your every pleasure. You may also choose to simply observe our riotous Roman festival. Whichever you choose, be respectful of others, and remember . . . when in Rome, do as the Romans do."

The recording had been timed to end precisely as they reached wide double-doors beneath an elaborate facade of a Roman building. The atmosphere, already, was nearly overwhelming.

"Should I be nervous?" she asked Damon once the voice had ceased.

"No," he said. "You should be . . . open-minded."

She stopped, looked at him. She'd decided she was ready for this—

whatever *this* was—back with Clodia, when it was more about a game of dress-up, but now she began to worry again. "What do you mean?"

His reply came in a steady, frank tone. "I mean you're going to be shocked at first by what you see—but then you're going to relax and enjoy. You're going to let yourself go. Just like you did on the Eiffel Tower. And in the gondola. And last night, with Jenelle. You're going to experience the most pleasure you ever have. It's that simple."

She stood speechless before him. It didn't *sound* simple.

Because up to now, with Damon, she'd always felt . . . as if she had a choice. About everything they'd ever done together. Their sex had only reached certain extremes because she had lost her inhibitions and wanted it to happen.

But this, now, felt more *thrust upon her* than anything they'd done. Whatever waited behind that door would be something she'd have to *endure*, could not easily escape. The fantasy was at once alluring and . . . intimidating.

"I'm a little scared," she said, deciding to lay it on the line. "I'm not sure I want to be here, want to do this."

He stayed quiet, but his dark eyes bored through her as he, again, placed his hands on her upper arms to gird her. "Have I brought you anything but pleasure so far?"

"No."

"Do you have any regrets?"

"No." Not even about Jenelle. Part of her had feared feeling remorseful or weird upon waking up this morning, but it hadn't happened.

"I never planned any of this, Brenna. But I like helping you discover the bad girl inside you. I like taking you deeper and deeper into that side of yourself. And this is just . . . the next step. The *ultimate* step. Don't you want to see what it is?"

When he put it like that, despite herself, she did. So, almost numb with wanting to please him—again, *always*—she felt herself nod.

Heard him say, "Good girl."

Then watched as he banged the large, gold, lion-headed knocker on the door of Caligula's palace.

Six

Maybe she had begun to form some picture of what took place here—a hedonistic feast, which surely included hedonistic sex. But she couldn't have imagined the elaborate scene that awaited her when the palace door opened. Damon again placed his hand at the small of her back to usher her inside the expansive room.

More murals framed every wall, making it appear as if they were indeed inside a grand palace, in a hall lined with large windows revealing well-manicured Roman gardens complete with fountains and the occasional horse and chariot passing by. Between the "windows" stood large tables laden with grapes and cheese and jugs of wine.

But the paintings and food were—by far—not the main attraction. In the middle of the space, Roman columns created a large circle. Between each rested a bed covered in white, strewn with metallic gold pillows, and most were occupied by people dressed as she and Damon were. In the circle's center were two small rectangular pools sprinkled with water lilies—and people, some immersed in their togas, others swimming naked. Between the two "baths" stood a grand dais on which a gorgeous blond woman took turns kissing two men, all three of them naked but for the golden laurels atop their heads and looking ready to do far more than just kiss.

Brenna wanted to stop, try to absorb it all from a distance before getting too close, but yet another toga-clad girl was leading them to an empty bed.

Looking around, she realized most of the beds' inhabitants watched the people on the center platform, but some were indulging in their own pleasure. One couple kissed, their hands between each other's legs beneath their togas, and she witnessed one girl seated behind another, reaching around to cup the second girl's breasts as a guy knelt between the same girl's legs, bending to eat her. On another, even two handsome, muscular *guys* made out.

"Relax and let yourself enjoy this," Damon whispered as they settled on the bed together. Not quite sure what to do, Brenna sat with her knees bent slightly before her, unable to deny how good—even comforting—it felt when Damon eased his arms around her waist from behind.

And for the first few seconds, she couldn't believe she was openly watching so many people have sex in a brightly lit room—and a stark embarrassment that bordered on shame bit at her.

But then something happened.

She realized that no one *else* was embarrassed.

They were simply enjoying the fantasy, the bacchanal, as the club was designed for them to do.

And she realized that it was impossible not to start feeling more aroused with each passing second. For everywhere her eyes fell, some-thing sensuous took place.

In the pool nearest her, a naked woman with a perfect hourglass body floated on her back while a nude man began to lick between her legs. A shapely woman in a toga emerged up the pool's steps, water sluicing off her dress to leave her ample breasts clearly visible, and her ass, as well, through the thin fabric. She lay down upon an empty bed, then motioned toward a toga-wearing man who stood nearby holding a tray of grapes. He went to her, dangling a clump of purple grapes just above her mouth, allowing her to bite one off.

In the room's center, the lovely blonde now positioned herself on her hands and knees on a plush divan as one man's cock entered her from behind and the other fucked her mouth. Brenna had never seen anything like it.

And although Roman-esque music could be heard—making her imagine a few of Caligula's subjects off playing lyres and lutes in some distant corner of the room—the melody was punctuated with the sounds of sex: moans, sighs, labored breath.

Brenna was—slowly—becoming more fascinated than stunned.

She leaned back to ask Damon, "How does this work? What are the rules?"

She turned to see a scolding grin. "I guess you didn't read what you signed."

Well, not closely, no. She'd seen the part about confidentiality and grabbed up her "quill," too uneasy to think very clearly. "Maybe not. So tell me."

"You can just watch if you want—or fuck whoever you came with. But the people who work here will do whatever you like—feed you fruit, fool around with you, or fuck you if you ask."

"Wow," she said on an amazed sigh at the "feast" of choices here. Then she looked to Damon again. "How do you know the people who work here from the ones who don't?"

"The armbands." He pointed toward the guy still dropping grapes in the mouth of the woman who looked like she was competing in a wet toga contest. A gold metal band circled his forearm and, scanning the room, Brenna realized many people wore them. The woman whose pussy was being eaten in the pool, for instance. And all three of the lovers on the dais.

When Damon saw her gaze resting there, he said, "Only the employees fuck on the center stage. They take turns all night to keep everyone entertained."

God, she thought—nonstop sex. All night long. What would it be like to work here? To fuck on that divan for a living? Up until this moment, she'd imagined every aspect of the sex trade as something dirty and debasing and undesirable, but for a split second, watching the woman being so thoroughly pleasured by two handsome Roman men with their muscular bodies and big, stiff cocks, Brenna thought maybe it wouldn't be so bad.

"What about . . . diseases?" she couldn't help asking.

"There are rubbers under every bed," Damon informed her. "And brand-new sex toys, too." As her eyes went wide, he added, "It's kind of like a minibar in a hotel—whatever's gone when you leave is added to your bill."

Unable to resist the temptation, Brenna leaned over the edge of the bed and pulled back the white covering. Indeed, beside a shallow bowl of condoms lay an amazing array of vibrators and other penis-shaped instruments—and a few things she didn't even recognize!

"Like what you see?" he asked when she rose back up, probably looking dumbstruck.

She bit her lip and answered honestly. "I like what I've got up here a lot better."

"Come here," he said, then pulled her into a kiss. Around them, sensual notes from the lyre still wafted through the room and more moans and groans echoed, creating their own erotic symphony, but in that moment, all she could see was Damon. And when his hand rose to her breast, caressing her as his kisses dropped to her neck, she didn't even care if anyone saw.

That quickly, somehow, she'd acclimated.

"Is this as horrible as you feared?" he whispered in her ear, his breath warm on her neck.

She found her gaze planted back on the threesome in the center of the room. The blonde now took turns sucking the men's cocks, and whichever one wasn't in her mouth was being worked by her hand.

"It's horrible, and it's . . . arresting," she said softly, trying to analyze her emotions. "How is it possible that I'm both appalled and . . . utterly captivated?"

"Because you think too much?" he suggested between kisses that now spanned down onto her chest.

She cast him a sensual smile in reply. "It must be great to be a man, to not have to feel so much and think so much."

"You've done pretty good at that this week, babe—and you should go back to doing it right now."

He was right, of course. She'd managed to discover a whole new sexual world with his guidance and her ability to turn off old Brenna this week. But being immersed in something so wholly shocking had threatened to take her back there.

Until this moment.

Because she wasn't going to let it.

Instead, she was going to close her eyes. Drink in the sensation of Damon's kisses across her chest, his thumb stroking her distended nipple. Soak up the sounds of pleasure all around her. And . . . eat a grape. That's what she wanted. To let a man feed her a grape while Damon kissed her. She wanted to be that daring. Take that step.

And it was just as she lifted her hand to wave over a darkly handsome guy wearing a gold armband and bearing a tray of grapes that Damon slipped the gauzy white fabric over her breast, baring it—and she didn't stop him.

She couldn't.

She had to keep going.

She held eye contact with the good-looking guy even as Damon's mouth closed over her nipple—and her cunt spasmed.

Oh God, she was doing this, really doing it. It somehow felt infinitely more wanton than anything else she'd indulged in this week.

The grape-bearer—who even *looked* Italian—approached, and she licked her upper lip, pointing toward a pile of green grapes. Lifting a small bunch, he held them over her parted lips, allowing her to pluck one free between teeth and tongue.

As the grape squashed in her mouth, the sweet juice flowing free, Damon suckled her harder and her pussy nearly exploded from the rush of pleasure, making her moan.

"More?" the handsome Roman asked.

It made Damon look up, realize what she was doing. His eyes went glassy with lust and she felt beautifully, thrillingly exposed with her breast glistening and naked between the two men. Being on display made her wetter still, made her feel hot and swollen beneath her tiny toga.

She was about to say yes—to more grapes, and maybe more everything—when Damon glanced up at the guy once more, and this time said, "Anthony?"

Oh God.

The Roman lowered his chin, looking confused at first, but then he grinned. "Damon—I'll be damned."

"I haven't seen you in forever, man."

"Whisky a Go Go in 2002, probably—because I've been in Vegas since then."

Brenna sat up a bit, pulling the fabric back over her breast. Her heart still beat between her thighs, but her sense of passionate abandon had been pretty much extinguished and she felt a little weird.

"Shit—I'm sorry, babe," Damon said then. "This is an old friend. Used to work at a couple of the clubs on Sunset and let me know about new bands." Looking up to Anthony, he said, "This is Brenna."

"Um, hi," she said, thankful—under the odd circumstances—that Damon hadn't mentioned her being Blue Night's newest A&R rep, even if it *would* remain confidential.

Anthony glanced down at her chest and smiled warmly. "Don't worry about covering up on my account, hon. When you work here, you see a lot of tits."

He spoke so sincerely that the comment actually succeeded in putting her somewhat at ease. "I can imagine."

"So," Damon said, "working at the most notorious sex club in Vegas, huh?"

Anthony shrugged in his toga. "What can I say? I started here a few months back, a couple nights a week. The money's good and the work's fun."

"I'll bet," Damon said.

Anthony glanced back to Brenna. "I'll let you two get back to what you were doing. But if you need anything, let me know and I'll take care of you right."

She understood that he meant food and drink, but knowing what he did here, she couldn't help hearing the offer a different way and letting the promise pool between her thighs.

"Sorry," Damon told her as Anthony walked away, then he lay her back on the gold pillows adorning the bed, letting his eyes fall half shut with lust. "Now, where were we?"

She thrust her breasts upward toward him, discovering, thankfully, that maybe the conversation with Anthony hadn't squelched her arousal as much as she'd thought. "We were *here.*"

In one swift move, Damon pushed the fabric from her breast again, closing his palm over her aching flesh. "I love that you called him over," he murmured between more neck kisses.

They trickled down through her so hotly that she could barely answer. "It was only . . . for grapes."

A sexy smile unfurled on this face. "Still . . . you got me even hotter than I already am." His hand shifted to her bent knee, gliding up her thigh as he bent to rake his tongue over her nipple. And in the center of the room, the blonde cried out her pleasure, and Brenna shifted her gaze to see one of the men pounding into her from behind, the other from underneath, and she was just comprehending that it meant one of them must be fucking her ass!—when Damon's hand slid between her legs.

"Ohhh . . ." she moaned, needing his touch there so badly now.

"Jesus God," he muttered, then pulled his hand back to flip up her skirt.

That's when she remembered—she'd shaved her pussy for him, and he'd just discovered it. In a far different setting than she'd envisioned.

Glancing down, she saw her smooth, pale flesh, the pink nub of her clit protruding from the bared slit.

"Oh *babe*," he said, sounding utterly in lust with her, "look at your sweet little cunt. Look what you did for me."

"Do you like it?" She even spread her legs a bit so he could look—and just like with her breast, realized she no longer cared about the other people in the room.

He let out a low groan in reply, then growled, "I have to lick you. Now."

"Oh . . ." she said, suddenly breathless—and ready. Meeting his gaze, she didn't hesitate to part her thighs farther.

After another ravenous look into her eyes, he refocused on her pussy and went down on her.

Leaning back into the pillows, she spread her legs still wider, wider, as far as she could, to welcome his hungry, wet tongue. She watched each long lick he made, fresh pleasure erupting inside her at every stroke. And she watched the trio still fucking on the divan, too. And she grew aware that *some* eyes in the room even watched *her* now. Watched her having her pussy eaten.

It should have horrified her, all of it—but it didn't. It only amped up her arousal, turned her crazed with lust, as she ascended to a sexual high that felt almost unreal.

Following her urges, she freed her other breast from the white fabric and began to massage both with her hands. Damon licked her deeper when he saw—and just over his head, on the dais, the scene had changed: yet another man had joined in.

The blonde straddled one of them cowgirl style while another fucked her ass from behind. And standing by the reclined head of the first guy was . . . Anthony! Thrusting his dick into her eager mouth.

Brenna had never seen or even imagined such a sight. And she couldn't have envisioned desiring that—so many men, inside her, at once—but the blonde appeared intoxicated with pleasure.

Brenna kept watching them as Damon's ministrations moved all through her, and she lifted to meet his mouth. "Yes, baby. Yes," she whispered, still molding her breasts in her palms and feeling the eyes in the room upon her, and—*dear God*—liking it.

At the same time, she let her own eyes wander farther, to couples and threesomes and foursomes all around the room. The place echoed with sobs and moans and immersed her still more fully into that sense of utter abandon. She yearned to shed her inhibitions like never before, and she fucked Damon's mouth harder, moaned louder, and returned her attention to the scene on the platform.

What was it like to have that many big, sturdy cocks inside you, pumping? How did a body take that much sensation? How did it feel to be the very center of an all-out Roman orgy?

Her pleasure multiplied, and she knew she would come soon. "Oh *baby*, lick me," she begged Damon, loving the sight of his beautiful dark eyes between her legs. "Lick my pussy."

Damon responded by latching his mouth around her swollen clit, making her cry out and squeeze her breasts harder. He sucked, pulling the hot nub deep, deeper, and just as the woman on the dais released Anthony's penis from her mouth to cry out in orgasm, Brenna's hit, too.

She heard her own hot sobs, not caring if she drew attention, only responding to the heavy pulses of pleasure arcing through her, again, again. And on the dais, two of the men came inside the blonde, thrusting and groaning, the three of them now undulating together in waves of flesh as Brenna's climax slowly faded.

As for Anthony, he didn't come. His cock was long, hard—almost pretty in that way a perfectly shaped phallus could be. And at first, Brenna wondered why he didn't finish, but then it occurred to her that most guys could only muster so many hard-ons a night and that maybe he needed to save it for the good of his job.

"How ya doin'?" Damon asked, crawling up beside her in the bed.

She felt positively dreamy, even with all the other sex acts still taking place around them. "Mmm—very well, thanks to your expert tongue."

Playfully, he leaned to flick it across one nipple. "My tongue likes you, too."

Just then, a toga-clad girl paused by their bed holding glasses of wine. "To parch your thirst," she said.

They took the wine, thanking her, and Brenna realized the employees must keep an eye on who was doing what if they were adept enough to deliver drinks after orgasms. The wine went down sweet and tingly, and when Brenna kissed Damon she tasted both Chardonnay and her own juices mixing together.

"I want your cock," she told him boldly—no hesitation.

"It's right here," he said, just as he had last night. "All you have to do is take it."

Glancing down, she saw his erection making a sizable tent of his toga. And she realized that, strangely, shockingly . . . she wanted something *more* than just his cock.

Something more extreme.

"I want you to fuck me *there*." She pointed to the dais in the center of all the beds, now occupied by two girls and a guy. Both females were topless, wearing only little white skirts and gold Roman-esque heels much like her own. One stood kissing the guy while the other knelt at his feet, reaching up under his toga, clearly preparing to give him a blow job.

"Really?" Damon asked, casting probably the most surprised expression she'd ever seen on him. He seemed not to even notice the goings-on in the middle of the room.

She nodded, not stopping to question it. "I don't know *why* I want it, and I can't *believe* I want it—but I want it. I want you to fuck me in front of all these people. I want them to see you giving it to me, want them to see me take it, want them to see our pleasure."

Damon's breath grew shallow—he clearly remained somewhere between shock and desire. "I'd *love* to fuck you there, babe—but, like I told you, only people who work here get to do that. The sex is orchestrated, like a porn movie."

In her lust, she'd forgotten the rules. And suddenly, being told she couldn't, Brenna grew desperate to live out this brand-new, unexpected fantasy. If she didn't, it would be like . . . like there was more of her wild journey yet to take, like she hadn't reached her full erotic potential, the potential Damon had uncovered.

Scanning the room, she spotted Anthony, who had put his toga back on. "Ask your friend. Maybe they'll make an exception."

Damon just blinked. "You really want this, don't you?"

She nodded, feeling outrageous and feral and ready—and also earnest. "I want to show you how dirty I can be, Damon. I want to be . . . the sex partner of your dreams."

He lifted a hand to her face. "You already are, Brenna."

Her heart felt as if it physically lifted. "I am?"

"I've fucked a lot of girls, babe, but . . ."

She bit her lip. "But what?"

"Most of them are . . . bad girls from the start. And how you let me . . . coax the bad girl *out* of you . . . well, that gets me hot in a way I've never been before."

Brenna had barely begun to process his words, let them seep into her skin—when Anthony walked by and Damon held up a hand to stop him.

"Listen," Damon said, his voice low, conspiratorial, "any way I can take my girl up there?" He pointed to the divan, where one woman now sat on the guy's lap, sliding up and down his dick with her legs spread, allowing the other girl to lick her.

Anthony looked back and forth between them, not one iota of judgment in his expression. "Sometimes," he began, "they'll let guests up there, but only with someone who works here. They know we'll keep the sex on track, make sure it stays visually exciting, you know?"

Damon nodded, then—cautiously—looked to Brenna.

She knew she should say, *Thanks anyway—I understand.* But instead, she said, "Maybe we could do that."

Damon blinked—and she knew that if she'd stunned him with her original request that it was nothing compared to how astonished he was by *this* suggestion. "We could?"

She lowered her chin slightly, feeling just a bit sheepish now. "If . . . if you wanted to."

"Me? Uh, yeah, babe—I'm fine with that. I just didn't expect *you* to be."

"Me either, but . . ." She lifted her gaze to Anthony. "You seem like a nice guy."

He shrugged, grinned. "I try."

Looking back and forth between the two men, she finally let her gaze land on Damon. "So . . . maybe we could . . . do it . . . with Anthony."

Seven

The thing that shocked Brenna the most was how easy it was.

How easy to let Damon and Anthony guide her up onto the dais when the previous threesome concluded. How easy it was to just focus on Damon and on her desire for him—more than that, her *love* for him—as she twined her arms around his neck and kissed him before the crowd.

Part of why it was easy, of course, was because even as they were the center of attention, so much else took place. Some people left and new ones arrived. Some of the surrounding beds held people fucking their brains out, and nude girls came and went from the "baths" at their leisure to simply stroll about the room, wet and slick-looking.

But part of why it was easy was because Damon had made it that way. He'd made it so that sin was . . . *good*. This kind of sin anyway. She refused to think of any *other* sins she might be committing this week—and concentrated only on the sins of the flesh, which, with Damon, no longer felt like sinning at all.

Soft musical notes from lute and lyre dripped through the air as Damon faced her on the dais—Anthony stood behind her, and she was glad, because even if she fucked them both, this was all about pleasuring Damon, *exciting* Damon, being his ultimate unleashed dirty girl.

Damon's gaze dropped to her breasts, the toga's fabric now covering her again, and reaching up, he molded them in his palms, making her sigh and arch toward him.

Behind her, Anthony's strong hands closed over her hips, then descended slowly, to massage her ass.

Oh God, she'd never been touched by two men before at once. And it was sort of like last night, when she'd been pleasured by both Damon and Jenelle—but better. Because both her lovers were men—hard, virile men. And because it felt as if the whole world was watching—watching her shed her every inhibition, for her lover.

Anthony's palms roamed her with skill from behind, skimming up over her waist and smoothly onto her breasts, kneading her. Her head dropped back as she suffered the strange, heady pleasure of letting a stranger touch her while Damon watched.

When Anthony curled his fingers into the swaths of fabric covering her chest and pulled downward, baring her, Damon bent to kiss, suckle her nipples. And as the pleasure roared through her, Anthony's hands traveled lower, one lifting her skirt, the other stroking boldly between her legs. She moved against his fingers involuntarily, still fueled by being in the center of the bacchanal.

And when Anthony untied the gold cord from around her waist and Damon slipped his thumbs beneath her shoulder straps to send the dress dropping in a rush to her ankles, she didn't even flinch over her nudity. Moreover, she basked in it. Her nipples puckered tighter; her pussy flooded with warmth.

With the guidance of Anthony's hands, she moved onto the divan, on her hands and knees, assuming the same position as the blonde who'd knelt here upon their arrival, the blonde who'd first begun to inspire her to desire such reckless sex.

Like the blonde before her, she boldly thrust her ass into the air, arching her back, and she gazed up at Damon as he let his own toga hit the floor. Her eyes then dropped to his tremendous cock, standing at full attention, looking so stiff and ready that she couldn't wait to feast on it. "Put it in my mouth," she said, peering back up into his dark eyes. She'd glimpsed Anthony rolling on a condom behind her.

She should be terrified. Freaking out. But she simply wasn't. The things she'd seen here tonight had freed her and, for this night only, her desire truly knew no bounds.

As Damon positioned his cock at her lips, she parted them and let him slide inside. He filled the recesses of her mouth, slow, deep, and she enjoyed all the eyes studying her in such an obscene state.

And as he began to move in and out, as she matched his rhythm, Anthony's hands closed back on her ass and his shaft nudged at her moist opening.

Again, part of her wanted to be repulsed, feel used and abused, feel like she'd made a horrible mistake. But she didn't feel any of those things. What she felt was ready. Ready to be fucked by two big, hard cocks. Ready to show the world—or at least the other people who'd come here tonight—how hungry she was, how naughty, how dirty.

When Anthony entered her, she groaned around Damon's cock. Oh God, she'd never felt so very *filled*. And she suddenly understood the blonde's joy from before. As Anthony plunged into her from behind, Damon fed her his cock from the front, both men making her feel more thoroughly fucked than she could have imagined possible.

They moved together that way, her lust growing, heat building, even as the sensation of having two large shafts inside her threatened to overwhelm her. She responded by fucking Anthony harder, sucking Damon more energetically. She gave it all she had, wanting to soak up every nuance of this moment, wanting to feel everything there was to feel.

Anthony drove into her with still more power, until she was forced to release Damon's cock in order to cry out as the strokes pummeled her. But she peered up into Damon's eyes the whole time, through every hard thrust from the man behind her, and—oh God—it was almost as if Damon were in front of her and behind her at once, because if felt far more like fucking Damon than fucking someone else.

"So good, babe," he whispered. "You're doing so fucking good." And she loved that he was as into this as she was, watching another guy do her as she gazed into his eyes.

But then Anthony eased off, going still, and used his hands to shift her position, reminding her—this was a show for the other patrons and she'd agreed to follow his lead even as he'd promised to keep things fairly simple.

Behind her, Anthony leaned back, resting on his knees on the divan, and he took Brenna with him, situating them both in an upright position, his cock still jutting up into her cunt. Oh—she felt it deeper this way, putting her weight on him. Her legs were parted, spread so that her calves stretched out on both sides of his, and he reached down, between her thighs, using the fingertips of both hands to spread the front of her pussy, as well.

Damon's eyes dropped briefly to her freshly shaved flesh, then rose to hers. He'd been standing at one end of the ornate divan, but now climbed up onto the upholstered bench on his knees, moving closer, closer, until his stiffened cock pressed directly between her breasts.

She sucked in her breath as Anthony's hands came around, pushing the two mounds of soft flesh around Damon's rock-hard length. She sighed with the pleasure it brought—pleasure she'd never before contemplated. And pleasure that grew still more intense when Damon began to slide his erection up and down between her tits, fucking them. Oh God, it felt so good. So good to have such powerful strokes buffeting her breasts while Anthony continued to fuck her pussy below.

Again, she moved with them, the three of them finding a common rhythm, then working it. Around them, moans of pleasure filled the air, some of them echoing from her and the two men enjoying her. And being on the dais continued to inspire her, make her more energetic, wanting to show everyone what it was to be a perfect bad girl.

As Damon's shaft pistoned upward, she stuck out her tongue, catching the tip at the end of each thrust. He let out a hot little groan with each lick she delivered, and finally, she bent forward, her mouth in the shape of an "O," letting him drive the head of his cock between her lips each time.

Making his cock wet again helped it slide more easily through the valley of her breasts, turning her skin slick, making them both move harder against each another. It was now *Damon's* palms pressing her tits around his thrusting cock; Anthony now used one hand to steady her hips over his as he fucked her and the other to rub hot little circles over her clit.

Together, the three of them gyrated, the pleasure deepening, deepening, until Brenna thought she would die of it. The rhythmic swirl of Anthony's fingers showed his sexual experience as he pushed her closer to orgasm with each circular caress. She shoved her clit against his hand even as she met his dick underneath. And her breasts felt swollen from Damon's hot fucking, larger somehow than they'd ever been in her life.

She heard her breath grow thready, louder, and knew she was close—and above her, Damon's breathing hitched, too. She looked up, meeting his gaze as the tip of his shaft entered her mouth, then heard him murmur, "Ah, fuck, I'm coming," just as hot, wet semen burst from the slit of his cock, arcing across her breasts in one, two, three, vigorous shots.

She sucked in her breath and orgasmed—the hot pulsing, pleasure exploding from her cunt and outward as Damon sensually rubbed his warm, white come into her breasts, making them slick and shiny, his obscene massage causing her climax to stretch, stretch, so long, longer than any she'd ever had.

As it finally passed, Anthony drove his cock up into her—hard, hard, hard—groaning with each stroke, his hands gripping her hips tight, and she knew he'd just come, too.

And as they all went still, the crowd around them seeming to quiet then, as well—making her think maybe a *lot* of people had just come *with* them—Damon did something no one else on the dais had done tonight after their performance. He took her face in his hands and kissed her.

Eight

They lay in bed in Damon's suite, cuddled together naked, on the verge of drifting off to sleep.

"Sure you don't want to shower?" he asked.

Her hair brushed against his shoulder as she shook her head. "No. Too tired. And I like having your come on me."

He smiled, exhausted and sleepy, but more gratified than he could understand. "I didn't think you'd like that. I even tried to hold it in, but I couldn't."

Another head shake. "I love it. It's like . . . wearing you."

Just like with his ejaculation earlier, *now* he couldn't hold in the low growl that escaped him in response. Just when he'd thought he'd taken her to the peak of her sexual willingness, she climbed higher. He'd hoped she would embrace the atmosphere of the faux Roman orgy—but he'd never dreamed she would *suggest* a threesome with another guy. It shocked him way more than their encounter with Jenelle had. Because it was one thing to kiss another girl, rub their bodies together—but to take in two cocks at once . . . hell, he was *still* surprised. And on the verge of getting another hard-on just remembering it, despite how damn worn out he was from a full week of wild, crazy sex with hot, beautiful Brenna.

"You didn't even get to fuck me tonight," she mused.

Damon thought about that for a minute, about how satisfied he felt anyway. "Yeah—but it felt like I did."

"I know. Isn't that amazing?"

He gazed down into her eyes, widened in wonder, in the dark. And recalled her being up on that platform, being so fucking dirty for all the world to see, such a contrast to the sweet girl next to him now. A contrast that made his heart feel like it was bending in his chest. "*You* are what's amazing."

She smiled over at him, cuddling a little closer. " 'Night, baby."

"Good night, my dirty girl."

THE SEVENTH NIGHT

"By that sin fell the angels."
—William Shakespeare

One

They slept until noon the next day. Although more than once Damon had woken up, found her soft body curled next to his, and ended up inside her, moving slow and deep, until finally he would come, then drift back into slumber.

"What's on our agenda for today?" Brenna asked over a late lunch at the California Pizza Kitchen at the Mirage.

"Not much," he replied across the table. "Just one club to hit tonight and that's it."

"Good, 'cause I'm pooped," she said on a laugh.

And he agreed. As much as he'd enjoyed their wild week together, little miss Brenna had worn him out.

Of course, even as exhausted as he was, he still wanted more of her. Couldn't seem to *quit* wanting more. Even now, just sitting across from him in a plain, fitted turquoise T-shirt and jeans, her hair pulled back into a ponytail, she looked as delectable as the pizza he ate.

Would he have thought that a week ago? If they'd been eating pizza, if she'd been dressed like this, plain and casual?

The truth was—no, he wouldn't have.

Of course, he'd known from early on that none of this was just about the way she looked. It was about *all* of her. And now that the week was drawing to a close and they were going home tomorrow . . . he just wasn't sure he was ready to say good-bye to having Brenna in his bed.

And maybe, just maybe, the idea of *not* saying good-bye was slowly becoming a little less scary to him—and a little more viable, real. Just like Brenna herself. Real.

Two

Brenna dressed down even more than last night—Damon had told her the club they were going to wasn't much more than a hole in the wall on the south side of town, so she took advantage of the situation, given that she'd already pretty much worn everything in her stylish new A&R rep wardrobe. Damon also asked if they could take her car tonight instead of a cab, which she didn't mind—but she let him drive, not particularly wanting to navigate the traffic on Las Vegas Boulevard.

When they walked into a small, dark building called Lefty's just after nine, she felt right at home in her simple black tank and jeans. Of course, Damon's usual jeans and vintage tee—tonight's featured the Doors—seemed to fit in anywhere. A few people at the club recognized him, but the beer-and-peanuts crowd was friendly and thrilled to have someone they considered a celebrity in their midst.

Over two Coors, they watched and listened to a band called the Outsiders, which featured a pink-haired girl with nose piercings, backed up by four garden-variety headbangers in their late thirties. The tip on the band, she learned, had actually come from Anthony, last night, while she'd been changing clothes, yet she and Damon quickly agreed that while the Outsiders were a decent bar band, they'd likely never find fame and fortune.

As they departed the bar only an hour after arriving, Brenna found herself reflecting on the previous night. Until Anthony's name had come up, the memory of Caligula's had seemed more like a dream than something that had really happened. The pleasure had been unsurpassed—and not just physical pleasure but the intense joy of feeling so bold and brave, so much like a free sexual creature, *set* free by Damon.

And as they drove through the darkness—the car soon leaving the retail and residential area for a landscape more sparse and empty—she thought about the fact that had she done something so spontaneous, so extreme, with any other man she'd ever met, she'd be swimming in doubt now, worried sick that he would see her differently than he did before, that he would no longer respect her. But with Damon, there simply *were* no worries.

She knew what they had was temporary, but she also knew it was more than purely physical, that he truly liked her and maybe even *cared* for her. And that he was sincerely *gratified* to see her reveling in her sexuality so completely.

"Um, where are we going?" she asked as the headlights cut through the night, revealing that they'd abandoned the city completely now— for the desert. On either side of the road, she saw nothing but dry earth dotted with low green-brown bushes, and a moment ago a tumbleweed had even gone rolling across the two-lane highway.

"Here," he replied lowly as he eased the car off onto a side road that was actually nothing more than a dirt path.

"Um, where *is* here? Since this kinda looks like nowhere."

He stopped the car, turning to peer at her, the dashboard lights illuminating his expression. She'd seldom seen him look so serious. "I guess I just . . . wanted to be alone with you tonight. Really alone. Not just in the suite, but . . . away from everything."

Brenna didn't answer, because she didn't know what to say. She'd worked pretty hard to keep the parameters of their relationship straight in her mind. Even though she'd fallen in love with him, she'd known it was going nowhere. Even if he did care about her, she'd understood that it was not romance.

This, though, sounded strangely like romance.

He let his gaze drop briefly, a slightly self-deprecating grin stealing over his face as he raised his eyes back to hers. "Is this weird? Or just . . . boring? After everything else this week, all the other places we've fucked? Is it strange that I brought you out here? That I want to be inside you with no one else around, no other distraction—just me and you?"

She swallowed, hard. She'd never heard him speak quite so tenderly—or ever sound even remotely sheepish. "No," she managed to whisper. "Not at all. I . . . like it."

Because he'd been right last night—no matter how wild or brazen she became, she would still always appreciate a loving, caring, romantic man.

"Come outside with me," he said. "I want to be outside with you, feel the night with you."

As Brenna walked with Damon into the stark desert landscape, she began to experience that *tiny* feeling, that way you could feel standing at the shore peering out over the vast ocean, the way she'd heard people felt at the Grand Canyon. It was like being immersed wholly in nature, forced to feel it, see it. Even in the dark, the rims of the mountains in the distance were visible in dim silhouette, the sky above just a shade lighter in midnight blue. A warm breeze stirred the night air around them.

She'd likened the "Grand Canyon feeling" to Vegas in a different way upon her arrival here, but this . . . this was so much deeper, better. She realized she wanted to be alone with him, too.

Finally, Damon stopped and turned to face her. "I like being out here. No lights, no noises—nothing but you." Then he lifted his hands to her face and pressed his mouth to hers. It was as hot and arousing as the first kiss he'd ever given her—in the closet at Fetish—and she immediately needed something else.

"Fuck me," she breathed more gently than she'd known such words could leave her.

And as Damon drew her to her knees on the desert floor, as he slowly pushed up her top and bra and kissed her breasts, as he gently peeled off her jeans and his own and eased his way into her warm, wanting body, she realized she'd never known fucking could be so sweet.

They moved together, slowly at first, but then harder—she lifted against his cock, her hips bucking, seeking that hot friction she loved.

And he kissed her as he slid in and out of her, kissed her and caressed her and made her feel worshipped from head to toe.

"Ah, God—you feel *so* damn good tonight," he said on a heated breath. "Your naked pussy's so soft and smooth when I slide in."

Mmm, she'd forgotten that she might feel a bit new, different to him now. It turned her on just to think about it.

"You feel better than anyone, ever," he went on.

And her chest contracted at his words. "Ever?" she managed. Now he fucked her slowly again, his erection seeming to stretch to impossible lengths inside her.

"Ever," he repeated. Then he whispered, "You're the only woman besides Angie I've ever fucked without a condom."

The statement left her stupefied—for multiple reasons.

He hadn't been wearing a condom. How the hell had she missed that? She'd realized, of course, that he hadn't, but why hadn't it alarmed her? Too much time married, feeling perennially safe in that way, she supposed. And she'd been too consumed by all that was happening this week. So what did this mean? Had they made a fatal mistake? And *why*? *Why* was he not wearing a condom?

"I'm on the pill, you know," she reminded him, peering up into those beautiful eyes, "but that doesn't protect from . . ."

He lifted one warm palm to her cheek, still moving ever so slowly inside her. "Don't worry, babe. I'm safe. Because like I said, I've always been careful. Always. And I know *you're* safe just because . . . I know you're safe." He smiled softly.

Beneath him, still soaking up the friction he created with his sweet cock, she bit her lip. "Why? Why did you not . . . ?"

He brushed his mouth across hers. "It was an accident at first. But after that . . . you felt so amazing, and I just . . . wanted to be that close to you. Nothing between us. Nothing."

She pulled in her breath, utterly amazed by the depth of his tenderness. And by what she could have sworn she'd heard in his words. The same thing *she* felt. *Love.*

Although maybe she was crazy. Maybe she was reading too much into it. Maybe this was just . . . his way of ending it. Tonight was their last night together, after all. Their last night in Sin City.

Yet she couldn't help remembering that tonight, he'd put a little *distance* between them and the city of sin.

"I don't want this to end," he told her, his voice deep, gravelly.

Oh God. Had she heard that right? "Wh-what do you mean?"

He combed his fingers through her hair. "Just because we're headed home to L.A. there's no reason we can't keep this good thing going, Brenna."

"But I thought you . . . I mean . . ."

Again, he kissed her. "Yeah. Well, usually I don't. But maybe now I do. I can't make you promises—I haven't been in a real relationship in a lot of years. But I don't think I can be with you and not want you. I don't think I can see you as just a friend."

Brenna feared her heart would explode through her chest. Had he really just made her dreams come true? Really just told her this wasn't ending? "You have no idea how happy that makes me."

"Then you feel the same way? You don't want this to stop?"

"God, yes, I feel *exactly* the same way. I . . . I love you."

Oh no, what had she just said? It had just come out, unstoppable! Stupid, stupid, stupid.

But then Damon's mouth covered hers again, and this time his tongue twined around hers, and her desire seemed to double somehow in that moment, making her pull him closer, wrap her arms around him as tightly as she could. And when finally the kiss ended, Damon leaned down near her ear and whispered the sweetest words she'd ever heard. "I think I'm falling in love with you, too."

"*Oh.* Oh God," she said, peering up at his beautifully handsome face.

And almost convulsively, she pumped against him, hard, needing to feel him still deeper. She didn't even care if she came—she just wanted to feel him, filling her up. "Come in me," she breathed, desperately begging him. "Come in me, hard."

She needed to make it happen, needed to draw that pleasure from him—and she needed him to leave part of himself inside her.

"*Oh yeah,*" he groaned. "Oh yeah—I can't stop. I'm coming in you. I'm coming deep inside your sweet little pussy." And he thrust *hard, hard, hard,* pressing her ass to the ground, somehow making her smell the dry scent of the desert more, feel the moonlight more intensely.

No sex in her life had ever left her more satisfied. In a different way than last night or the night before. That had been so physically intense, and the mental part had been about *her*, about her daring, about her feelings for Damon. But *this*—*this* was about *him*. About him loving her. And about her wanting to give him pleasure so very freely, without any want or need of her own.

Although a moment later, he apologized. "I'm sorry, babe. I didn't make you come."

"I don't mind," she whispered, smiling up at him. "I couldn't feel any better than I do right now anyway."

Three

Damon handed off Brenna's car to the valet, then led his beautiful girl through the front door of the Venetian, hand in hand. Jesus, he couldn't believe it. He'd told her he was falling in love with her. And more than that, he'd meant it.

This wasn't over. He was going to have more Brenna—not just as a colleague, but as . . . everything. A friend, a lover, and . . . that strange melding of the two that he didn't even know a name for.

He hadn't quite realized he wanted that until he'd heard the words leaving his mouth—hell, a *lot* of unplanned words had left his mouth tonight. He hadn't even known why he wanted to take her out into the desert until they'd gotten there. He'd actually thought maybe it would be a nice, quiet place to fuck, a nice way to end their affair. But the moment he'd stopped the car, he'd understood that he couldn't end it. Just couldn't.

And he wasn't sure where it would go from here, but . . . he couldn't remember ever feeling this great. Like there was more to life than music and sex. And music and sex—well, hell, they'd both been very good, but . . . maybe it was time to start making some changes in his life. He hesitated to think of it as "settling down" so decided to think of it more as "making a closer connection" and maybe having someone to lean on, depend upon, when he needed it.

At the moment, he felt totally carefree. He didn't even care if Claire

Starr sued him. If she did, he'd get through it. With Brenna's love and support.

With her, he had the whole package. A scintillating sex kitten. A sweet, loving companion. An intelligent friend. An insightful coworker. No wonder he was in love with her.

And if Claire sued, or if the tabloids persisted, or if more rumors abounded—he simply knew he and Brenna would get through it, together, and everything would be okay in the end because he'd still have *her*. He'd always thought his job was the only thing that really mattered to him, the thing he couldn't live without. But he'd just made room for something else—*someone* else—in his life, and Claire Starr and nasty accusations aside, the world felt pretty fucking perfect right now.

"Happy?" he asked as they walked down the hall toward his suite, still holding hands.

She smiled up at him, biting her lip. "Very. Happy and . . . dusty," she said, giggling. They were both covered with a fine sheen of desert powder.

"The price of fucking in the dirt," he said with a grin, remembering how he'd moved on top of her, in the dreaded missionary position—which, suddenly, had felt a lot more intimate than dreadful—and how much he'd *welcomed* that intimacy this time. "How about this?" he asked. "I'll run us a nice, sudsy bath in the Jacuzzi, and we'll make sure you get that orgasm, after all."

Four

Damon had disappeared into the oversize bathroom, and now she heard water running. "I'm getting naked," he yelled out to her. "Don't keep me waiting."

She called back, "I'll be right there, baby—just want to check my messages first." Because the moment they'd walked in, she'd seen her cell phone blinking. And it had reminded her of . . . everything.

The horrible lie, the threat to Damon's job.

And she wasn't sure exactly what she was going to do, but she wasn't going to let anything ruin this, what the two of them had. She was going to work this out somehow. She was going to convince Jenkins that no matter what Claire Starr did, Damon was too valuable to let go. And she would figure out a way to tell Damon the truth.

Standing in the bedroom, listening to the tub filling and anxious to get to her man, she quickly retrieved the missed call.

"Hey, girlfriend, it's just me." Kelly. What a relief! No Jenkins. "I just called to see how your big week with Damon Andros went, but I guess you're not back yet—I wasn't sure exactly when you were coming home. Anyway, I can't wait to hear all about it, and I hope I find out you came to your senses and fucked that man's brains out."

Brenna flipped the phone shut, smiling to herself and rolling her eyes. Kelly was going to be thrilled. Not that Brenna was going to tell her *everything*. Some things were so private that she could share them only with Damon. But still, her friend was going to be very pleased to hear how things had worked out.

"I'm waiting," Damon called playfully from the bathroom.

"On my way," she replied, starting toward him—when her cell phone rang, still in her hand. "In a minute," she added. "Let me grab this call and I'll be right there—promise." Then she flipped the phone back open and put it to her ear. "Hello?"

"Hello, Brenna."

Shit. *This* time it was Jenkins.

Her heart pounded as she walked briskly out through the dining area, across the living room to the windows that looked out on the Las Vegas lights. "Hi," she said, sounding terse.

"I know it's late, but I just got some news I thought would interest you."

Oh God. "What?"

"Claire Starr is going to file suit first thing tomorrow morning. Which means Damon's out. As soon as he gets back here tomorrow, I'm going to call him into the office and give him the bad news. So I hope you learned the ropes this week."

Brenna let out a sigh. She'd really hoped to broach this in the office, without having the Claire Starr thing feeling like the *definite* threat it did now, but . . . well, she'd just take a different approach. She'd get into the heart of the matter—Damon being indispensable—later, but for now, she'd just speak in terms Jenkins could understand without a long-winded discussion. "Listen, I've learned a lot, but not enough yet. So I think it would be unwise to fire Damon right now. I'm coming home tomorrow, too, so before you call him, please wait. I'll come straight to the office and we'll talk about this, okay?"

"No," he said. That simple.

"What?"

"Brenna, I understand your trepidation about having the job dropped in your lap this quickly, but I just can't have Damon associated with Blue Night any longer. We're being *sued* because of him. Firing him is the only way to send a clear message that Blue Night doesn't turn a blind eye to sexual blackmail. So repeat after me: *Damon is fired, and I'm taking his place.*"

Brenna let out an exasperated sigh. "Yeah, yeah, I know. Damon is fired, and I'm taking his place. I've been in on the plan from the beginning, remember? But I still—"

"No buts, Brenna. It's late and I'm tired, and I'm gonna have a media circus to deal with tomorrow. So we'll talk when you get back. After Damon's been let go. Good night."

The line went dead. And Brenna flipped the phone shut, still peering out on the neon display twenty floors below.

And it was just when she realized that the water had stopped running at some point that she turned—to find Damon standing naked behind her.

But instead of focusing on his nudity, her attention was drawn to his eyes—which told her he'd just heard her terrible secret. Her horrendous betrayal. Because she'd been stupid enough to actually talk with Jenkins about this while Damon was in the next room.

"Oh God," she said, her body deflating as she stepped instinctively toward him. "Damon, this wasn't my idea, I swear." She shook her head. "And I didn't want to do things this way. At all. You have to believe me."

"No," he said quietly, anger blazing from his eyes. "I don't."

She suddenly felt as if she couldn't breathe. "I promise you, I didn't want to take your job, and I was planning—I'm *still* planning—to go to Jenkins tomorrow and tell him firing you would be a terrible mistake."

"Be quiet, Brenna," he said, sounding too calm, only his eyes relaying his emotions, "and leave."

She drew in her breath. This couldn't be happening. "Damon, please. Let me explain. Let me make you understand."

"You can't." He pointed toward the door of the suite, his voice turning harsher. "Now get the fuck out of my room."

Brenna's heart physically hurt—her eyes, too, as tears began rolling down her cheeks. She reached out to touch him, but he pulled away. "Please, Damon," she begged. "Please. Give me a chance."

"I already did. And you used it to steal my fucking job, to fucking lie to me." He shook his head. "You had me fooled, that's for damn sure. Here I thought you were so sweet, so . . . so fucking *genuine*." He laughed without mirth at what he probably thought was irony.

She held her hands out in front of her, helpless, beseeching. "Everything *was* real. Everything between us. I swear, Damon."

But again, he just pointed to the door. "I don't need any more lying, deceitful bitches in my life, Brenna. Get out. I mean it. I don't want to hear another word from your lying mouth."

Brenna didn't know what to do. She feared her chest would burst. Her eyes ached, her nose was running from crying, and her legs had grown weak. And Damon wouldn't listen to reason, wouldn't even let her try to make him understand.

"Now!" he yelled, making her flinch.

So, like a frightened puppy with its tail between its legs, she scurried toward the foyer, picking up her purse on the way, stopping only to look back at him when she'd reached the double doors.

"Get out," he said one more time, low, menacing, as if he couldn't believe she was still there, still trying to hang on to him.

She had no choice but to open the door and walk out, letting it shut behind her. Leaving behind the man she loved, the man who, miraculously, had loved her, too—until he'd found out about her lie.

She'd known from the start that this was a bad idea. But she couldn't have imagined how much she'd have to lose when it was over. And she felt as if she'd just lost . . . everything.

THE WAGES OF SIN

"Great eagerness in the pursuit of wealth, pleasure, or honor, cannot exist without sin."
—Desiderius Erasmus

One

Brenna was exhausted. She'd barely slept in days. Maybe weeks. She'd returned from Las Vegas both physically and mentally wiped out, and rest had been nearly nonexistent in the two weeks since.

She sat at her desk with her head in her hands. Her *new* desk, at the Blue Night offices, which was shoved into a tiny corner. She'd decided to keep working from the office, despite the fact that Damon had worked from home, because she currently spent about half of each day putting out fires Jenkins' new administrative assistant couldn't yet handle and—Brenna feared—maybe never would.

Just then, the new girl, Collette, rounded the corner. "Brenna, the copier is jammed again. And that reporter guy I told you about called again for Jenkins, and I don't think he believes me when I say he's not in."

Brenna just sighed. Then fixed the copier. And explained to Collette to simply keep lying to the reporter, explaining, "It doesn't matter whether or not he believes you." Of course, *she'd* never had to lie about Jenkins not being in—only since the shit had hit the fan two weeks ago had that started. But unlike her, she didn't think Collette *minded* lying—she just wasn't very good at it.

Upon returning to her own desk, Brenna contemplated how to handle the rest of her day—minus future interruptions from Collette. She'd quickly learned that having such an unstructured job made it easy to put off doing the less desirable parts.

Like calling back Blush's new manager. She supposed it was smart of them to hire one, but why had they had to go and get a heavy hitter like Tommy Max, the toughest guy in L.A.? He'd been a thorn in her side for a week, making demands she had no idea if she could fulfill.

She also had a message on her desk from Malcolm Barstow, whom she'd inherited from Damon—and who was none too happy Damon was gone. He was threatening to leave the moment his contract was up and she hadn't the first idea how to convince him not to, especially now that he was big enough to go with one of the majors if he wanted.

She'd once thought being an A&R rep would give her a feeling of importance, security. Ha! All it had given her was a constant headache. And a broken heart.

Strange—she'd only had a week with Damon, but she couldn't get used to sleeping without him again. The bed had felt lonely after her breakup with Wayne, too, but this was different. More of a guttural need than a plain feeling of loneliness.

She hadn't seen Damon or heard from him since the night she'd left his Las Vegas suite in tears. And she hated—just *hated*—knowing he thought she was *that* kind of person. The conniving, manipulative kind. The entertainment business was full of them, though, so under the circumstances, she couldn't really blame him.

She just wished . . . well, she wasn't sure *what* she wished exactly.

If she hadn't agreed to Jenkins' plan in the first place, she never would have gotten to know Damon. And if she'd been honest with him at any point in their week together, it would have changed *everything*. He wouldn't have fallen for her—she knew that much.

She just wished . . . that she was still in Sin City, with Damon, learning more and more of those new ways to sin.

When someone came whizzing around the corner to her desk, she expected Collette but instead looked up to find Kelly in a stunning coral suit. "Hey," her friend said. "How's it going?"

Kelly, of course, knew everything that had happened. Well, not about Rendezvous or Caligula's, but she knew about the sex, and the love, and the heartbreak. She knew it had ripped Brenna apart to have Damon fired and to see news about Claire Starr's lawsuit splashed all over the entertainment headlines. And she knew Brenna was finding his A&R shoes challenging to fill.

Brenna just shrugged. "So-so." But then she reconsidered. "Although I'm afraid of Malcolm Barstow and Tommy Max, so I can't bring myself to return their calls. So maybe a more accurate answer would be . . . sucky. It's going sucky."

Kelly winced. "Sorry. And maybe this isn't the best time to tell you this, but . . . I just got a press release announcing that Damon is starting his own label."

She sat up straighter, stunned. "You're kidding."

Kelly shook her gorgeous blond head. "He found a few investors who believe in him, and he's back in business. He's calling the label Inspiration."

"Oh, that's *so* great!" Brenna said. Music was Damon's life, and she was thrilled to hear he was carving out a new place for himself in the industry this quickly.

"Great?" Kelly looked aghast. "No, it's *not* great. It's *awful*. We don't need this kind of competition right now." Kelly hissed in her breath slightly, making a face of regret. "No offense, but . . ."

Brenna nodded matter-of-factly. "But I don't know what I'm doing. I agree. So you're probably right. This is terrible news for Blue Night. Still . . . I'm glad for Damon. He didn't deserve what happened."

"Oh, and here's your mail." Kelly dropped a small handful of it into the in-box on the corner of Brenna's desk. "Collette saw me walking this way and asked me to bring it. Lazy ass. I worry about her, Brenna. I don't think she's catching on."

Brenna sighed. "Yeah, I know. The whole place is crumbling around us."

"And I get to handle the PR nightmare of it all. Yippee for me." Kelly pointed over her shoulder toward her office. "So I'd better get back to it. But . . . speaking of Damon, how are you doing in *that* way? Getting over him a little by now, I hope."

Another large sigh left her, which she supposed answered Kelly's question. Added to everything else, the very thought of him—of *them, together*—made her feel as if her chest was being crushed.

"Oh, hon," Kelly said, reaching down to squeeze her hand. "Want to get drunk after work?"

Never in her life had Brenna purposely set out to get drunk for the sake of escaping problems or pain. It just wasn't in her makeup. So as tempting as the offer was, she said, "Thanks anyway, but I'm gonna try to tough it out sober."

After Kelly departed, Brenna picked up her fresh stack of mail, gasping when she saw the return address on the first piece. It had come from the freaking *Playboy Mansion!* Ripping into the expensive stationery, she found an invitation to one of the place's famed pajama parties. *Oh God.*

It was her worst nightmare come true. Exactly the sort of thing she'd dreaded. Because she *should* go. Because she *needed* to meet more people, get to know others in the entertainment industry and L.A.'s party scene.

But she couldn't.

Only not for the reasons she would have expected—not because she was horrified by the very thought, or would feel underconfident or embarrassed. She simply didn't want to go anyplace with that kind of sexual aura without Damon at her side.

And—what if Damon was there? With some other woman? Or more than one? She didn't think she could handle that. The wounds were too fresh.

Oh, who was she kidding? She wasn't sure she'd *ever* be able to take that.

So you can't return phone calls from your artists.

And you're willingly turning down A-list networking opportunities.

Yep, you're doing a real bang-up job here, Brenna.

Just then, the phone on her desk rang and she snatched it up, praying it wasn't Tommy Max or Malcolm. "Brenna Cayton."

"Uh, yeah—hi. This is Austin. Austin Cole. I met you a few weeks ago."

Oh, wow! When Damon's firing had hit the airwaves, Collette had taken a message from Austin's mother canceling their meeting. Brenna had been deeply disappointed, figuring they'd decided to go with the other label, but she'd been dealing with so much that she hadn't pursued it further.

"Yes, of course. Hi, Austin. I'm happy to hear from you. I hope I can meet with you and your mom again soon."

"That's the thing," the boy said. "She's pretty set on me going with the other guys. But it's mainly because of Damon getting fired and all that. So . . . I guess I'm just confused. I don't really want to write off Blue Night until we talk some more."

"Like I said, I'd *love* to talk more. And I can understand your mother's concerns, but . . ." She sighed, not sure how honest to be, yet given that honesty was her natural inclination, she went with it. God knew *lying* hadn't gotten her very far. "Just between you and me, Austin, I can tell you that Damon is innocent in all this—he's just getting a bad deal. So please don't base your decision on what you hear in the media."

On the other end of the phone, Austin sighed again, and she could *feel* his confusion. God, he was only a teenager, not even out of high school. How could he be expected to know what to do, how to make the right choice? And his career might well ride on that decision.

Her heart nearly beat through her chest when she realized what she was about to do, but she couldn't stop herself. Because it was right. It was the most right thing she'd done in a couple of weeks now. "Austin, can I give you some advice, from the heart, just between you and me?"

"Yeah, sure."

"Damon just started a new label—called Inspiration. And despite everything that's happened to him, he's a good guy, and in my opinion, the best guy to handle your music. If I were you, I'd go with Damon."

When she hung up the phone fifteen minutes later, she plunked it down, then plunked her head on her desk. She'd just given away her chance to build something at Blue Night, her chance to make a mark in the industry.

Shit.

But she still knew it was right. For so many reasons.

So instead of beating herself up for it, she just prayed Jenkins would never find out, then picked the phone back up and dialed Kelly's extention.

"Kelly Mills, Blue Night PR."

"I've changed my mind. It's almost five. Let's go get drunk."

Two

"Thanks, Mrs. Cole. And Austin, I'll see you next week, as soon as school's out. We're gonna have to cram a lot of work into a short time, so be ready."

Damon smiled as he walked Austin Cole and his mother to the door of his condo—which was his current place of business until he moved into the office space he'd just secured.

Austin lifted a hand in a so-long wave, and said, "Don't worry, dude. I'll be *so* ready."

"I'm counting on it, and I'm glad this worked out. I think it's gonna be a great move for all of us."

He closed the door on them, feeling more energized than he had in a while. Austin had just signed a contract making him Inspiration's first artist. He couldn't imagine a more promising start for the company, and he knew his investors would be pleased.

Of course, now that his visitors were gone, he found himself reflecting on an earlier conversation with the boy.

"How'd you hear about the new label?" he'd asked.

He'd merely been curious, making small talk, so it had surprised him when Austin had cringed slightly and said, "Uh, it's kind of a secret."

Damon had looked up. "A secret? What do you mean?"

The kid had appeared nervous, then said, "The person who told me about it said she thought my best move was to go with you, but she, uh, works for Blue"—he'd stopped abruptly then, correcting himself—"another label."

Of course, there'd been only one person he could think of, but he couldn't imagine she'd want to give up Austin. "It wasn't Brenna?"

The boy's features froze, and even when he said, "I'd rather not say," Damon knew the answer. He just didn't know why Brenna would do that.

Maybe it was her way of apologizing, and if so, he'd take it, but it didn't change the way he felt about her. He'd meant what he'd said that last night. He didn't need another deceptive person in his life. And to find out that Brenna, of all people, fell into that category—hell, he couldn't deny that it had been fucking devastating.

The hell of it was—today was probably the first day in weeks that he hadn't had her on his mind 24/7. He'd been so focused on getting Austin to sign with him today that nothing else had entered his brain—nothing. Until her name had come up.

And there for a few minutes, he'd been back in Vegas, back . . . inside her.

But it was high time he resumed focusing on business around the clock. Given that he was mired in the work of getting Inspiration off the ground, God knew he should have enough to occupy his mind. As luck had it, a handful of his previous Blue Night clients were up for contract renewal in the next few months, so he'd made some phone calls and felt confident all of them were going to come over to Inspiration and let him keep taking their careers in the right direction. So things were going well. But there was the office move to worry about, and staff to hire—and he planned to be very hands-on in developing Austin and maybe other new acts, too.

And, of course, there was the lawsuit to contend with. Claire had filed two of them, one against Blue Night and a separate one against him. He was trying to keep it off his mind as much as possible, letting his lawyer handle most of it, and having the new company was a great distraction.

So he simply didn't have the time to waste on thinking about Brenna. Even if she *had* unknowingly helped him name his company.

He'd told her once that she inspired him, and he'd meant it. She'd made him feel things he never had before; she'd taken him to emotional highs—and lows—that had forced him to examine who he was and what he wanted out of life. He wasn't sure he had *everything* he wanted now, but he had a promising label to build and, whether he liked it or not, she *had* inspired him—sexually, emotionally, and even professionally, given the way he'd lost his job to her.

Part of him hated her. He'd never felt so deceived, so much like a gullible fool.

Yet part of him kept remembering all those moments together. The really dirty ones. And the really sweet ones. And every one in between.

Shit, even now, it was still hard to believe she'd lied to him—he'd been utterly blindsided, simply hadn't seen it coming.

But as far as he was concerned, it was a hard lesson learned. Trust was a valuable commodity, and he wouldn't give it away so easily in the future—even to someone who seemed as totally guileless as Brenna had. Damn, he'd have thought he'd learned something about that from Claire Starr. But Brenna had been a whole different animal. A wolf in sheep's clothing.

He'd given some thought to her parting words, her promise that everything between them had been real. He didn't know *what* to believe—so he'd simply chosen not to believe . . . anything.

He had a company to build, and he'd just signed Austin Cole, so that was a great start. From now on, it was back to music and sex. He didn't need anything more—and, amending his earlier thought, he decided he didn't *want* anything more.

Three

It was the third time in a week that Jenkins had summoned Brenna to his office—and she knew she was in trouble, just from the sound of his voice over the phone. What had happened *now*? Had Malcolm complained to him directly? Had he heard the tapes from Blush's first recording session? It hadn't gone as well as hoped, because the producer kept asking her for input as he'd done with Damon in the past, and she simply didn't have enough experience to help.

She pushed through the closed door without fanfare, missing the days when her boss thought she did good work. "What now?" she asked.

Jenkins stood up, steam practically coming out his ears. Oh boy, whatever this was, it was bad. Really bad.

"I just heard what I hope is a nasty rumor."

God, she hoped it was, too. "What?"

"Word on the street is that Inspiration just signed a hot new kid named Austin Cole. A kid you and Damon scouted in Vegas. And further word on the street is that *you* sent the kid to *him*, saying he'd do a better job for him than we could."

Her options here were simple. Lie. Or tell the truth.

And she'd had enough lying.

"It's not a rumor. I did it."

Jenkins slammed a book down on his desk, making papers fly. "What the hell were you thinking?"

She raised her voice, just as angry as he was. "That Damon *will* do a better job for him than I can! Because I've been thrust into a job I'm ill suited for with little to no experience! And that Austin Cole has one of the best sounds I've ever heard and, frankly, I thought he deserved better than I can give him. I didn't want to ruin his career, so I sent him to Damon."

Jenkins stood before her, red faced, shaking his head. "Damn it, Brenna..."

She hated this. It just kept getting worse and worse. It was supposed to be a dream job, but it sucked. She'd never been more miserable in her work.

Just then, Collette stuck her head through the open doorway. "Um, Brenna, when you get a chance, the copier's jammed again."

"Screw the copier," she snapped, making Collette flinch, then disappear back through the door.

After which she turned back to Jenkins. "And screw you, too. I can't do this anymore. I'm a smart, likable, professional woman—and *I* deserve better. I quit."

RETURN TO SIN

"Had I not sinned, what would there be for you to pardon?
My fate has given you the opportunity for mercy."
—Ovid

One

Oh God, she'd quit! Really quit!

Three days had passed, but each time she thought about it, the news felt brand-new—and just as horrible. She had a little money saved—she could pay the rent this month and next, and her car payment—but she needed another job fast.

Now, she sat in a park not far from the Blue Night offices—Kelly was picking up sandwiches and meeting her there for lunch. While she waited, she cautiously reopened her old book, *You Don't Need a Man to Be Happy.*

Because it was high time she convinced herself of that, once and for all. Damon, of course, had put a big dent in that belief, but at the same time, *after* Damon, she couldn't imagine finding another man who could really make her happy. He'd taken her places she'd never gone before and would likely never go again without him—and any normal guy just wouldn't compare.

Scanning the area around the park bench, she found she was alone, so figured it was safe to start her affirmations. "I don't need a man, I don't need a man, I don't need a man."

"Oh, Jesus Christ, not that again."

She looked up to find Kelly—today in a striking suit of dark fuchsia that only she could pull off. She handed Brenna a large Styrofoam container, which she presumed held her lunch.

"Well, I'll tell you what you *do* need," Kelly said, taking a seat next to her, her own white container perched in her lap. "You need a vacation."

Brenna simply sighed. "I just took one. Remember? Sin City? Lots of sex? Broken heart? Ring any bells?"

Kelly shrugged. "That was work. Kind of."

"Speaking of which, that was also paid for by Blue Night. And girls without jobs have no business taking vacations."

"Maybe not, but you're in a funk, and I intend to get you out of it. And if you ask *me*, you need a little hair of the dog that bit you."

Brenna just blinked. "What?"

"Let's go to Vegas. Just for the weekend. I'll drive, and I'll even spring for the room."

"*Vegas?* You want me to go to *Vegas?* After what just happened to me there? Are you crazy?"

"That's the hair of the dog part, dummy. You need to go back to Vegas, have a good time, and quit associating it with him. Otherwise, the place will be ruined for you forever, and Vegas is far too fun and far too nearby to mark off your list of weekend getaway destinations."

Brenna shook her head. "No."

"I insist."

"The last time you insisted upon something, I ended up with a tattered heart."

Kelly rolled her eyes. "I told you to fuck him, not fall for him. Big difference, girlfriend." She opened her sandwich box and popped the top on the soda can she'd tucked inside with the food. "Now I'm not taking no for an answer. We're going to Vegas for a girls' weekend. I'm picking you up at five thirty on Friday."

TWO

"How's the office?" Brenna asked Kelly as they drove across the Mojave Desert.

Kelly let out a slightly hysterical laugh. "In shambles. Trust me, this getaway wasn't just for you. I need it, too—bad."

They discussed the various disasters occurring at Blue Night for a while longer, but both concluded it was a downer, so decided to turn on the radio. From which blared Malcolm Barstow's latest hit, which made them both grimace, so Brenna turned it back off. And peered out over the flat brown landscape. "Did I tell you Damon and I fucked in the desert?"

Kelly looked over at her with a sly smile. "No, you didn't. And honey, I have to tell you, that man was *so* good for you. Even if you only had him a week."

Brenna cast a wry grin. "Why—because I can say 'fuck' now without flinching?"

Kelly wore a satisfied expression as she looked back out the windshield. "Well, that, too—but mainly . . . you're just a more confident person now. You're more outgoing, you don't let people push you around, and you don't dress like a schoolmarm."

Brenna hadn't really thought about it—she'd hardly had time, given everything else being juggled in her brain—but maybe Kelly was right.

"I guess maybe I . . . *feel* better. I definitely feel like my divorce is long behind me now—like it happened in another lifetime. And . . . I *was* brave enough to quit that so-called dream job, *wasn't* I?"

"I think he just . . . showed you parts of yourself you'd never seen before."

"You can say that again," she replied, clearly thinking of sex, and they both laughed.

She still thought this girls' weekend in Vegas was a generally bad idea, but for Kelly's sake, she decided to try and have fun, or at least to *pretend* she was.

Kelly tended to drive like a maniac on the open road, so they turned onto the Las Vegas Strip just after ten o'clock, which flooded Brenna with recent memories. Her heart beat harder just seeing the hotels she and Damon had toured together, the streets they'd walked—and the Eiffel Tower, of course.

But she nearly passed out when Kelly veered onto the drive leading to the Venetian.

"What are we doing *here*?" she asked.

"Um, sleeping. Maybe some eating. And possibly partying, as I hear they have some great clubs here."

Brenna passed her friend a dubious look. "This is where Damon and I stayed."

Kelly blinked. "Oh. I guess you mentioned that at some point—I must have forgotten. But hey"—she shrugged, smiled softly—"hair of the dog, remember? And it's a gorgeous hotel. And I got a great deal on the room, so we're not going anywhere else."

Brenna didn't like it, but she supposed it wouldn't kill her to be here. Even if everywhere she glanced she found another memory. Yet she tried to push that aside as they checked in and headed up a familiar elevator where Damon had once rubbed his hard cock against her ass. She tried to push it aside as they rolled their suitcases into a room very much like the one Brenna had stayed in—even if she'd ended up not spending a great deal of time in it.

"So," Kelly said, "ready to hit the town?"

Brenna simply blinked. "It's late. Aren't you tired?"

"No way—the night is young. And Vegas never sleeps. I'm ready to go dancing, or maybe do a little gambling. Have I ever told you how lucky I am at craps?"

"Uh, no. But even if *you* aren't tired, maybe *I* am."

Kelly lowered her chin and stabbed her fists into her hips. "O-ho-ho no you don't. You are *so* going out with me. I'm betting you were out 'til the wee hours every single night the last time you hit Sin City, so no way are you going to just put on your jammies and go beddie-bye." Kelly grabbed her wrist, saying, "Come on."

And before she knew what hit her, they were back in the elevator.

Given the prime-time hour, it was crowded, people coming and going on various floors, and Brenna wasn't paying much attention until Kelly latched on to her arm again and dragged her out into a quiet hallway. "Where are we?" she asked.

"One of the lower floors. I think there's a dance club around the corner."

"I don't hear any music," Brenna said but followed Kelly anyway, thinking the area looked vaguely familiar—and finally recognizing it when they exited through a pair of doors that led out to the lush pool area. "Oh, this leads to the pool. We're in the wrong place," she informed her friend.

But Kelly pressed onward anyway. "Well, while we're here, I may as well check it out, scope out my chair for tomorrow—since I intend to spend at least half the day working on my tan."

Brenna followed behind silently, not particularly wanting to revisit the pool, either, but forcing herself to be tolerant. *Hair of the dog, hair of the dog. I don't need a man, I don't need a man.*

The area was bathed in darkness, but the surrounding neon lights of the city illuminated the place enough for her to make out the columns and arches, the potted trees, and the alluring beds at various points along the pool's edge.

Which was when she noticed . . .

Was there someone lying on one of those beds?

She squinted, figuring she was seeing things in the shadowy darkness—but then she froze in place.

Oh God—it was Damon.

Wearing his usual T-shirt and jeans, he stretched out along the elaborate poolside bed, his head propped on one fist. His grandmother's cross glinted in the moonlight. And his eyes sparkled, sexy as ever.

He met her gaze, looking wholly seductive, and curled one finger slowly toward him, beckoning her.

Beyond shocked, she couldn't quite process what was happening, and she glanced to Kelly for help.

"Go on already," Kelly said, giving her a light shove forward.

Brenna peeked over her shoulder, once more, at her friend. "But . . ."

"I'll be downstairs at the craps tables if you need me—but I don't think you will." She concluded with a smile, then turned and walked away—and Brenna understood in that moment what a really wonderful, priceless friend Kelly was.

Then she turned back to Damon.

Who she couldn't believe was really here.

"Lie down with me, Brenna."

Cautiously, she approached the bed that had drawn her into fantasy the first time she'd seen it. Slowly, she climbed up onto it, reclining beside him. "Does this mean . . . you don't hate me anymore?"

"I never hated you," he said. "Not really. I was just . . . angry. I felt betrayed."

"Of course—I understand. But . . . you don't feel that way any longer?"

"I called Kelly and we met for coffee, talked for awhile—about you. She convinced me that the you I'd fallen for was the *real* you and that the you who lied wasn't."

"That's so true," she said, leaning toward him. "I *hate* lying. I didn't *want* to lie. But I felt my job was on the line if I didn't." She glanced down. "Of course, I eventually ended up without it anyway, but that's another story."

"Come work for *me*," he said, "at Inspiration."

She let out a heavy breath. "That's a generous offer, Damon, but . . . I've concluded that I'm not really cut out to be an A&R rep."

"Yeah," he said, "Kelly told me that part of the story, too. But I'm not offering you an A&R position—I want you to run the office. I need good people, and I figure you're a great place to start. Although I would also welcome your input on music, babe—you're good at that, I promise. I've also offered Kelly a PR position, and I think she's going to take it."

She sat up a bit. "Really?" Running an office she could do. And to be there working alongside her best friend and her . . . well, she started to think *lover*, but she wasn't sure where they stood yet. "I . . . I would love the chance to do that, Damon, but . . . do you think it's a good idea for you and I to work together?"

"As a matter of fact, I do. We managed to mix work and play pretty well before, didn't we?"

"Is there going to *be* . . . um, play?"

He went deadly serious then, reaching out to cup her cheek. And to be touched by him, after all this time—oh God, the sensation raced all through her. "Brenna, we both made a big mistake here. Yours was lying to me. But mine was not giving you a chance to explain. I . . . hadn't ever really opened my heart to a woman before, not since I was a teenager, so thinking you'd used me to get a job hurt pretty damn bad. I didn't deal with it very well—I just shut down. But I want to start over. Or, more accurately, I want to pick up where we left off.

"Like I told you that night in the desert, I can't make you promises. But I know I want you. I know I've been damn lonely without you. I know that for the first time in my life, I need more to satisfy me than music and work and random sex." Then he grinned. "I need sex with *you*. And I need you *next* to me, in bed, and at work, too. I need you in my life, Brenna."

There were a great many things Brenna could have said, but the simplest way to reply was to slip her arms around his neck and kiss him.

God—it was so good to have his mouth back on hers, his sweet, hot tongue kiss drizzling through her like warm icing.

"Ah, *damn*, babe," he breathed afterward, peering into her eyes. "I've missed kissing you. Fucking you. I've missed feeling your sweet little cunt around my cock."

"Oh—me, too. So, so much. Fuck me now, Damon. Please."

When she'd first met Damon, she wouldn't have *dreamed* of having sex out here by the pool—even at night, because workers or anyone else could wander in to the area, just as she and Kelly had—but now, after all she'd experienced with Damon right here amid the neon lights, she didn't even hesitate to reach for his belt buckle.

"*Oh*. Oh Jesus," he moaned when she unzipped his jeans and slid her palm down over his temptingly hard erection. She massaged and stroked him, fueled by the feel of him in her hand, utterly amazed he was back in her life.

Damon reached to unzip her jeans, too, and soon eased them down, along with her panties. And when his fingers sank into her pussy, she practically howled her pleasure.

She next pushed his shirt off over his head, then removed his jeans, wanting him completely and beautifully naked, and she shed her top and bra, as well. "Fill me," she told him.

And he complied, parting her legs, positioning the head of his large cock at her oh-so-ready pussy, then plunging inside. Like always, they both moaned at the entry, then began to move together in a familiar rhythm that nearly took her breath.

"You feel so good in me, baby," she purred up to him between hot kisses. "So, so good."

"Get used to it," he told her, "since I plan to be here often."

Soon, he pulled out and instructed her to get on her hands and knees, entering her from behind. As usual, she felt him more that way, and each firm stroke made her cry out her pleasure. She didn't care if anyone heard, or even if anyone saw—she just wanted to be with her man, right here, right now, in one of the places where he'd first begun helping her shed her inhibitions to become the woman she was meant to be.

"Fuck me," she demanded through clenched teeth. "Harder. Harder."

Thick pleasure poured over her with each drive of his stiff shaft, and she held nothing back, arching her ass to meet his thrusts, sobbing her joy as each one echoed through her.

A few minutes later, they lay resting on their sides, Damon's dick still inside her from behind, and she rolled to her back, lifting one leg over his hip so that his cock remained snug in her pussy, but she could look into his eyes, touch his chest. "I love you," she told him, no longer shy—about anything, even that.

He lifted her hand from his chest to his mouth, kissing the back of it. "I love you, too, Brenna."

And their new position made it so that one of his thighs lay stretched between hers, and when he began to move in her again, it stimulated her clit in just the right way. She lifted instinctively to rub against him, seek more pleasure—and seeing her response, he began to saw his thigh more rhythmically across her wet slit. "Is that good, babe?"

"Mmm," she whimpered. "Yes, baby. Yes."

And driving his cock deep inside her, sliding his thigh across the nub jutting from the front of her flesh, he took her closer and closer to heaven, until . . . "Oh God—yes, yes, yes!" The orgasm washed over her like a tidal wave coming up out of the pool, taking away all feeling but utter and thorough pleasure. She bucked against him, drinking it in, reveling in the hot joy of it.

"Oh, Damon—that was nice."

He altered their position just enough to lean in and kiss her. "You can get used to *that*, too." Then he rolled her to her back once more, positioning himself atop her and proceeding to fuck her slow and deep, making her feel each long thrust, and peering deeply into her eyes, until he said, "Oh shit, babe—I don't want to come yet, but I'm coming. You're making me come."

And then he pounded into her, pummeling her with each hard stroke, making her feel the intensity of his climax—until he finally went still but didn't move from inside her. He simply lowered his body to rest atop hers and kissed her sweetly, their tongues sparring playfully.

"How did I make you come?" she asked, smiling up at him. "I mean, I . . . wasn't really doing anything."

"It was from looking into your pretty eyes."

She practically gulped at his reply. "Really? That's all?"

He gave a short, direct nod. "That's all it takes, apparently, after being away from you for a few weeks. Something which, by the way, I don't intend to let happen again."

As he rolled off of her and onto his back, she peered up through the vine-covered wrought iron that crisscrossed the bed to the dark sky above. She couldn't see stars here—too much light—but she could see the moon and feel the breeze, and just like in the desert, experiencing even such simple things with Damon made her feel alive.

"I'm so happy," she said. "I have you back, and we're going to work together by day, and fuck each other's brains out by night, and all will be right with the world."

Next to her, he laughed.

"Although, I feel bad for Kelly. She went to so much trouble, planning all this with you and convincing me to come—and here I am, ditching her for a guy. No offense," she said, rolling onto her side to look down at him, "but that's a major girlfriend sin, at any age."

Yet Damon merely chuckled, pulling her naked body to his. "Don't worry about Kelly. She's taken care of."

Brenna blinked. "What do you mean?"

"Tomorrow, Anthony will be joining us at the pool. And if he and Kelly hit it off, he's going to take her out for dinner and a night at Rendezvous."

Brenna threw her head back in a laugh. "Oh my God, she's going to be in heaven." Then she gazed playfully down into her lover's eyes. "And where will *we* be tomorrow night?"

"Wherever you want. I don't care. As long as I'm with you."

She tilted her head, thinking. "Maybe we'll . . . revisit the gondolas. Or the Eiffel Tower. Every time I think about either one, I get wet."

Damon replied with a low growl of arousal. "Then we're hitting both. And you're not wearing panties. And you're going to shave your pussy before we go out, and I'm going to watch. And by the time we actually get to fuck, you're going to be crazed with lust, just like the first time we hit the gondolas."

She nuzzled closer to him, letting the fresh heat invade her and bring out the dirty girl inside. "I can't wait."

"And once we get Inspiration in good shape—get a few more acts signed, get Austin's CD in the works, get the office up and running—I'm taking you on a trip."

Her eyebrows lifted. "Really? Where to?"

"Paris. And Venice."

She sucked in her breath, falling more in love with him every minute. "*Oh, Damon.*"

"I want to float along the real Grand Canal with you, Brenna. I want to look out on the lights of Paris with you from atop the real Eiffel Tower."

This was the man who had been so clear about not doing relationships, not letting sex turn into romance. Now, she couldn't imagine a more romantic guy. And if he was a little sex-crazed, too—well, she definitely considered that a perk, one which she expected to keep her life extraordinarily exciting from this point forward. "Although when we get up on top of the real Eiffel Tower," she teased him, "don't be expecting a blow job."

He grinned, his eyes sparkling on her. "We'll see about that."

She couldn't help smiling in return, her voice filled with flirtation, when she said, "Yes, we will."

A month ago, the very idea of that would have been unthinkable— but with Damon, she'd learned, anything was possible.

I do need a man, I do need a man, I do need a man.

And now I've got one—forever.

Lacey Alexander invites you to a hot day at the beach for her next sizzling erotic novel…

The Bikini Diaries

On sale February 2009

Read on for a sneak peek….

You always see those girls at the beach—the ones who somehow make you feel inferior even when you're usually a fairly confident person, perfectly happy with who you are. Killer tan, killer boobs, and those long, silky to-die-for legs, all strapped into some sinfully tiny bikini that has Fuck Me written all over it.

I'm watching one of those sex-goddess types approach even as I write this. God, she's beautiful. I kind of hate her—for making every other woman on this beach look so dreadfully normal, for making married men and dads stop talking with their wives or building sand castles with their kids in order to stop and stare.

What is it like to be her?

Is this really who she is—a woman who's so comfortable with her sexuality that she's happy to advertise it, a hot chick looking for a good lay and that's all? Or does she work so hard to look so perfect because she secretly harbors low self-esteem and she's trying to cover that with physical beauty? And is it sex she wants, or is that just a trap and she's really looking for love?

I prefer to think the former, I suppose, since even though I'm intimidated by her, I also envy her. The sexually comfortable her. The her who wants to get laid and nothing more. And even though I like myself just the way I am most days—right now, for just a moment, just a brief little second, I want to be her.

Wendy Carnes closed her journal and set it atop the beach bag next to her lounge chair, then laid the pen on top. She kind of hated that she wanted to be that woman, the one she'd just watched walking up the shoreline, all tan and perfect, hard nipples jutting through the two white triangles covering her breasts, long blond hair blowing behind her in the sea breeze. She kind of hated it, but she could accept it. It was only natural—everyone wanted to be beautiful and desirable.

And maybe . . . maybe everyone secretly wanted to know that sort of power. Because that's what the bikini woman possessed—power. Over all the men on the beach. And some of the women, too.

Of course, she couldn't forget to factor in pleasure. One glance had told her the blond bikini babe *knew* pleasure—how to give it and how to take it. Her eyes had nearly sparkled with it.

Beauty, power, and pleasure. What was there *not* to envy?

But then she shook it off. Because she was here for *business*, not pleasure. In fact, she was surprised at herself for letting Miss Bikini Babe distract her so much. To think she'd even started writing about it in her work journal—that wasn't like her.

Then again, her work seldom led her to places so posh and intoxicating as the Emerald Shores Beach Resort, edging three miles of pristine white sand along Florida's panhandle, also known as the Emerald Coast. The word *emerald* got tossed around a lot here, with good reason—when the sun hit this particular edge of the Gulf of Mexico, the pale sand underneath turned the water a nearly electric shade of green.

No, her job usually led her to a downtown Chicago office building, where she served as administrative assistant to Walter Carlisle, a wealthy real estate investor with holdings all over the country, and a genuinely pleasant guy to work for. Walter was serious and stalwart when it came to business—he had to be, to rack up so much money over the years—but he was also a fair and friendly employer who liked to go boating, play Texas Hold 'Em, and spend time with his wife and their young grandchildren.

Wendy had been truly stunned when Walter asked her to go to Emerald Shores on what in the office they called a "scouting mission." Even when Walter had chosen to permanently relocate his usual "scout," Marie Hill, in Seattle to oversee his large collection of property there, Wendy had assumed he'd hire someone new to take over Marie's position. And who knew—maybe he still would. But at least for now, Walter had elected *her* to take on the task of coming to Emerald Shores to determine whether he should sink significant money into the place.

And maybe the job wouldn't be so daunting—if Emerald Shores had been your run-of-the-mill beach resort. But it was far from it—it was, in fact, an enormous, upscale self-contained community. In addition to thousands of high-rise condo units stretching along the beach and the adjacent bay area, Emerald Shores boasted abundant shopping, nightlife, restaurants, and even a full-scale grocery and pharmacy—along with biking, golf, tennis, and a free shuttle to get you wherever you needed to go. It was a world of luxury that also came with all the conveniences of home, and that was the charm of the vast property—for vacationers, for full-time residents, and for Walter Carlisle.

When one of the resort's largest investors had pulled out last month, the Emerald Shores executives had begun vigorously courting Walter. And as a result, she found herself sitting on a pristine white beach, digging her bare toes into soft, warm sand, and ... well, now wondering what it was like to be sex on a stick.

Because even though White-Bikini Babe was out of sight now, she remained in Wendy's thoughts. She'd felt both ... intimidated and rebuffed by the woman's very presence.

So why did she also *envy* her? Did she secretly long to be intimidating, to make other women feel bad about themselves? No—she was a nice person and liked people. Mainly she just kept wondering what it was like to be an object of pure sexual desire, plain and simple.

Focus, she told herself. She wasn't here to watch girls, or guys—she was here to check out every aspect of Emerald Shores, from both a tourist's and an investor's perspectives, and talk with the resort executives about what she felt needed to be changed or updated to garner Walter Carlisle's money; then, based on their responses, she would share her findings with Walter when she went home next week, and make a recommendation that he invest—or not.

After taking a sip of the frozen mango daiquiri, complete with umbrella, that a Hawaiian shirt–clad waiter had just delivered, she lowered the drink to the sand and took up her journal and pen again—and this time made notes that mattered.

> *Umbrella drinks—too expensive. People may be willing to pay $12 for a drink, but I'm sure they resent it. Lower the price by 25% and you still make a profit, people will be likely to drink more, and they won't feel ripped off.*

She'd examine later whether that was actually an issue worth presenting to the Emerald Shores execs, but she'd decided to bring a journal, keep it with her as often as possible, record anything that occurred to her, and then sort through it all afterward.

As for why she'd written down her thoughts about White-Bikini Babe—she supposed she'd been venting. And no one but her would ever see the journal, so she could use it however she wished.

It was when she abandoned the journal once more, taking another sip of her mango-and-rum concoction, that she noticed a vision in white in her peripheral sight. She looked up to see that—lo and behold—White-Bikini Babe now glided back down the shoreline in the opposite direction. This time her hair blew around her face a bit, making her look more windblown-and-sexy than sleek-and-hot, but the effect remained the same. As those lithe, tan legs moved smoothly over the sand, Wendy could feel every guy in the vicinity watching—just as she was. Just like before: dads, husbands—young men and old.

But this time a group of twentysomething guys who had just arrived to start tossing around a football all stopped to gape, too. And something about *that* got to her on a deeper level. Because the guys were cute. Hot, even. And now two of them had abandoned the game completely to boldly approach White Bikini, and Wendy watched as they spoke, flirting visibly. Suddenly *she* wanted to know how to flirt like that. Because she suddenly wanted such cute beach guys to notice *her*, to want *her*.

And as the conversation ended—maybe with plans for later?—and the white bikini sashayed on up the beach still looking enviably hot, Wendy finally understood her strange fixation with the woman. In fact, it hit her like a ton of bricks.

Wendy was thirty-four years old. And if there was a window of time in her life to ever look that good or act that way—to openly advertise herself sexually—it was probably past. And that meant she would never know what it felt like to fuck a drop-dead gorgeous guy for no other reason than pure physical pleasure.

Unless . . . unless she grabbed it right now.

She bit her lip, stunned at her last thought.

Wendy wasn't normally a sexually aggressive person—she saw herself as mild-mannered and pretty-in-an-ordinary-way, and she hadn't dated since getting her job with Walter Carlisle two years ago. It hadn't been a conscious decision, but . . . well, she'd been through a number of relationships with dreadfully average guys who were crazier about her than she'd been about them, and she supposed at some point she'd decided they just weren't worth her time. Given that her job came with long hours. And that the guys she seemed to attract just weren't very exciting to her.

Of course, at night, in bed . . . well, she occasionally allowed herself some pretty wild fantasies about fabulously hot guys—and in them, she was always stunningly sexy. Which, now that she analyzed it, probably meant that she had needs and desires she was shoving under the rug, bored and irritated with the offerings in her life.

And now, suddenly, for the first time ever, as she glanced at the round, firm ass of the girl moving away from her up the beach, she wondered—was it even conceivable? Could she, Wendy Carnes, ever *pull off* stunningly sexy? Could she wear a skimpy bikini like that one? Other sexy clothes?

She didn't see herself as overly prim, but she generally tried to be *appropriate*. When she went to Myrtle Beach in South Carolina every summer with her sister and three nieces, she always wore a conservative two-piece suit—the same she wore right now. She wasn't twenty-one anymore, nor did she have the body she'd had then. What a crime that when she *had* been twenty-one, she hadn't the guts to wear something skimpy, and would have felt slutty and afraid of sending the wrong message. Now that she *wanted* to wear it, *wanted* to send a different message than she ever had before—just once, just for this week—she feared her body was probably too imperfect. A classic catch-22.

Still, it was a pretty decent body for her age. God had blessed her with good boobs and, so far, only one small spot of cellulite on the back of her right thigh. She worked out regularly, so that helped. And she'd just gotten a new hair color, which everyone said looked sexy, although that hadn't been the goal—she'd gone from her regular medium brown to a coppery hue with a few blonde streaks.

She stared out at the ocean, pondering the unthinkable. Except that, to her surprise, it had suddenly become thinkable.

Could she pull it off? Could she become like that woman? Could she become . . . someone else?

About the Author

Lacey Alexander's books have been called deliciously decadent, unbelievably erotic, exceptionally arousing, blazingly sexual, and downright sinful. In each book, Lacey strives to take her readers on the ultimate erotic adventure, and she hopes her stories will encourage women to embrace their sexual fantasies.

Lacey resides in the Midwest with her husband, and when not penning romantic erotica, she enjoys studying history and traveling, often incorporating favorite destinations into her work.